Mowzl's story takes the reader on
a child or a grown up, this tale, lik
ages. From the very start, you will
are transported into the magical w
The story is deftly woven between
of Mowzl, some long time in the f
charms his human friends and brir
confronting them with the painful

much they have lost touch with nature they find the courage to be transported within,
to a deep understanding of healthy, abundant nature.
This is a story of hope and encouragement. I most earnestly recommend it to you.
Rick Vick Artistic Director, Stroud Festival

*Mowzl is ace and I wish I could meet him really truly and I want to learn purling, so
I can talk to animals. I like stories of our world and Mowzl's all mixed up. It's lots of
levels and fun and challenging. Thanks Mowzl!*
Will Beckwood (12)

*Mowzl's story is packed full of imagination and adventure, it's so unique and will
stick with me for ages. It's different, you'll love it. I made a Top Trumps game with all
the characters for a school project!*
Lucy Richmond (12)

*Dear Paul, I very much enjoyed Mowzl's story and I am writing to you to say a few
things.*
1. The book is very good and it leaves a nice cliffhanger at the end.
2. There is a lot of excitement and suspense in the book.
3. I really think that lots of children would like it.

To Mowzl,
*You play a big part in the book and you certainly like chocolate very much.
Good luck with the rest of your adventures.*
From Matthew Gardner (10)

"Pippee," says Mowzl. "If you's to be ritin' mi story, you's avin' to be lernin' again
ow to feel feelin's like wen you woz littl; I's come to elp you, n we's learnin' you ow
to burro inside."

Thank you, everyone, for your interest in the Mowzl books and for your reviews.
If you would like to review, or comment, you can email Mowzl from his website at
www.mowzl.co.uk

Paul Thornycroft

Also by Paul Thornycroft
**The Adventures of Horatio Mowzl,
Volume Two, 'First Purlings'**

The Adventures of Horatio Mowzl

Volume One
Little Humans

The Adventures of Horatio Mowzl
(Volume One: Little Humans)

By Paul Thornycroft

First published in 2017 by Arkbound Ltd. (Publishers)
This second edition published by MowzlPrint Publishing 2019
ISBN: 9781916198104

All internal illustrations by the author
Cover illustration by L H Trevitt

***

MowzlPrint
PUBLISHING

For my grandson, Rufus,
for all children everywhere and the wild web they share;
for all living things whose habitats are disappearing.

Volume One

Little Humans

Contents

Chapter One

Typhoon

The *Wreckless* heaves and rolls as the typhoon tears at her rigging. With a crack loud as cannon, the top of the mainmast snaps, crashing through the deck into the hold below. Cutlass Kate and Emmy are there, on sentry duty, and now have to hold on for dear life as the wind sucks at them through the hole in the broken deck.

The wind tugs at Emmy's body as he clings to a rope fixing a stack of barrels. He tries to wrap his tail round the rope, but the wind is too strong and it pulls him upside down.

"I can't hold on much longer!" he screams, but Cutlass Kate can't hear him over the howling wind. *Oh, my goodness,* he thinks, *my time has come.*

The *Wreckless* heaves, lifted by a huge wave, only to crash down shuddering and creaking; the barrels wriggle free from their restraining ropes and disappear up through the hole in the deck; Emmy shrieks as he loses his grip.

The wind is so strong he can't breathe, and in fear of suffocating he thinks he is sure to die. In his mind's eye, he sees the faces of his family and friends and as everything begins to go black, he sees Flimsy's face just for a moment before he passes out.

When Emmy comes to his senses, he is able to breathe again; the wind has eased, and when he looks about him he sees that he has been carried high into the sky. Looking down, he sees the spiralling clouds of the storm below covering much of the ocean world. He had been sucked up by the spiral wind and spewed out at the top, along with the barrels and broken bits of wood. These things are tumbling all around him, but slowing down now, and Emmy realises with alarm that he will soon begin to fall all the way back to the sea, along with everything else.

He inspects his tail, his limbs and body, amazed to find no wounds or damage except a bit of fur missing here and there. He has some aches and bruises, but nothing too bad considering what has just happened. While he is examining his tail for a second time, a scrap of seaweed floats towards him, wrapping itself gently around his body. Emmy watches in surprise as more seaweed strands come to him, wrapping him more and more thickly.

"Hallo, seaweed, what are you up to?" asks Emmy, curious, but also worried in case the seaweed should cover him up completely and then digest him, as some plants do. To Emmy's delight, he realises that it is not smothering him; it is making a kind of bag that comes up to his armpits.

"You're making a pouch! Why are you doing that? It does feel very nice. . . and look! I'm not falling — I'm floating!"

Emmy looks around to see what's happening to the barrels and bits of wood. Most of these things are falling away from him, but some are not. He looks at the nearest thing that isn't falling and has to rub his eyes and look again. He sees a fish that is also being wrapped in seaweed.

"Hallo! You look like a fish out of water!" he calls. "I see you're growing a seaweed pouch like mine!"

"Yes, you're quite right, I am a fish out of water," says the fish out of water. "My name is Baloop. Look at my seaweed bubble!"

"Hallo, Baloop, my name is Emmy and I'm a mouse. What is this seaweed doing, do you think?"

"I don't know, Emmy, but I have been feeling so much better since the seaweed wrapped me up. A fish out of water doesn't live very long, and I was sure I would die before falling back to the sea; it's so far away down there. Now I feel peaceful, and seem to be able to breathe, even though there's no water for my gills."

"Yes!" agrees Emmy. "I'm feeling good too now that my seaweed pouch has finished growing. Do you think we are dead

already and that's why we are floating and feeling good?"

"Emmy, you don't have to be dead to feel good."

"I know, it's just all so strange."

"Hmm. Dead! Maybe we are," muses Baloop wistfully.

"Why aren't we falling, like those bits of wood over there?" says Emmy, perplexed.

"It's the seaweed. It's magic."

"How do you know? You're just saying it aren't you?"

"Why don't you ask it?" suggests Baloop.

"Ask the seaweed?"

"Yes, ask the seaweed."

"Alright," Emmy clears his throat. "Hurrumm. Hallo, seaweed, my name is Emmy and I am a mouse. What's your name?" But the seaweed doesn't say anything or give any sign that Emmy notices.

"No answer, Baloop, but never mind, I'm feeling happy now! This seaweed bubble is really snug. It's more of a pouch than a bubble, so I'm calling mine a pouch. Ha! Hallo, Pouch! No, you are special and need a special name; I'm going to call you Snug . . . erm . . . Snugweed! Hallo, Snugweed!"

There is still no reply.

"Did you hear anything, Emmy?"

"No, Baloop, but I think Snugweed squeezed me a bit."

"Squeezed you! How nice. Try again," cries Baloop excitedly.

"Hallo, Snugweed, thank you for saving me and Baloop."

Emmy definitely feels the pouch give him a little squeeze.

"Yes, Baloop! Another little squeeze! Ha!"

"A day full of surprises, I wonder what will happen next?"

A strange voice calls out at that very moment; Emmy and Baloop look all around but see nothing nearby. The voice continues in a very slow and drifty sort of way.

"Hallo, please could you tell me the way to some land?"

Emmy sees the bird first.

"Over there, Baloop, and up a bit, look!"

Already wrapped in seaweed the bird drifts towards them, it's face bearing a sad expression and its long, narrow wings hanging down like broken things dangling.

"Hallo," calls Emmy, in greeting. "My name is Emmy and I'm a mouse, and this is Baloop. There's no land in the Ocean world except the Island of Mist. What sort of bird are you?"

"I am Wandering Wings. Sadly, I don't know what sort of bird I am. I have been flying for as long as I can remember searching for another bird of my own kind and now I am tired, and the storm was too much for me; I need to rest."

"I hope your seaweed bubble is holding you well," says Baloop.

"Hmmm, strange sort of nest, don't you think? I would have preferred something in white."

"Not a time to be choosy, p'raps."

"True enough, Baloop. Hmmm. Are you a flying fish?"

"No, no, just a fish sucked out of the sea by the monster wind and spat out into the sky. Without the seaweed bubble I would die because I cannot breathe air without water for my gills.

"Hmmm. Very strange. Emmy Mouse, please speak more of the Island of Mist."

"Wandering Wings," replies Emmy. "If you have been flying for a long time over the ocean, you will have seen many strange things. You will have seen the blue ocean covering the whole Earth, from west to east and south to north."

"Yes," says Wandering Wings, in his slow way. "I have seen strange and marvellous things. I remember seeing a ship with human sailors who tried to catch me, but I kept out of reach. I followed that ship for a long time, until I decided that they didn't know where to find land."

"I know that ship!" cries Emmy. "It's called the '*Wreckless*' and it's always looking for the fog. Have you ever seen the fog?"

"Fog? Oh yes, I remember seeing fog."

"Well," Emmy explains. "If you want to find the Island of Mist, you must first find the fog and then go inside it; then, and only then, the Island of Mist will be revealed. Well, so I am told. I have never been there myself."

"How do you know all this, Emmy?" asks Baloop.

"I was on board that human ship, before the great wind, and my friends on the ship told me about the fog and the Island of Mist. We were planning to go there. The humans go to the Island of Mist to hunt for food and collect fresh water, and they go there to look for treasure, but they never find any."

"What use is treasure they never find?" cries Baloop.

"Maybe they believe they'll find it one day," says Emmy. "The great wind broke open the ship and I was sucked up into the sky. My friends are on that ship and I want to find them. I hope they are alright, and not sunk to the bottom of the sea."

"Let's go and find them — and the Island of Mist!" cries Baloop cheerfully.

"Hmmm, we could. Yes, we could," agrees Wandering Wings, uncertainly. "But how do we move?"

"Oh! I seem to be moving already," cries Baloop. "Look!"

Wandering Wings and Emmy watch as Baloop drifts away.

"He's going down!" cries Emmy. "Let's go too — but how?"

"It seems to just happen to Baloop," says Wandering Wings.

"Maybe we have to ask. Snugweed? Can you help? May we please follow Baloop and look for the *Wreckless*?" Emmy feels a slight squeeze from the pouch as he begins to move.

"I'm moving! Wandering Wings, are you moving as well?"

"Hmm, yes, I seem to be moving. Who is Snugweed? You spoke to Snugweed."

"Snugweed is my seaweed pouch, and I think it's alive. Are you alive, Snugweed?"

Emmy doesn't feel a squeeze from the pouch, but he does have the strangest feeling, a feeling that someone has just said something to him, but he hasn't quite heard — except inside, a feeling inside.

"I'm sure Snugweed is alive, but I don't know how."

"Hmm!" says Wandering Wings. "Very strange indeed."

They move downwards, slowly, following Baloop.

"Let's try and catch up with Baloop!" cries Emmy.

They get faster, little by little, as they learn to relax and let their pouches do the moving.

"There's Baloop! Look, down there," says Wandering Wings, pointing with one of his long, skinny wings.

They shout out to Baloop, who waves a fin.

"Ha! Ha! This is fun!" he cries.

They get closer to the sea and soon can see the waves moving, but there is nothing else to be seen in any direction. Their pouches carry them fast now, lower and lower until they are skimming just above the waves, close enough to taste the salty spray. All day they fly like this, and when night falls the sky is bright with stars. Emmy recognises the Southern Cross constellation that Whip-Tail Jack had told him about during his days on board the *Wreckless*.

"We're going Eastwards," Emmy declares.

"Ha! It's all water to me!" says Baloop, laughing.

"Don't you want to get back to the sea, Baloop?" asks Emmy.

"Not yet! I'm loving this."

Wandering Wings has very good eyesight, and when the first sign of dawn appears over the eastern horizon, he sees something far away.

"That might be fog."

"Where?" asks Emmy.

"Far, far away . . ." says Wandering Wings. He turns towards what he has seen, and Baloop and Emmy follow. They move faster and faster now, the sea becoming a blur; they see the cloud of fog getting closer, looming ever larger.

Anxious about his friends, Emmy has been looking out for the *Wreckless* but has seen no sign of it at all. He will just have to follow the others into the fog and hope for the best.

The three pouches slow down, moving gently into the fog. The further into the fog they go the darker it gets until it's black as pitch and they can't see anything at all.

"Hallo, are you there? Emmy? Wandering Wings?" Baloop calls, anxiously.

"Hmmm, here I am," says Wandering Wings. "No need to worry, Baloop, we just go where the seaweed nests take us."

"You sound far away," shouts Emmy. "Where are you, Baloop? Wandering Wings?"

"Over here!" they call back, their voices fading.

"Oh, no! You sound further away than ever! My pouch is taking me somewhere else! Goodbye, Baloop, goodbye, Wandering Wings! I'm very glad we met!"

"Goodbye, Emmy!" they call back, but they are already far away, and the fog deadens the sound of their voices, Emmy can only just hear them.

"Oh dear, that was so sudden, I'm feeling so sad. What's happening, Snugweed? Do I have to go somewhere else?"

"Yes. Somewhere else."

"Snugweed! You can talk!" cries Emmy.

"You feel the unwords inside."

"Snugweed, I don't get it. Why can I understand you now when I couldn't before?"

"Feeling unwords is slow to happen. When you are with other creatures you are not feeling unwords, but you will learn how to."

"So, when I was with Baloop and Wandering Wings I couldn't feel what you were telling me — because I was listening to them?"

"Different listen, yes."

"I hope I can learn, Snugweed. Where do we go now? Do we go to where Uncle One-Eye found the light?"

"YesNo."

"That's not very helpful, Snugweed. Oh look! The fog's thinning, I can see a bit of sky showing through. Where's the Island of Mist?"

"Purling first, much purling."

"What's purling?"

"Flying like this."

"Why is it called purling?"

"Because one day you will name it so," explains Snugweed.

"What? One day? Me?"

"We go . . ." declares Snugweed.

Suddenly Emmy is purling at great speed high into the sky, and then yet higher, beyond the atmosphere and into space. Slowing down at last, Snugweed turns so that Emmy is facing towards the Earth. It is very beautiful, and Emmy gazes in wonderment for a long time; he becomes aware of the Earth's slow turning and of the other planets moving in their orbits around the sun. It is exquisite.

It must be Snugweed telling me all this without any words. This must be the unwords, he thinks. He notices that the Earth has a strange shadow, or reflection, as though there is an invisible mirror hidden in space behind the Earth; this shadow-earth has a shadow-earth of its own, and that shadow-earth has a shadow, and then another, and another. . . Emmy is seeing the many worlds revealed, like a rainbow reveals the many colours of light.

He notices that he *feels* these worlds; some feel familiar, some do not, some have life happening and others have none. With the unwords, Snugweed tells Emmy about the isness of each of these worlds. He explains to Emmy that only the invisible ones can see the many worlds happening. Emmy has to interrupt when he hears that!

"How come I can see them happening then? I'm not an invisible one!"

"The invisible ones are revealing to you the isness of the many worlds. The isness you are feeling now is the Ocean world."

"Did we just come from there?"

"Yes."

"Are you an invisible one, Snugweed? And why are you, I mean they, showing me these things? I don't understand."

"It is not the time for you to understand, but to see, and feel, the isness of the many worlds."

"Hmmph," says Emmy, feeling a bit of a headache coming on. He wonders why Snugweed hasn't answered his question about being an invisible one.

"This is the human world," announces Snugweed.

The human world feels familiar to Emmy, but it's not quite like his own world. There's something about it that makes him feel uncomfortable. Very uncomfortable.

"And this is your home world, Mowzl Emmy."

Emmy feels proud when he hears Snugweed use his name, and he feels reassured. For a moment, he is curious about how Snugweed could possibly know his Mowzl name, but with all the excitement, and feeling his home world close by, he is distracted. Looking upon his home world he feels its isness; he is thrilled to feel this, so familiar and loved is it to him, and he longs to see his loved ones and the loved places where his heart belongs.

"Listen to the colours, Mowzl Emmy," instructs Snugweed.

"Listen to colours? How do —," Emmy's ears suddenly pop, and he hears singing that tells him of the isness of the colours, and because each world has its own colours, the singing tells of the isness of each world. Emmy is listening to a rainbow of sound.

"Snugweed, this is so beautiful I could stay here forever, listening, but when I hear the singing of my home world I want to go there and my heart leaps towards it."

"It is not yet time for you to return to your home world, Mowzl Emmy."

"Oh, no, what is it time for, Snugweed?" Emmy asks anxiously.

"It is time to go back to the fog."

"And to the Island of Mist! Hooray!" cries Emmy. "Will I find Scraggy?"

"Maybe, one day."

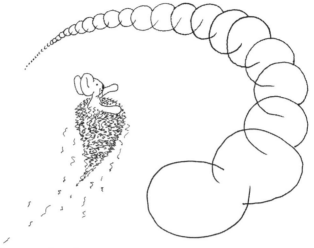

Snugweed carries Emmy back towards the world of ocean and fog where the *Wreckless* is and maybe the Island of Mist, and as he gets closer, the other worlds disappear one by one until there is only the world of ocean to be seen. He is purling fast through the sky and over the sea, and around the world until, suddenly, there is the fog.

Snugweed slows down, entering the wispy, swirling fog. Little by little the fog thickens and the light fades.

"Are we going to find the Island of Mist, Snugweed? I want to find my friends from the *Wreckless*, and I want to see Baloop and Wandering Wings again, but most of all I want to find Scraggy!"

A few moments pass before Emmy feels Snugweed's reply.

"Know this, Mowzl Emmy; the Ocean world is where the many Worlds meet. There are great mysteries here, which we have glimpsed when seeing the many worlds happening. There will be much more for you to learn. Now, tell me, what is in your heart?"

"I'm feeling sad for my friends and my heart is heavy. I'm not going to see them yet am I, Snugweed?"

"Not now, Mowzl Emmy. What else are you feeling?"

"I'm being pulled, like a string is tied to my tummy button; I'm being pulled, but I don't know why, or where to. It's getting quite strong now, Snugweed, we'll have to go along with it."

"Snugweed cannot come with you, Mowzl Emmy. Snugweed cannot leave this world."

"You mean I'm leaving this world? Where to? Snugweed? Oh, no! Not again!" cries Emmy, truly alarmed.

"It is your journey, Mowzl, Snugweed cannot be with you. Listen carefully now; remember all that you have seen here, remember the isness of the many worlds that you have seen, remember Baloop and Wandering Wings, remember all your friends from the *Wreckless* and remember your home world; and remember, Horatio Mowzl, this is now your name. But you will forget all that you remember, and you will remember all that you forget."

"Snugweed, you are talking in riddles, you remind me of Uncle One-Eye. I'm not going home, am I?"

"No, Horatio Mowzl, you are not."

Snugweed begins to unravel; separate strands of seaweed detach from Mowzl's pouch, floating off into the fog and drifting down to the sea. Mowzl is pulled steadily faster through the fog by an invisible thread.

"Am I going through another porthole?" Mowzl cries out, anxiously. "How can I remember if I forget? Snugweed?"

"All that you have seen will make your heart wise, even when you forget. The invisible ones will always be with you, and you will find your way."

"I'm being pulled, Snugweed! Oh dear, I'm being pulled, and not to my home world. Is it the invisible ones pulling me?"

"You are pulled by a human."

"A human? Why? What?"

"Be trusting, Horatio Mowzl! Snugweed can go no further."

"Goodbye, Snugweed, thank you for saving me in the sky, and for everything!"

Mowzl is pulled faster and faster, frightened now that Snugweed has gone. The thick, foggy air rushes by, wetting his fur and making his eyes sting.

Suddenly, with a flash of light, the fog and the Ocean world disappear.

~

Mowzl is no longer wet and bedraggled. There is no fog, no ocean, nothing that he recognises. He examines his body only to find that it isn't the body he is used to at all. Now it is made of soft stuff that's woolly and squashy; he has no bones, but even so he can still move a bit, and he can see and hear and smell, but most of all, his heart is full of fright. He can definitely smell things, all sorts of new smells he's never smelt before, and some are not very nice new smells.

Looking around he sees that he's in a pile of soft creatures a bit like him, but different shapes. There's a rabbit and a badger, a blue tit and a dog, all quite the wrong sizes, because the dog is the same size as the blue tit.

"Hallo, blue tit, have you been purling too?" Mowzl asks, but the blue tit doesn't answer, and none of the other soft creatures say anything, or move, or do anything at all. "Oh dear, are you all dead? Maybe you haven't been alive yet, poor things. I hope you are all alive soon."

Mowzl looks around a bit more, seeing all sorts of creatures that he's never seen before.

"Can any of you talk?" he calls out. His voice doesn't go very far because there are so many soft things soaking it up. There's no reply. Nothing moves.

He pulls himself up through the other soft creatures, so that he can see around better. He sees that he and the other soft creatures are jumbled up in a big bowl. Now he hears noises: rattling and banging, and then voices, and then a rhythmical thump, thump, thump. Suddenly a human appears, just two hops away. Mowzl is terrified. He's never seen a human before. He keeps very quiet.

The human switches on a machine and presses a button, a drawer slides open and she fiddles about for a bit before pushing the drawer closed again. She walks around rearranging things on the shelves and, to Mowzl's alarm, she comes to the bowl of soft toys that he's in and rummages about, rearranging them. She picks Mowzl up to have a good look at him.

"Hallo! You must be a new line, I've not seen you before. You're really cute." She kisses him on the nose and puts him down again on top of the pile in the bowl. Then she goes away. Mowzl hears the rhythmical thumping as she goes back down the stairs. He hasn't understood a word that she said.

He's wondering what to do next, when he hears more noise coming from wherever the human went. He can hear more voices, and a bell that rings every once in a while, and soon he hears the sound of humans thumping up the stairs. They come very close, huge and looming, so big that Mowzl can't understand how they can be strong enough to move their enormous bodies about. The humans wander about looking at things, sometimes picking something up, turning it over and putting it down again, then picking something else up, examining its bottom, and putting it down again.

The she-human that had said Mowzl must be a new line, comes back to stand by the till machine. A shopper chooses a paint box, goes to the till to pay, and with the purchase safe in a bag goes back down the stairs and out of the shop.

Oh-oh, Mowzl thinks, *I'll have to catch one of these humans and get out of here, but which one? I don't like the look of any of these.*

He waits and watches, learning what he can about humans. It's all very puzzling. A little later there's a quiet time and no humans come, so the she-human by the till machine goes downstairs to have a chat with her friends and make a coffee. While she is doing that, another human comes into the shop and up the stairs to the toys section. Mowzl sees straight away that this he-human is different. He looks different, yes, but most importantly he feels different. He's a bit scruffy, he's wearing a woollen hat, he's got glass things in front of his eyes, and he has a hairy face; Mowzl quite likes the feel of him and thinks that he wouldn't mind if this human comes over and picks him up and takes him out of the smelly shop. But he doesn't come over.

The human rummages about for ages and doesn't even look at the bowl of soft creatures. Mowzl realises that the human doesn't know what he's looking for and is just turning things over in his hands without feeling anything in particular. Mowzl decides there and then that this is the one he must catch, so he calls him with his heart. The human moves about some more and then stops, turns slowly, and comes towards Mowzl's bowl of soft creatures. The human's eyes have a sad, faraway look, and Mowzl calls with his heart again; the human's eyes are not seeing Mowzl, but he holds out his hand as he passes by the bowl of soft creatures. Mowzl leaps into his open hand, and the human's sad eyes light up. He smiles, and straight away goes downstairs to pay.

The human doesn't want a bag to put his purchase in, so when he has given the money and got his change, he puts Mowzl in his coat pocket. Mowzl scrambles up to poke his head out, and as the human walks out of the shop into the street Mowzl feels the cold air and can breathe again. He feels a surge of excitement.

"I've just caught a human!" he says out loud, in Mouseze of course. "Oh, my goodness gracious me!"

"What was that?" says the human, reaching into his pocket and lifting Mowzl out. "I thought I heard you squeaking, but that's just silly of me. You look as though you might be alive, little mouse, but you're a soft toy, aren't you? I'm glad I found you; I have a strange feeling we were meant to meet. I wonder if you have a name? I'm sure you'll tell me when you're ready. My name is Pip and I'm a human, more's the pity."

He puts Mowzl back into his pocket and walks on through the light rain. Mowzl pokes his face out of the pocket and breathes the fresh air. *I wonder what he said,* he thinks to himself. *I shall have to learn human speak. Hmm, I'm a bit peckish. I wonder what I can eat in the human world.* He snuggles down for a well-earned rest.

Chapter Two

Allo!

Sitting in a small bowl on the kitchen table in Pip's house, Mowzl bends down to breathe in the smell of chocolates put there for him specially in case he should get hungry.

Mowzl is thoughtful today. He woke up in the night feeling that something special is going to happen today, something big. It is four winters since he arrived in the human world and he is desperate to find his way home again, but to do so he needs to remember what happened, which he can't — yet. He has made a big effort to learn human-speak and is ready now to tell his story, and for this he will need your help. Yes, you! Mowzl needs you to be imagining his story so that he can remember.

He stirs himself, sits up straight and takes a big, deep breath. He's ready now, ready to say hallo.

~

"Allo! Mi name iz Oratio Mowzl n I's a mouse. I's been ere nearly four wintaz so I's nearly grow'd up. Truly I's much more old, coz I's lived in uvva world before I's magic'd ere. There's not any oomans in mi ome world, but ere oomans iz all evry where.

"Ow I's comin' ere's a mystree, xcept me's kno-in' I's pulled bi a thread through a fog. So, wot appns iz, I's wakin' up in world ov oomans in a bowl ov fingz in a smelly shop, n all of a sudden I's not a real mouse, I's a toy mouse, but wiv an 'eart n real feelin's.

"Course, I's not talkin' ooman fashion bak then, not like now me's learnin', nor could I rite ritin' bak then, not like now me's learnin' from Pippee who's mi scribbla frend. Pippee's notta mouse, e's an ooman.

"So, wot appns iz, oomans iz clumsyin' about n I's feelin' fright inside, coz I's avin' feelin's ov real mouse coz I's real mouse bak ome. N wot appns iz, an ooman comes in n e's a bit scruffy lookin' n I's likin' im, but e's lookin' all evry way, but nevva mi way, so I's callin' im wiv mi 'eart. I's feelin' straight n away I's goin' wiv this ere ooman n not no uvva.

"Wot appns iz, 'is dull eyes comes around n sees Mowzl n they's lightin' up, n I's jumpin' into 'is open 'and. E gives some munnee so e's not stealin', n we's all ov a suddn outside, n I's pockited in an ooman's pockit finkin' *I's just caught an ooman! Oh, mi goodniss grashus me!"*

Mowzl bends down for a lungful of chocolate fumes.

"Mmm! Choklit foomz! Mowzl's favrit. Where woz we? Ah! — I's merembrin' — I's caught an ooman, n you'sll be wantin' to kno a bit 'bout who this ooman iz. Well, I's callin' im Pippee, n e's a bit ov a greybeard, meanin' e's 'ad lotz ov wintaz. E's a bit scruffy lookin' so's a bird might fink ov nestin' in 'is 'at.

"Pippee 'as a speshl frend called LuLu, n we'sll be meetin' 'er later. I's lovin' LuLu, like I's lovin' Purl, who's mi sista bak ome. I's avin bowl ov choklitz at LuLu's place too, so I's livin' wiv LuLu too.

"Oh-oh! I's earin' Pippee comin'. Let's be seein' wot appns!"

Mowzl sings a little tune: "Laa la laa la laaa laaa."
Which looks a bit like this:

"Oh, there you are, Mowzl!" says Pip, coming into the kitchen. "I've been looking everywhere for you. It's nice to hear you singing! Do you know, I woke up this morning feeling that something special is going to happen today, but I don't know what it might be. Come on, shall we go for a walk to the woods?"

"Ha! Pippee, I's been tellin' you to be 'comin' on' since four wintaz bak, wen you's inventin' Mowzl."

"Invented you?" Pip sounds surprised. "But it was you that jumped into my hand in that shop!"

"You wouldn't ave bin there evva at all if you wozn't lookin' for Mowzl." He looks at Pip with a look that goes right inside. "Why's you inventin' Mowzl, Pippee? Why's you pullin Mowzl through the fog?"

Pip glances shyly at Mowzl. "We've talked about this before."

"I's needin' to be earin' all again," insists Mowzl.

"Mowzl," says Pip, scratching his beard. "I didn't know that I was looking for you, and I didn't know then about the thread that pulled you through the fog — I didn't know it was me pulling the end of the thread!"

"Now you's kno-in', so be tellin' Mowzl wot's in yor 'eart."

Pip is quiet for a long time, and when he speaks his voice is far away. "What's in my heart?" he murmurs. "Sadness, Mowzl."

"We's simila, Pippee, mi 'eart iz sad too, coz I's sick for ome."

"I can understand that you are homesick, Mowzl, because you've been magic'd away from your home world and you don't know how to get back, but why should I be feeling homesick and lonely when I am here in my home world already?"

"Pippee, everyfin' you's luvin' iz in yor 'eart, but you 'as a bad abbit, you's lettin' foughts of sad get bigger'n wot's in yor 'eart."

"Em, this talk is making me feel bad. Can we go outside please? I need to be outside, let's go out to the trees and birds."

"Pippee, I's needin' you to be talkin'. It's four wintaz n we azn't rit 'Wot Appnd'. You's sidle steppin'."

"You're right, Mowzl. I promise to try harder. Let's go to the woods and get some air and talk there."

"Oh, orite," says Mowzl, sighing. "Let's be goin' owt n abowt!"

Pip tucks Mowzl into the rim of his hat, as he always does, and they set off down the road to the paths that lead out of town and away to the woods. Pip climbs a steep slope towards an old larch tree at the top of a grassy clearing; he sits at the bottom of the tree leaning against the trunk. From here they can see over the tops of the trees growing on the slope below, right across to the other side of the valley.

A buzzard mews as it circles overhead. Mowzl jumps down, settling himself on the bed of needles fallen from the larch tree.

"Mowzl, do you remember when the buzzard hunted you?"

"Scary, wozn'it."

They sit quietly, remembering how the buzzard had been circling above the valley, sometimes swooping down closer to the ground and sometimes finding a wind to carry it back up high. On one of the swoops down, Mowzl had realised that the buzzard was coming straight at him. He was about to become the buzzard's dinner! 'Pippee — Buzzard!' Mowzl had shouted, and Pip snatched him up in the nick of time, for the next moment the buzzard swooped by, inches away, screeching in disappointment.

"'E would've been un'appy if e'd tried eatin' me."

"Yes, Em, I know you're a real mouse in your home world, but in this world you're a stuffed toy and not good food for a buzzard! He might have choked on you!"

"We's nevva wantin' that."

25

After a long quiet — not just one quiet but two quiets because they are both quiet, and two quiets is very quiet — Mowzl says:

"I's sadly sick for ome, n I's needin' you to elp me get 'Wot Appnd' rit, coz it's only way to be seein' through fog n findin' mi ways ome. Ere in yor world I's only a toy mouse, but I's avin' an 'eart n real feelin's n I's urtin' for ome. Pleez be elpin', Pippee . . . pleez."

Pip's heart aches for Mowzl. "Mowzl, yes, I'm trying to learn from you how to write your story, but I don't know what happened to you, and I don't know about your home world. I'm so sorry, Mowzl, I don't know what I can do."

"Pippee, pleez be quiet. Wot 'as to appn iz, inside you must ave emptiniss."

For a moment Pip is stung by Mowzl's words, but he tries to be quiet. In his heart, he knows that Mowzl is not meaning to upset him, and little by little he settles down feeling quieter inside.

"How do I make myself empty inside, Em? I can't imagine it."

"Oomans nevva iz empti, so Mowzl's findin' ways to be elpin'. Be tellin' again, wot's in yor 'eart?"

There's another quiet before Pip answers. "Sadness, Mowzl."

"Be tellin'."

"Your asking the question helps me to feel it, to be aware of it; I'm feeling that I'm sort of, er, hollow, or missing something, missing... the middle of me."

"We's made simila! Iz you stuffed toy like Mowzl?"

Pip doesn't find Mowzl's joke very funny. "So, what do you mean, 'the feeling in my heart'?"

"In yor 'eart lives all wot you luvz, it's a luv battree wot's powerin' you."

"So why are the sad feelings happening?"

"Coz you's missin' fingz you's luvin', you's not livin' in yor 'eart, you's livin' in yor foughts ov sad."

"Can you help me change that, Mowzl?"

"I's avin' to elp, coz I's needin' you empti ov sad, I's needin' you to elp me get ome."

"We must help each other to get home! You to your world, and me to my heart!"

"Yip, n wot 'as to appn iz, you be empti inside so Mowzl's ome world iz floatin' in yor imaginin'. Let's be avin' a go!"

"Alright, Mowzl, I'll have a go right now. Is this what you mean?" Pip concentrates really hard, frowning with the effort of trying.

"Pippee, you's always lookin' like that! You's not empti 'nough, you's avin' to stop finkin'."

"Oh, dear me, how do I stop thinking? I'll never do that!"

"It's nevva a doin', Pippee, it's a bein'. Foughts iz like fingz, n tween fingz iz no fing. Tween foughts iz emptiniss, n that's where the 'eart iz."

Pip closes his eyes, listening to Mowzl's voice, trying to relax and be empty, whatever that might mean.

"Good, Pippee, you's doin' betta, keep tryin'. Oh, mi goodniss grashus me! Oh, me oh mi!"

"What's happening, Em?"

"You's gettin' betta, relax a littl, ree-lax, reee-lax."

"How can you tell, Mowzl? How can you tell if I'm 'empty'?"

"Coz I's seein' wiv mi 'eart, Pippee, n you's doin' good!"

Pip is feeling very strange, like he is floating along like thistledown in the wind. It's lovely one moment and frightening the next. He likes the lovely feeling better than the frightening feeling. Not a very difficult choice, but you try telling those little fear voices to be quiet! They won't listen. Pip has to let them be, and pretend he is thistledown on the wind.

"Pippee, I's seein' you's goin' deep. Oh yes! Pippee! You's seein' Purl! You's seein' Purl! You's gettin' it. Hooray!"

"How do you know I'm seeing Pearl? And who is Pearl anyway?"

"You's seein' wot I's seein' in mi 'eart, n I's seein' Purl, who's mi sista. Orite, Pippee, oh mi goodniss grashus me, you's feelin' great wave now. You be relaxin' a littl more."

"Em, if I relax any more I'll disappear completely!"

"Wot's you seein', Pippee?"

"I'm seeing some strange writing, like hieroglyphs. What does it say, Mowzl?"

"Wot you's seein' iz Mouseze, you's seein' mi cousin Scraggy talkin', n wot e's sayin' iz: *'6 or 7 days bak me goes fishin' n caught one this big! It was Whaley! But e got away'.* Pippee, if you's lettin' it come, you'sll be seein' Scraggee n Mowzl fishin'. I's in a boat fishin', n Scraggz iz sittin' on rivva bank tellin' stories."

"Yes, I see them, I mean you, Mowzl!"

"Now you's seein' wot's appnin' in mi 'eart, n you's seein' mi ome world in yor imaginin'. Scraggz iz mi cousin . . .

"Oh eck, Pippee? Wot's appnin'? Pippee? Calm down! You's

lookin' poorly sorted. Oh dear — Pippee? Wot's appnin'?"

"Where am I, Mowzl? I'm lost. I feel like I'm floating, but I can't see myself anywhere. I'm frightened, Mowzl — help me!"

"You's done plenty, Pippee, n you's nevva done nuffin' like this before."

"Never done anything like this before? Em, this is the scariest thing, ever!"

"You's to be comin' bak, Pippee, pleez be comin' bak to where we woz. Meremba wen buzzybird 'unted Mowzl wen we woz sittin' unda larch tree?"

"Yes."

"We's truly sittin' unda larch tree rite now, coz we azn't moved.

If you's imaginin' where we's iz we'sll be findin' ourself's. Iz you seein' Mowzl sittin' ere? Iz you seein' Mowzl?"

"Er — oh! Yes, you're a bit blurred . . . Em, is that you? Yes! I can see you! What a relief. Hooray!"

"Pippee, I's so appy wiv wot you's done."

"It was spooky just now — ooooo — I feel sick."

"You'sll be orite inna mo."

Pip's eyes are as big as saucers; he sits under the larch tree feeling dizzy and not understanding what has happened. Mowzl keeps watch in case the buzzard should return. He la-la's his little tune: "Laa la laa la laa laa — laa la laa la laa laa."

"Erm?"

"Pippee? P-I-P-P-E-E?" Mowzl spells out, but there's no reply. "Pippee? Iz you talkabl?"

"gurblburblmanglewurzl."

"Ah! Good tri, av anuvva go."

"splooddittumneedoonitay."

"OMG, wot ave we ere appnin'? Ah! Mowzl's kno-in' wot 'as to appn. Pippee, wot you's needin' iz a list. We's now makin' list ov fingz to be doin' — ere goes:

one	be stood up
two	meremba Mowzl
three	run ome
four	be eatin'
five	be drinkin' water
six	meremba Mowzl's brekky
seven	ave a lie-down
eight	get nuvva list rit

You's got a list ov fingz to be doin', Pippee!"

As Mowzl is saying all this, Pip's eyes slowly stop spinning like Catherine wheels, and begin to sparkle again. He stands up, whisking Mowzl up in his hand, and sets off down the hill as fast he can go.

"Yikes! Oratio!" yells Mowzl, as they crash down the hill.

"You'sll be orite now, Pippee!"

After running down the hill, Pip slows down to catch his breath, stopping to lean against an old wall. He puts Mowzl on the mossy wall.

"Em, that was the scariest thing that's ever happened to me. Where was I? I disappeared — gone. I was truly frightened; I'm still frightened!"

"You woz empti, Pippee. I's finkin' you'sll nevva be abl, but you woz. I's finkin' we's needin' somethin' speshl, so let's be goin' to LuLu's, coz she'sll be elpin'."

"Ah, but I've got things on my list. I've got to go to my place and eat something and drink some water."

"You's a list monsta! Orite, let's be goin'."

Pip tucks Mowzl into his hat and walks on. The rhythm of the walking is soothing and the feel of the ground underfoot and the smells of the woodland are soothing too. By the time they get home he's ready to eat something, and he soon feels better.

"Em? What's on the list now?"

"Ave a lie down."

"I don't need a lie down, Mowzl, I feel lots better now, thanks to you."

"Get list rit."

"Let's just go to LuLu's, like we said."

"Yippee! Pippee, you's feelin' betta!"

Scooping Mowzl up, they set off for LuLu's place. On the way Pip thinks about the questions queuing up in his mind. How could he have been able to see Mowzl's world so clearly? Was it a dream? He doesn't know. He still can't think straight.

"Wakey up, Pippee, we's ere."

When LuLu comes to the door, she looks them up and down a little suspiciously, but welcomes them with her soft voice.

"Hallo, you two, what have you been up to? Mowzl, have you been looking after Pip? He looks a bit green."

"E's green orite, LuLu, e's ad a frite n we's needin' yor elp."

"Come in. Muffin has settled in the other room, so let's sit in the kitchen."

Pip sits down at the kitchen table, taking Mowzl from his hat and putting him in the small bowl that LuLu keeps on the table, just for him. Pip stares at Lulu, seeing her as if for the first time, feeling, as he does, like he has just come back from the moon.

She is looking like a spring day. LuLu usually wears beautiful dresses and shawls, and today she is wearing green, and her dark brown hair has a red glow in it.

"Is Muffin alright today?" Pip asks.

Muffin is LuLu's cat. She is so old that she has become very thin, and she seems to glow, like amber, purring even though she is very ill. Muffin's fur is lots of colours mixed up; there's white and black and ginger — a tortoiseshell cat.

"She's been very restless and wouldn't settle in the night, but she's asleep now," says LuLu softly. "She wants company, and she likes me to be present, really *here* for her."

LuLu is quiet, tears welling up in her eyes. She sighs. "I'm going to miss her so much, I can't bear it."

"LuLu, our 'eart's iz achin' for Muffin, you's kno-in' ow we's lovin' 'er, n we's powerin' you wiv our 'earts too. I's sorry to be sayin' it, but we's needin' yor elp, pleez."

"Alright, Mowzl, what can I do?"

Mowzl tells LuLu about what has just happened, as best he can. Pip listens eagerly too, almost as if he hadn't been there. When Mowzl is finished, Pip says that after seeing Scraggy and Mowzl fishing, he felt frightened. He didn't know where he was or who he was, it felt like his body didn't have a middle, and even now he feels lost and frightened.

"Pip," says LuLu gently, "I know you're feeling terrible now, but remember how long it has taken for this to happen! This is a very special day! It's taken a long time and a lot of practice but now it's happening. But you must both be very careful; you must protect yourselves, because when you are empty like that you are very vulnerable."

"Vulnawotzibl?"

"Vulnerable, Em, it means that you could be easily hurt, because you are not protecting yourselves; that is what empty means in a way, it means being open to everything, so we need to protect you from harm."

"LuLu, you's like Purl, she's kno-in' fingz too. Wot's best to be doin'? Iz you kno-in', LuLu?"

"Yes, Mowzl, and it was your sister, Pearl, who told me. Do you remember when we found a mysterious parcel in the bowl of things at Christmas? It was all ragged and written over in funny words and pictures. Well, inside were the presents from Pearl and the others in your home world. There was a note, it's in your bowl of things now, Mowzl, and it said: 'dear mowzl please come home quick we's missin' you luv from us xxx'."

"I's merembrin' perfiklee, n afta parsl come I's feelin' big sad n woz in big urry to get ome."

"I know, Mowzl, it was hard for you. But the presents in the parcel will help you to get home! Pearl sent me some very special wool — well, I think it's wool — and she sent a little drawing of what I should make. Let me show you, I'll fetch the wool and the drawing; you two relax. Pip, you look very pale."

"Ha ha! You should've seen im urlia, LuLu!"

"Did he look bad?"

"Me's finkin' e'd nevva be comin' bak."

"I'm here you know!" Pip protests, feeling a bit overlooked.

LuLu fetches the wool and drawing, putting them on the table.

"Pearl's drawing looks like a little pocket, or pouch, made from wool," she explains. "I think it's meant to be crocheted, because there's a broken crochet hook that came in the parcel too, made from a bit of twig. It's too small for me to use, so I'll use my smallest one."

"LuLu, I's merembrin' . . . I's seen wiv mi eyepeeps a pouchee fing before, but I's not kno-in' where or wen."

"I'll make a pouch for you, Mowzl, but what about Pip? He's much too big!"

"LuLu, pleez be makin' two pouchiz Mowzl size. Me's seein' wot 'as to appn."

"Alright, Mowzl, I will when I have time. Just look at this wool! It's amazing! It's plaited from three threads, which are all two-ply, and they are so fine I can't believe it! It's very beautiful. Right, two pouches you say? I'll make two pouches Mowzl sized."

"I'm a bit lost with all this," says Pip.

"Laa la laa la laa laa! Pippee's lost! Ha! ha!"

"Oh, Em, don't tease him so much! Do you think this wool is special? What could it be? Maybe the pouches will have the power to protect you, but you will have to find a way to be inside them."

"You's rite, LuLu, we'sll be dreamin' into our pouchiz. Purl's givin' us magic wool wot's spinnd bi Freeda n Ping Ling — I's merembrin'! LuLu? Iz wool 'nough for three pouchiz?"

"If they are all the right size for you, Mowzl, there should be just enough for three."

"Pleez be makin' three, LuLu, coz you's comin' too."

"Oh, Mowzl, thank you! Where are we going?"

"We'sll be seein'."

"I need a bit of a lie-down," says Pip, yawning.

"Why not both of you go and have a rest," suggests LuLu. "I'll make the pouches, but don't rush me! I am not going to hurry them. Oh, Mowzl, who are Threeda and Ping Ling?"

"Freeda's Uncle One-Eye's sista, so she's mi aunt, n Ping Ling's mi grannee coz she's mi dad's mum."

"Blimey," says Pip. "What strange names!"

"You'sll be earin' all bout evry one wen we's gettin' 'Wot Appnd' rit."

"Plenty of time for all that," laughs LuLu. "Now off you go!"

And off they go.

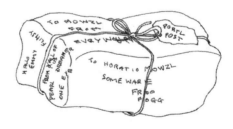

33

Chapter Three

Time Capsules

After leaving LuLu's house Pip is quiet and thoughtful. He doesn't understand what has happened, he doesn't comprehend how he could have seen Mowzl fishing in his home world or how he could have heard Scraggy telling stories.

Mowzl tries to cheer him up, teasing him, singing and laughing, but Pip gets quieter and quieter. He keeps remembering the feeling he had when he disappeared and was seeing Mowzl's home world as though he was actually there.

"Mowzl, I don't want a lie-down, I'm too restless. Let's keep walking, let's go to the woods again."

"You's needin' to be gettin' over yor sadniss, Pippee, n I's avin' idea! Let's be goin' to seaside n cliffs n wind."

"Mowzl, that's a really good idea. Yes! We need the sea! But it's a long way away, we'll have to drive."

"We's avin' to be tellin' LuLu."

They go back to LuLu's and tell her of their plan and she agrees that it's a good idea. She says the pouches will be ready by the time they come home.

Back at Pip's, they collect together the things they will need, like boots, a rainproof jacket and a backpack with food and water — and chocolate! When they're ready, Pip drives the many miles to the seaside, where the cliffs are high, and the wind blows the wildness of the sea over the land.

They walk along the cliff tops with the wind whistling and sea birds screaming. Pip hasn't said a word since they left home. Bit by bit his worrisome thoughts are blown away. As usual, Mowzl is tucked safely into the furry rim of Pip's hat, and they walk — or Pip walks and Mowzl enjoys the ride — for a mile or two. Pip calls out to Mowzl, shouting over the wind:

"Em! I need a rest!"

"Empti tummy!"

"Picnic-stop coming up!"

"Oooray!"

Pip finds a place to climb down to a ledge where tufts of sea-pinks grow in the springy grass. They can sit here, sheltered from the fierce wind. Taking off his backpack, Pip sits on the grass with his back to a rock. He takes Mowzl from his hat, settling him comfortably into a tuft of sea-pinks making sure that a sudden gust of wind won't blow him away — it's a long drop down to the sea.

Opening the backpack, he gets out a bottle of water, an apple, cheese, a box of dried fruit and a small box of chocolates.

"What do you fancy, Em?"

"Pippee, you's always askin' n you's kno-in' perfiklee well, Mowzl's only avin' choklit."

"I know, Em, but it can't be healthy only eating chocolate."

"Really I's eatin' nothin' at all, coz me's a toy mouse in yor world. I's smellin' choklit n I's livin' on choklit foomz."

Mowzl sniffs the box of chocolates and breathes in deeply. "Mmm!"

Pip drinks some water and eats a little food; they listen to the wind and to the waves crashing on the rocks below. They're quiet for a long time, listening and watching the ocean moving.

"Mowzl, I need to talk about what happened."

"Ha! Xaklee!"

"Well, Em, what you mean by 'Wot Appnd' is your story, and I know we need to talk about that, but I mean what happened just this morning, when I disappeared and saw you and Scraggy in your home world. I've not felt right ever since . . ."

"You's poorly sorted orite, Pippee. Be tellin' Mowzl wot's appnin'?"

"Do you remember you kept on saying to me that I must be more empty?"

"I's merembrin'."

"And I said I felt like I had no middle?"

"Yep, I's kno-in' wot you's meanin'."

"I'm hurting, Mowzl," Pip complains.

"Me's deeplee sad you's urtin, Pippee, but you's learnin'."

"I want to feel better."

"Learnin' iz not ow to be feelin' betta, but ow to be betta at feelin'."

"Oh," says Pip, disappointed and a little offended.

They are quiet again. Clouds have hidden the sun for a while, but now they are thinning and moving away; the sun is strong on their faces and sparkles the sea. Wind brings a fine mist from the waves and Pip can taste salt on his lips. His eyes are watering.

"Mowzl, I know you are sad and homesick, and that you are hurting too."

"You's rite. I's wantin' to be wiv the wunz me luvz, but I's not kno-in' ow. You n LuLu's in mi 'eart n I's livin' n real, xcept I's still a toy mouse."

"Did you feel alive when you first arrived in the human world?"

Mowzl is quiet for a while before he speaks, gazing out to sea.

"Mowzl woz feelin' deaded. I's avin' body ov toy mouse wot's not real, n I's feelin' frit n thin."

"What do you mean 'thin' Mowzl?"

"Wot's joinin' me to ome woz stretchin' so thin I's feelin' empti, no Mowzl inside, just thin n frit."

"I think I understand, because that's how I was feeling when we were seeing Scraggy. I was feeling no me inside, and I was frightened. Oh, Em, I'm so sorry for you. I love you with all my might, Mowzl — you know that, don't you?"

"Mi 'eart iz not so full ov frit no more coz you's lovin me, n LuLu's lovin' me, n coz ov bowl ov fingz."

"What's 'bowl of things'?"

"It's where I's puttin' speshl fingz. I's puttin' in all the world but it nevva quite fit, so I's puttin' littl fingz wotz preshus, n feelin' big in mi 'eart, n lov'd fingz n lov'd wunz n lov'd mo-mentz. Bowl ov fingz iz a battree ov livin' feelin', it's a luv battree."

Pip is silent, floating in his imagining. He pictures in his mind the bowl that Mowzl is talking about at home, full of pebbles and feathers, and all sorts of lovely things that Mowzl has collected. He can't quite see how this could be a battery of living feeling.

"Pippee . . . If you's to be ritin' 'Wot Appnd', you's avin to be learnin' again ow to feel feelin's like wen you woz littl. I's come ere to elp you, n we's learnin' you ow to burro inside."

Pip doesn't say anything. Mowzl looks at him and says:

"Pippee?"

"Yes, Em?"

"Ha! Laa la laa la laaa laaa!"

"Oh! Mowzl!"

"You n Scraggz iz made simila, n LuLu n Purl iz made simila. You n LuLu pulled Mowzl ere, you's rescuin' Mowzl wen e's lost in fog afta tyfoon."

"What typhoon, Mowzl? Whatever happened to you?"

"Wot appnd iz lost in fog, n you's avin' to get mi story rit. Wen you's rit story we'sll be seein' through fog togevva."

"Mowzl, I'll do my best, you know I want to help you. But how can I write your story if you don't remember it?"

"You'sll be elpin' us both, Pippee, I's merembrin' wen you's imaginin', like wen you woz littl."

"Is your world like this world?"

"Mi world iz same only it's got no oles n not no oomans."

"What do you mean, 'no holes' Mowzl? And what do you mean, 'not any humans'?"

"Ooman world iz all oles n life skin iz all raggid n torn, coz oomans appnd."

"So, if humans hadn't happened, would this world be the same as your world?"

"World's iz same. Mowzl's omeworld iz ooman world in foocha."

Pip's jaw drops, he stares at Mowzl with wide eyes.

"In the future! *Whaaat?* How do you know that?"

"Coz we's findin' ooman fingz wot's very old, n we's keepin' em in Mouseum bak ome."

"Do you mean 'museum'?

"Me's meanin' Mouseum, n you watch out you izn't loozin' letta 'O', coz we'sll be needin' it, n you watch out letta 'O' izn't rollin' ova cliffs into oshn."

Pip smiles, wanting to know more about this mysterious little mouse and his world.

"What human things have you found in your world?"

"We's findin' all ov ooman kno-lij."

"What?"

"We's findin' wot oomans iz callin' 'time capsules' wot woz berrid fowsandz ov wintaz bak. We's 'ad skolar mouses wotz decipherin' meanin', n gettin' it all rit in Mouseze, n we's learnin' in skool."

Pip sits quietly trying to take this in, wondering if it's all a joke. What a ridiculous idea it is.

"Mowzl?"

"Yip?"

"Just how much in the future is your world?"

"Eight fowzand wintaz, n a bit."

"Oh, my goodness," says Pip, shocked. "This is unbelievable. This is impossible."

"Pippee?"

"Yes?"

"Ha haa! Laaaa la laa la laaa laaaa! O em gee!"

"You rascal, Mowzl! You're teasing me, aren't you? It can't be true! Eight thousand years?"

"Laaa la laaa la laaa laaaa! It's troo, it's troo, no teez!"

"Mowzl, what happens to the humans?"

"oomans iz makin' too mennee oles."

"And?"

"Wild web iz gettin' poorly sorted, n wild fingz iz deaded n life skin iz deaded n it gets very ot. It's all rit in time capsules. Undreds ov wintaz ov ungry n poorly sorted oomans n deaded creachaz n bombz n warz."

"What happened to the humans, Mowzl?" Pip asks again, his voice trembling.

"We's not kno-in'. Mowzl nevva 'as seen oomans, nor 'as Old Ones evva seen oomans."

"Who are the 'old ones'?" asks Pip, not really able to take in what Mowzl is saying; he can't quite believe it, he doesn't want to believe it.

"Mennee wintaz bak, clevva mouses, wot we's callin' 'Old Ones', iz findin' time capsules wen they's burrowin'. Over mennee jennerayshunz ov mouses we's learned, coz we's wantin' to be understandin' ow oomans could evva ave been so clevva n so stupid at same time."

"What did the old ones think happened?"

"Oomans woz xtinctin' mennee creachaz n livin' fingz, coz oomans izn't feelin' inside till too late. P'raps they's 'earts woz broke, p'raps they's avin' no luv battreez. N coz they's not feelin' great wave, they's finkin' they's speshl, n not like uvva creachaz."

"The great wave? You've said that before, what is it?"

"Wot's birfin' all fingz."

Mowzl gazes out to sea.

"You's urtin, Pippee; you's urtin' coz yor 'eart iz feelin' wild fingz dyin', you's urtin coz oomans iz too mennee, n too greedy, n you's urtin coz you's not able to be stoppin' it appnin'."

Seeing Pip's face, Mowzl realises that he has upset him. It's time to stop talking, time to walk again, and enjoy the ocean.

"Let's be movin'," says Mowzl, trying to sound cheerful. "Let's be goin'!"

Pip remains silent as he packs up the picnic things and tucks Mowzl into his hat. They set off along the cliff path once more.

"Pippee!" yells Mowzl, against the wind.

"Yes?"

"Oomans appnd, it's nevva yor fault, oomans appnd."

"But what can I do? I have to do something!" cries Pip.

"Be feelin'. You's nevva kno-in' wot great wave iz bringin'."

Pip walks and walks. He doesn't know whether to believe Mowzl or not. Deep down he knows, because in his heart he believes Mowzl, but the words worry him and hurt him. What does it all mean?

"Pippee?" yells Mowzl, over the wind.

"Em?"

"You's carryin' eavy foughts. You's avin' to let wind blow 'em away. Let's be goin' for miylz n miylz!"

And they walk for miles and miles.

Chapter Four

Home Oak

Pip and Mowzl spend a few days walking the cliff tops by the sea, staying the first night in a barn getting very cold. The next night they stay at a farmhouse B&B, where they warm up again and have a big breakfast. Well, Pip has a big breakfast, but Mowzl has to make do with the fumes of chocolate from Pip's backpack. On the third day, when they've had enough walking, they make their way back to the car and set off for home. Pip doesn't say very much. Mowzl hums and sings a bit, but Pip says less and less.

By the time they get home Pip is very quiet. For the next few days he doesn't want to do anything at all, he doesn't even want to visit LuLu, and one day he doesn't even get out of bed.

Well, that's not quite true, because he gets out of bed when he needs to get something to eat or to drink. And he gets out of bed when he needs to poo or to wee. But otherwise he just stays in bed and doesn't say anything at all.

Today Mowzl is on the windowsill, sitting in what Pip calls the Egyptian Boat, a small wooden thing that's a bit boat shaped and looks a bit Egyptian. The 'Gypshun Boat', as Mowzl calls it, is always on the windowsill and he likes to sit in it to look outside and watch everything going on out there. He can see the street and the houses along the other side, joined together all in a row, their windows reflecting little bits of the houses on his side.

One window across the road, an upstairs window, has 'frosted' glass so you can't see through it very well. It's probably a bathroom. Mowzl can see the pale shape of a model sailing boat with a mast and sails; he sees it through the wiggly glass, a bit like seeing a ship through fog. The sailing boat reminds him of when he was on a ship, and it reminds him of the fog, and of how sad he feels because he can't remember what happened. Maybe telling stories will help — but how can he tell stories if he can't remember what happened?

Mowzl sits on the windowsill watching his thoughts run about like chick-henschasing each other in a farmyard. He slowly feels more himself as his thoughts slow down. He can think more clearly now.

He is thinking about how to get home to Pearl and Scraggy and everyone else in his home world. He must find out what happened to him when he was in the fog, and he needs to know how he got into the fog in the first place — and why did he arrive here in the world of humans? To find out all this, he needs Pippee to write 'Wot Appnd', and for Pippee to write 'Wot Appnd', he has to learn to understand Mowzl's heartspeak, he has to learn how to dream into his pouch — well, when LuLu has made them!

The trouble is, Pippee's not strong enough yet. When he did that disappearing trick it really un-knitted him, and all that talk on the cliff-top about deaded creatures has made him very sad.

What to do?

"I's 'ad an idea! I'sll be tellin' stories!" Mowzl says out-loud without meaning to, but Pip doesn't wake up. To tell stories about his home world he needs Pip to be like a book with empty pages, somehow the stories will come and fill those empty pages. Well, Mowzl hopes the stories will come; he must be trusting of the great wave and the invisible ones.

He wonders if Pip is strong enough yet to listen to a story. If LuLu has finished the pouches she could bring them over and that would help, and she could listen too! *Good idea,* thinks Mowzl, *I'll call her with my heart.*

"Pippee," says Mowzl out loud, "I's wontin' to be tellin' story 'bout mi ome world n me's finkin' you'sll be lovin' it n gettin' betta kwikka. Iz you wontin' story Pippee?"

Silence. Then a little groan, then a sigh. Pip turns over in his bed, but his eyes stay tight shut.

"Mowzl, yes . . ."

Mowzl waits.

"I would love you to tell me a . . .story but . . ."

Mowzl waits some more.

"I won't be able to listen for long."

"You's poorly sorted orite, Pippee. I's 'ad an idea 'bout that, n it's for you to be 'oldin yor pouch in yor 'and. It'll be elpin' you."

"What pouch?" says Pip in a faraway voice.

"You's merembrin' we's askin' LuLu to be makin' pouchiz, n LuLu says she'd ave em done wen we's bak from oshn?"

Pip just lies there, all dull and flat.

"Pippee?"

"Mm."

"LuLu's comin' wiv pouchiz, pleez be stayin' wakeful."

"Mm."

"I's been finkin' 'bout wen we's bi oshn. I's sorry, Pippee, to be sayin' fingz wot's urtin' you."

"It's not your fault, Mowzl."

"You's avin' mor sadniss."

"Mm."

Mowzl thinks about being on the cliffs by the sea, listening to the wind and the birds. It reminds him of another place where there is a high rock, though in that place there is no sea but a river down in a valley. Mowzl is remembering! It's called Eagle Rock and it's in his home world!

There's a tap at the door. LuLu comes in.

"Hallo, Mowzl, I've brought the three pouches. Oh, dear! Pip's not looking good, is he? I should have come sooner . . ."

"E's poorly sorted orite, LuLu. I's avin' idea to be tellin' stories to elp im get betta, but we's needin' pouchiz coz e azn't got 'nough energee to be listnin'."

"Good idea, Mowzl. Here's his pouch. Where shall I put it?"

"Pleez be puttin' 'is pouch in 'is 'and."

"Hmm, that feels good," says Pip sleepily, feeling warmth flow from the pouch through his hand and into his body.

"LuLu, pleez be puttin' Mowzl's pouch in bowl ov fingz wotz bi Pippee's bed."

"Can I listen to the story, Em? Muffin is sleeping, so I've got some time."

"I's opin you's listnin', coz it'll elp if you duz. Pleez be oldin yor pouch n settlin' comfy. LuLu, I's feelin' Muffin in mi 'eart."

"Thanks, Em, I know you are."

"Fankz for makin' pouchiz, I's seein' they's perfik. You's clevva, like Purl."

"You're very welcome, Mowzl," says LuLu, sitting down in the chair by the window.

"Orite, Pippee," says Mowzl, trying to keep Pip awake. "LuLu iz ere n you's avin' yor pouch in yor 'and."

Mowzl sits quietly gazing out of the window waiting for the story to arrive.

"Bein' bi oshn iz merembrin' me ov Eagle Rock, wot's in mi ome world. I'sll be tellin' a story I's callin' ''Ome Oak'.

"'Ome Oak iz a tree growin' where Mowzl iz livin' wiv all frendz n familee. I's merembrin' Eagle Rock, n birdz wot's flyin' over forrist, n I's imaginin' bein' high in the sky like a bird, lookin' down n it's green forrist az far az eyepeepz iz seein' in all direkshnz. Be imaginin' you's a bird, weelin' round n round n divin' n flyin' n comin' closer to the treetops. . ."

Pip and LuLu listen to Mowzl's familiar voice, and with the eye of their hearts they see the sky and the wildwood that Mowzl is describing and they are flying like birds! Lulled by Mowzl's voice into story-sleep, they are hearing Mowzl's heartspeak. It is the magic of the pouches that helps them to understand his heartspeak, even though it is Mouseze.

Are you beginning to see it too? Are you seeing like a bird and looking down? Let the eye of your heart imagine that you are a bird flying high in the sky looking down upon the wide world; you see the wildwood going on forever like a blanket of green. You glide down closer to the treetops, and you see there are hills and valleys, rocks, cliffs and rivers.

You feel the air rushing over your wing feathers as you turn in the air. Looking down you can see a rock, still some way away, where you like to perch to rest and look out across the river valley below. You see a young mouse scrambling under the bushes towards the rock. You swoop closer.

Where the terrain is steep and craggy the trees and plants have only a little soil to grow in, so they don't grow very big and many different sorts to grow side by side. In the summer when the sun is hot, making the rocky ground warm and dry, there is a wonderful scent of thyme and marjoram and wild sage. Close to the river gorge there are rocky out-crops sticking up above the height of the trees and bushes. You fly down towards your favourite rock and land there, folding your wings and ruffling up your feathers as you settle. Relaxed now, you watch the valley below.

Now close your bird-eyes.

You are looking at the bird on the rock, you can see every detail of the beautiful feathers; when it turns its head from side to side, as it watches movements in the valley below, you can see its fierce eyes and sharp bill. You are peering between the stems of the marjoram tuft that you are hiding in. The body that your eyes are looking out from is trembling — it is the body of a mouse. The mouse moves very carefully, turning away from the bird, creeping into the undergrowth as quietly as possible.

The bird is a peregrine falcon, one of the fastest hunters on the wing in the whole world, but this bird is not hunting at the moment, it is resting. Even though it hears the mouse in the scrub it doesn't turn to look, and the mouse is in no danger.

The mouse moves away from the rocky place and back into the woods from where it had come. She is a young mouse, and this adventure, especially the encounter with the falcon, has made her wish to be back at home and that is where she goes — as fast as she can. She sees the familiar oak tree growing close to a mossy cliff and scampers towards it, diving between two great buttress roots and into the entrance of the burrow to her home.

Remember, you are still seeing through the eyes of the mouse! In the burrow it's dark, and she can't see much at all, but she can find her way easily enough, because she has long sensitive whiskers that tell her where the walls of the burrow are, and she can hear the echo of the sounds she makes; as well as these senses, she can smell the damp earth of the tunnel and the familiar smells of her family home, and soon she can hear friendly voices.

Rounding a corner in the burrow she sees a faint light that grows brighter with every step; in another moment she steps from the burrow into a chamber that has a high ceiling of rock, and walls of rock — it's a cave! In one wall of the cave is a small window letting in a warm rosy light.

"Ah! There you are, Nettl," Pearl calls in greeting. "We've been wondering where you were. Are you alright?"

"I was worried, Pearl, and a bit frightened, but now I'm home I'm feeling better. I'll tell you all later."

"Why not tell us now, Nettl?" asks her brother BillBill.

"May I, Pearl?"

"Yes, of course, if you want to."

Nettl tells the story of her morning and how she went out towards the cliff-top to look down at the river, as she loves to do, and how the bird frightened her, and how fast her heart was racing as she turned away, running home as fast as she could go.

Listening to her with eyes wide are some of Nettl's brothers, sisters and cousins.

When Nettl has finished, Pearl says, "I think you have been very brave, and we are all glad that you are safely home, but, Little Garnet, it would be good if you didn't go so far from the burrows all on your own."

Pearl uses Nettl's full name to show how serious she is. Of all the young mice, Pearl is the oldest, except for Beechnut and Acorn, who are Pearl's sister and brother, all born in the same litter. Today, it's Pearl's turn to keep an eye on things, and to make sure that Burrow Cave is kept tidy. Burrow Cave is the name that the mice have given to this cave. It is the heart of their home! It is not only a classroom, but also where all the mice gather to talk and have their meals and their parties; it is the place where everything happens. Sometimes the young mice work on their homework, and other times they do important chores such as cleaning and sorting seeds and nuts ready to be stored in one of the larders. And, of course, there is always tidying to be done, but their favourite activity is when Pearl takes them into the Mouseum, where there are hundreds, no, thousands of interesting things that have been found under the trees of the wood and in the ground, collected together over many winters; and they take some time before choosing something to take back to Burrow Cave, where they will talk about it, write stories, and draw pictures. Some of the treasures are thousands of winters old and one of these treasures, made of coloured glass, has been used to make the window in Burrow Cave.

Sometimes the older mice teach them. They are taught where the burrows lead out from the cave and into the wood, and they are taught which ways to go in an emergency, such as when an owl or weasel comes a-hunting. They are taught how to keep perfectly still and silent when danger threatens and there is no burrow nearby to dive into. Gradually, the young mice learn about the wildwood and the trees that grow the nuts and seeds they need to eat.

Something that all the mice help with every day is gathering and storing food. The older, stronger mice that like being outside go into the woods to find food and bring it back. Younger mice, and the mice not happy to be out in the wilds for too long, work closer to home, and even in the safety of Burrow Cave. Nuts and seeds are brought in, cleaned, and graded. Graded means that every seed and nut is looked at very carefully, in case there is a bug inside, or a crack in the shell. Bad seeds will not keep through the winter and might make other good seeds go bad too. The seeds that don't pass the test are eaten straight away or returned to the wildwood, and the good seeds are spread out to dry before they are taken to a larder to be stored away. There are lots of larders — dry little caves, which open into the burrows leading away from Burrow Cave — and in the autumn these larders must be cleaned out and filled to the top with new nuts and seeds.

One of the mice who loves exploring the wildwood to find food is Pearl's younger brother, Mowzl. He had not been in Burrow Cave when Nettl ran home from her encounter with the scary falcon; he had been out in the woods on his own, quite a long way from home.

While Nettl is telling of her adventure at Eagle Rock, Mowzl is wondering if he knows the way home or not. He sort-of knows the way home and is not frightened, but he's almost frightened in an excited sort of way. Finding new nut bushes and other useful things has become Mowzl's special job, because he is good at exploring, and good at finding his way home.

Feeling nearly lost is a good feeling, because he feels that he is part of the Earth and he loves the wildwood; he knows that it will lead him home. The idea pops into his head of climbing a tree to have a look over the tops of the bushes. He manages to get high enough to see over the smaller bushes, and he notices straight away that there are big trees dotted about. Each tree has its own particular shape, and Mowzl realises he will be able to learn to recognise these shapes and know one tree from another. He is pleased that he has come across a new way of exploring the wildwood and he will enjoy climbing trees until he knows them like the burrows in his own home.

From his lookout in the tree he can see a big oak tree that looks very familiar — it must surely be the one growing nearest to home. Mowzl memorises the direction as best he can, climbs down to the ground and scampers home. He reaches Burrow Cave safely and, although he is tired, he feels very pleased with himself. He has learned a bit more about how to find his way around the wildwood.

~

It has been a hard winter, and spring is slow in coming. There are mild days when the hazel catkins come into flower, filling the air with their yellow pollen, and the little red nut-flowers sparkle in the sun like tiny rubies. But these warm days are a trick, because then the weather changes and the cold returns, freezing everything once again.

The mice like to go foraging outside even though the weather is still cold. There isn't much food to find, but they love to be out in the fresh air running around. A lot of time is spent inside, safe and warm, where they play all sorts of games, have their lessons and listen to stories. One day, Mowzl explains to his sister, Pearl, about his adventures climbing trees, seeing from high up which way to go to get home. Pearl wants him to make a drawing, and they use a stick to scratch the floor of Burrow Cave, which is just hard earth. Mowzl starts to draw little trees in the positions where he remembers them to be. He and Pearl get quite carried away and begin to make up things that aren't there just to make the drawing look better.

"It would be really good if we could keep this drawing," says Mowzl. "Then I could add a bit to it each time I come back from exploring, but it's on the floor in the busiest place in the burrows. It'll get trampled to bits!"

"We could draw it on one of the walls," suggests Pearl. "It would be useful when we teach the little ones. The trouble is the wall is made of stone and too difficult to make scratch marks. We would have to make marks with something else."

"We could ask Uncle One-Eye for help," suggests Mowzl.

"Yes! Good idea, Mowzl! Let's see if he's in his den now."

Pearl and Mowzl set off down the main burrow, which goes from Burrow Cave into the hillside sloping gently uphill. There are openings, left and right, in places where the rock is crumbly, and the mice have made little chambers for bedrooms, larders and junk rooms. Of course, all this burrowing has taken a very long time, as Burrow Bill is only too happy to recount whenever the storytelling urge comes over him. Burrow Bill is Nettl and BillBill's father.

Pearl and Mowzl keep going along the burrow, and as they go further the light from Burrow Cave gradually fades. They don't mind a bit, because their other senses are so good that they can 'see' with their skin and their whiskers, with their noses, their ears, and their whole bodies. Soon, they come to the opening of a chamber which they know, by the smell, to be Uncle One-Eye's. Now, this doesn't mean that Uncle One-Eye stinks and is badly in need of a wash, it means that everybody has a smell that is their very own and not like anybody else's, so if you learn which is which you can tell who's who, just with your nose.

A glow of soft light ahead of them tells Pearl and Mowzl that they are getting close to One-Eye's chamber, and as they move further inside the glow grows stronger until, when they reach the inner chamber — what Uncle One-Eye calls his den — the light is strong enough to read by. The glow is coming from something hanging from the ceiling, above the table where Uncle One-Eye is sitting.

Pearl calls out, "Hallo, Uncle One-Eye, are you at home?"

One-Eye looks up from what he is doing and, seeing the two young mice coming into his den, he smiles a broad smile.

"'Allo, dear niece, 'allo, dear nephew! T'is nice to see thee . . . sit yourselves down . . . would you like . . . what can I do bein' for thee? . . . oh, my word! . . . which ones be ye? . . . it's my memory you see, t'is all full up."

"I'm Pearl, and this is my brother Mowzl. We've come to see you to ask your advice about something, is that alright? Are we interrupting you?"

"Interruptin'? Nooo, not likely my dear, I ree-tired from doin' do you see? Heh-heh! I just be, I 'appy be! Now then, Pearl, now then, Mowzl, what can I do bein' for thee? Eh?"

"You tell the story, Mowzl," Pearl says to her brother.

"Uncle, you know that I go out looking for new trees and bushes where we can collect food . . ."

Mowzl relates the story, with Pearl chipping in whenever she can, until Uncle One-Eye gets the message.

"*Ahaa!* You're needin' a map! I's been tryin' to remember what I's teachin' for my next lesson, 'n now I'm rememberin'! Thank ye! I'll be teachin' all 'bout maps in my next lesson."

"Oh, Uncle One-Eye! That's not fair! Please tell us now!" Pearl pleads with him.

"We-e-e-ll . . . I s'pose 't'would be good practice. Hmm, let me see now — the thing is, what exactly is a map? Let's be 'avin' a look at a map, shall us?"

Uncle One-Eye goes over to a corner of the room where books and boxes are crammed onto shelves that cover the walls from floor to ceiling. It's almost dark in that part of the den, because the soft glow from the mysterious thing hanging from the ceiling doesn't reach that far. He rummages about, returning with two long, round things that look like small logs. He puts them down on the table where they rock gently before settling. In one end of each is a plug, like a cork.

Pearl and Mowzl have never seen anything like this before and are jumping up and down with excitement.

"What's inside? Can we open them?" says Mowzl.

"Patience, ye rascals, be waitin' a little. What's inside be fragile 'n precious, so we wouldn't want to be 'armin' 'em now would we? This time I'll be showin' thee 'ow 't'is done, so then ye'll be knowin'."

Uncle One-Eye picks up one of the tubes, grips the cork, twists, and gently pulls it out of the hollow tube.

"Look inside, children, what be ye seein'?"

"It looks like the tube is made with a hollow plant. It's got very thick sides; I bet it's very strong. Inside I can see something rolled up. Is that the map Uncle?"

"Aye, Mowzl, that it be. The tube is an 'ollo' plant that we's callin' bamboo. 'Tis giant grass! You get the map out by tappin' the tube to see if the map be slidin' out, so you can get 'old of it with your fingers, but if 'e won't budge, you 'as to get your fingers inside, ever so careful, and wind the middle edge o' the map around, makin' the roll a bit smaller, then you can slide 'im out — like so!"

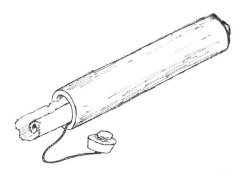

Uncle One-Eye does as he describes, and as he pulls the roll out he holds the tube flat and close to the table. The roll springs open when it is freed from tube but doesn't unroll completely because it has been in the tube for a very long time and is in the habit being rolled up.

"What we 'as to be doin' now is use little stones to be 'oldin' down the corners, so we can be lookin' at the map lyin' nice 'n flat. Pearly, would you be fetchin' some little stone 'eads from the bowl there?"

Pearl does as she is bid. She can hold four of the 'little 'eads' if she cradles them with her hands against her body. The little stones have a shape, but not what she thinks of as head-shaped. When she gets back to the table, Uncle One-Eye has carefully unrolled the map and is holding it down on the table so that it doesn't roll up again.

"That's right m'dear, put an 'ead on each corner 'n we'll see if they's 'eavy enough. If they ain't we'll 'ave to 'ave two. Ah! We 'as another map 'ere, Mowzl please be gettin' some more little 'eads, lad."

"Right-oh."

While picking up stones Mowzl sees other things in the bowl: unfamiliar seeds and coloured pebbles, and spiralling shells much bigger than any he has seen before. He wants to look at everything and, forgetting what he is doing, he gazes into the bowl of things and slips into daydream. He has no idea how long he daydreams while looking into that bowl of things, but suddenly he snaps back, aware of the room again and Uncle One-Eye and Pearl looking at him silently. Mowzl hurries back to the table with the little heads.

"Lose thyself, eh?"

"Er — yes, Uncle, I'm sorry."

"No need for sorry, lad, 'tis full o' magic, that there bowl. Nothin' like spells nor troublesome things, but dreams that show the way. But let's be gettin' back to what's in 'and, plenty of time for all that 'nother day! Now look-ee 'ere, young 'uns, this 'ere is a map. Most be sea, with marks showin' where islands be, and names be writ 'n signs mark'd tellin' of what ye may find, beach or reef or island — like where is to be found sweet water, or good food, or if the folk be fierce or fair. So, if ye be sailin' in those there seas, ye can navigate isle by isle and be knowin' where ye be."

"Uncle, what's navigate?" asks Pearl.

"Navigatin' is findin' your way by stars 'n sun 'n map, so you's steerin' your ship 'n not be lost in the great ocean."

"How do you use a map to help you steer the right way?"

"You've 'it the nail on the 'ead my young scholar! The map 'as got to 'av a top 'n a bottom, a right 'n a left. Well, the top we're callin' North 'n the bottom be South. Where the sun rises be East — that be on the right-side o' map — 'n where the sun be goin' to bed be West — that'll be on the left side o' map. On this 'ere map there be an arrow pointin' sort of up: 'n there's a big N. What be that meanin' lad?"

"North!" cries Mowzl.

"That's it. Some maps be showin' North only, so you 'as t'be remembrin' which way around they be! This 'ere map 'as 'em all writ, 'cept for W what's got torn away, or burned, 't'is very old. So be learnin' straight ways: We's Never Eatin' Snakes, WNES, what be West, North, East 'n South. Stand facin' North, we's never eatin' snakes, W on your left hand, N straight ahead, E on your right hand, 'n S sneakin' up behind ye! Get it? So, little by little we be findin' our selfs. Next, you makes your first mark of a place — I's been thinkin' 'bout your trees 'n the wildwood 'n all — you be sayin' the oak what's near Burrow Cave be a special shape, 'n it be 'ome, so make your mark for 'Ome Oak in the middle of your map. This be your first mark."

Silence.

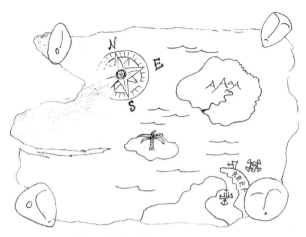

"Erm, Uncle?" says Mowzl.

"Yep?"

"There's nothing to make the first mark with, and nothing to make the first mark onto. How can I make a map?"

"Ahh! I shall be givin' ye such things lad, don't fret 'bout that now. What you 'as to be thinkin' on now is 'ow to set about makin' your second mark on your map. Tell me what you're a-thinkin' now."

Pearl is grinning, looking pleased.

"Uncle! We need to find out what our next mark is first — and where it is. Would it help to imagine seeing the wildwood with the eyes of a bird flying high in the sky?"

"You be right, Purly, it would be 'elpin' to see like a bird. A map is tryin' to be like the woods you be walkin' in, but little and tiny, like a bird would see from on 'igh. 'Ow to mark your second tree? What 'ave you to be findin' owt?"

"Well, we need a name for the second tree, so we don't get muddled up," suggests Mowzl. "and we need to find out how far away it is from Home Oak — oh — and which way."

"Good, Mowzl, good, 'n ow's ye findin' out?"

"I don't know, Uncle."

"What's you reckonin', Pearly?"

"I've been thinking, wouldn't it help if we knew which way up the wood is?"

"Which way up the wood is? What do you mean, Sis?"

"Well, if you could stand underneath Home Oak and say, 'that way is North', then we would know which way up the wood is, and then we would know which way up the whole wildwood is."

"Pearl, you're a genius! Uncle, how can we find out which way up the wood is?"

Uncle One-Eye's one eye sparkles; he is enjoying how the young ones are taking on the challenge he has set them. He wants to help them, but he mustn't give too much away otherwise they won't think it out for themselves.

"Tell me all ye be knowin' about North, South, East 'n West."

"The easiest is East and West," says Pearl. "because we can see where the sun gets up in the morning and where it goes to bed in the evening. We can put arrows up at the bottom of Home Oak pointing to East and to West."

"Ah, yes, Purl, good; 'n North 'n South?"

Mowzl remembers a school lesson about this. "We've learnt in school that warm places face towards the sun and cold places face the other way, and never get the sun on them. I think I remember someone saying that the warm direction is south, but I don't know why."

"Good, Mowzl. We'll be 'avin all this in school again. The sun be shinin' in the southern sky 'cos we's livin' in the north part o' the world; if we be livin' in the south part o' the world the sun would be shinin' in the northern sky. What's next with your map?"

"We can stand underneath Home Oak and see which way is south by the direction of the sun," Pearl is feeling confident that she understands now. "If we choose another tree not far away, one we can see from home, we could say, well, that tree is between north and east and it is so many paces away."

"Ha-ha! You're goin' to be great explorers! Well spoke, Pearl, what you've called 'tween North and East' we's callin' North-East. What 'bout how far away it be, 'so many paces'? Who's doin' the pacin'?"

"It would work if the paces are all the same size! We could call them Mowzl paces."

"Alright, that'll be doin' for now, we'll be comin' back to that. So, what's next?"

"I think I get it," says Mowzl. "Are we ready to go and do it?"

"Always in a rush, you young 'uns. You be waitin' a mo! Let's be seein' what can be found to 'elp."

Saying this, Uncle One-Eye goes over to the shelves again to do some more rummaging. He finds the things he wants and brings them back to the table.

"Mowzl, be tryin' this for size, 'n you, Pearly, be tryin' this."

He holds up two old backpacks, and Mowzl and Pearl put their arms through the straps while Uncle One-Eye helps to tighten them up.

"Thanks, Uncle! It fits me well! I like it," Pearl is pleased.

"Mine fits too, Uncle," says Mowzl. "It's just right; it'll be useful for carrying things to keep my hands free for climbing."

"That's what I's been a-thinkin'," says Uncle One-Eye. "'N 'ere's some o' the things you'll be a carryin'."

He shows them a small tube with a cork in the end, a roll of wafer thin birch bark, another, even smaller, tube, and some pieces of charcoal stick to write with. He explains that the charcoal will be a bit messy and will smudge but not to worry, because they should come back to see him, and he will show them how to make a proper map using ink that won't smudge.

Pearl is very curious about all these unusual things, and she asks, "Uncle, how did you make all these things?"

"I's makin' some of 'em, lass, but not all, you see. Lots o' these treasures be comin' from far away, 'n some are older than the wildwood itself. When I was young as ye be now, I was off adventurin', 'n a ship took me far away. I learn'd me the ways o' the sea, findin' me sea-legs in a storm when the ship is 'eavin' 'n rollin', 'ow to navigate by the stars, 'n 'ow to make all manner o' things, 'n splice a rope 'n dance the 'ornpipe — talkin' of it now brings me back to it, 'n I do be missin' the old life."

One-Eye is silent for a moment, looking into the distance with a misty eye. His voice is suddenly stern when he speaks again.

"Let me alone now. Be off with ye! Leave me to my memories!"

While talking, One-Eye has been putting the birch bark and

charcoal back into the bamboo tubes, pushing the corks firmly into place and putting the tubes into the backpacks that Pearl and Mowzl are wearing. He hurries the two young mice out of his den, gruffly saying, "Now be off with ye, 'n be comin' back tellin' 'ow your maps be goin'!"

With that, he turns away, disappearing back into his den.

Pearl and Mowzl are very surprised by One-Eye's sudden fierceness as he pushes them out of his den, leaving them in the darkness of the tunnel once again. They keep still while their senses adjust to the dark.

"I meant to ask about the light," whispers Pearl. "How does that thing make such lovely soft light?"

"I don't know, Pearl, I meant to ask about that too. There were so many things I want to know, but I didn't know where to start. Those little heads, and that bowl of things!

"And what did he mean 'a ship took me far away'? What ship?" asks Pearl.

"I don't know, Pearl, maybe now we've started talking with him he'll tell us more, bit by bit. We must visit him more often!"

"Yes, we will, but now let's go and do some . . . umm, what did he call it? Map making?"

"Alright, but I need to get something to eat first — and I'm thirsty!"

"Me too!" cries Pearl. "Let's get something to eat!"

And off they go.

Chapter Five

Pouches and Things

After telling the story of Home Oak, Mowzl sits quietly in the Gypshun Boat on the windowsill in Pip's bedroom. Through the window he watches two wood pigeons perched on an electricity cable stretched between tall poles. One of the pigeons is sidling along the cable towards the other pigeon, which jumps up and flies a short way along before settling again. Her admirer starts his courting all over again, sidling towards her, and up she flies again. Mowzl smiles, but his thoughts are with his family in his home world and his heart aches with the missing of them.

LuLu and Pip are asleep, so his thoughts run free while he waits. He thinks about the things that he wants to talk to them about. He wants to talk about the pouches and about dreaming and about the bowl of things — but this is all too much for Pip, or has been until now.

It might be different now because Pip and LuLu loved the story. Mowzl could tell they loved the story from watching their faces while he was telling it. Pip had been lying very still and his face began to light up, even to smile, instead of being dark and closed; and LuLu was smiling all the time! LuLu wakes up first.

"Mmm, Mowzl, what a lovely story. It's so nice to hear about your world and about your family; I'd like to write down all of their names, so I don't get muddled up. Uncle One-Eye is very mysterious! I'd love to know more about him."

"I's appy you's likin' story, LuLu, n we'sll be gettin' names rit wen Pippee's ritin' 'Wot Appnd'."

"Let's hope that happens soon, but now I must go because I've left Muffin alone for too long already. I'll come back later with something for Pip to eat. Thanks for the story!"

"Be tellin' Muffin we's feelin' 'er in our earts, LuLu, n pleez be movin' Pippee's pouch to bowl ov fingz; n LuLu — be merembrin Mowzl's tummy!"

"I'll have to see if I can find some nuts for you to eat."

"LuLu!"

"I know, Mowzl, don't worry!"

~

Mowzl feels tiredness pulling him down into sleep. He scrambles over to the bowl of things on the chest of drawers and climbs into his pouch. This is the first time that he has touched his pouch, and snuggling into it now, he feels the warmth of the wool and the curious softness of it. Well done LuLu!

He thinks of Pearl, who sent the parcel of wool with the drawing of the pouch, and he thinks of Auntie Threeda and Granny Ping Ling who spun the wool; he feels very happy to be wrapped in something that they made with their own hands.

He drifts off to sleep dreaming of Pearl, and of oak trees and Burrow Cave, and of Uncle One-Eye's bowl of little heads. He dreams of oak trees again, seeing a woodland scene with sunlight streaming down through the canopy of leaves lighting the branches. Clinging to a branch is a woodpecker moving in a jerky way looking for insects. He moves as though held to the tree by a magnet and, even though he is often upside down underneath a branch, he shinters about quite happily.

Mowzl is interested. His interest makes the woodpecker come closer, or so it seems; in fact it is Mowzl moving closer to the woodpecker! The woodpecker notices Mowzl straight away.

"Upon my word!" he exclaims. "Never before have I seen anything so strange! A mouse floating in mid-air! What sort of a creature are you?"

"Allo, mi name iz Oratio Mowzl n I's a mouse. Iz I really floatin' in mid-air? Iz you a woodenpecka?"

"Hallo, Horatio Mowzl! What a splendid name! My name is Rattltap and I'm a woodpecker, yes, but please, not a wooden pecker; and yes you are floating in mid-air and you seem to be wrapped in something — it reminds me of a cocoon."

Mowzl is floating in his pouch! He is here in the woods with Rattltap and at the same time he is asleep in the bowl of things in Pip's house! He is so surprised that he starts to wobble and feel dizzy, because he is so high up.

"Oh, mi goodniss! Iyz fallin'! Yikes!"

"Steady, Horatio Mowzl, I've got you."

Rattltap flies to Mowzl and, holding a thread of the pouch in his bill, he tows Mowzl to a nook in a branch and settles the pouch safely there.

"Fankz, Rattltap, I's feelin' giddee, I's nevva been in mi pouch before."

"Hmm. I should think it takes some getting used to. Mowzl,

it seems to me that you are not quite like other mice that I have had the pleasure to meet. Where do you come from?"

"Rattltap, I's first avin' to be askin', iz we in ooman world?"

"Yes, we are in the human world, you are correct, Horatio Mowzl."

"I's from uvva world where no oomans iz, n me's a real mouse in mi ome world. In yor world I's a toy mouse, but I's avin' an 'eart n real feelin's."

"I have no doubt that what you say is true! Why have you come from another world?"

"I's pulled bi a thread through a fog, n all iz mystry."

"I see," says Rattltap. "What have you discovered about this world?"

"I's needin' wild talk wiv creachaz, coz oomans 'as forgot, n oomans iz all evry where, n too mennee, n wild web iz urtin'."

"Mowzl, you are quite right. If you want wild talk, I know the creatures will be glad to tell you what is happening, and I will help you to meet them. Look! I see Priklstik down there now; let's go and say hallo to him!"

Rattltap flies from the high branches, and with a 'Tchak — Tchak' he swoops towards the tree nearest to Priklstik, settling on the trunk close to the ground.

Mowzl floats away from the branch in the tree above, his pouch moving by itself — or so it seems. He is beginning to feel the soft way of the pouch and to understand that the pouch moves as his feelings move. His worry has gone now, and he feels a great surge of joy! He is feeling the invisible ones — beings from before time who are wise and see the many worlds happening.

Mowzl is glowing with wonder and delight by the time he reaches Rattltap and Priklstik.

"Ah, Mowzl, I see that you are no longer frightened of your cocoon! Let me introduce you to Priklstik; Priklstik — Mowzl."

"Allo, Priklstik, mi name iz Mowzl n I's a mouse."

"Hallo, Mowzl! I'm very happy to meet you, and what a surprise! I think there's some magic here with your cocoon. What fun! I'm a hedgehog, as you might have guessed."

"I's meetin' edj oggz in mi ome world, Priklstik, n they's yor cousins. Ow I's come ere to yor world iz mystry, but now I's ere I's seein' big urt appnin', coz wild web iz breakin'. I's wantin' to be learnin' from creachaz 'bout wot's appnin'."

"You're right, Mowzl, the wild web is being torn by what

humans and their machines are doing. I've got a lot to say about it, if you've got the time to listen, and I'm grumpy about it I can tell you. Everyone I know is cross too, wouldn't you say, Tappers?"

"Rattltap, if you please! Yes, indeed, we creatures have been trying to tell the humans for a long time about what they are doing, but they don't seem to hear us . . ."

"I's avin' idea!" Mowzl interrupts. "Xcept I's only feelin' it appn this minnit so I's avin' to wait a mo."

Rattltap and Priklstik wait patiently for Mowzl's idea to arrive.

"I's avin' a plan to be bringin' littl oomans to be learnin' from creachaz."

"A noble idea, Master Mowzl," declares Rattltap. "But the human cubs no longer understand the wild talk."

"He's right, Mowzl, we've tried and tried," grumbles Priklstik.

"Pouchiz iz bringin' magic wot'll be elpin' ooman cubz to be learnin' wild talk. Pleez be elpin', we's needin' oomans to be wakin' up. Pleez be elpin' wen Mowzl's bringin' littl oomans."

"What fun! Ha-ha!" says Priklstik, laughing delightedly. "Yes of course you can count on us, Mowzl. Oh! I do look forward to some fun. Make sure it's soon, as I'm preparing to sleep for the whole winter."

"I agree with the hedgehog," said Rattltap solemnly. "I will help whenever I can. But now I must go to my beloved Tattlrap who calls me. It is an honour to meet you, Horatio Mowzl, goodbye for now! Tchak!" And off he flies.

"I's feelin' I's avin' to be goin' too, Priklstik, fankz for everythin'."

Mowzl begins to look a bit see-through; he gets fainter and fainter, finally disappearing with a little pop.

"By the bristles on my back! Never have I seen anything so strange! Ha! What fun! Goodee! Ha-ha!" Laughing and muttering to himself, Priklstik shuffles off into the dry leaves and undergrowth looking for tasty morsels to eat.

~

Mowzl wakes up in his pouch in the bowl of things in Pip's bedroom. He feels wonderful! He has loved purling in his pouch and talking with creatures and feeling the invisible ones so close has filled him with happiness. The storytelling is working!

He thinks of Pearl and of the memories that the story of Home

Oak has awoken in him. He's been longing for home, but now he has the feeling that he knows what to do; he doesn't know quite what it is, but it feels like he's got a compass inside him and it's saying, 'this way'!

Pip starts to fidget.

"Pippee, iz you sleepin'?"

"Yes."

"Oh . . ." Mowzl pauses a moment.

"Iz you likin' story?"

"Yes, Mowzl, thank you. Loved it . . ."

Mowzl waits for Pip to catch up with himself.

"I feel so sad for you, missing your home so much. There's so much I want to ask, so many questions . . ."

"There's no urry, Pippee."

Mowzl smiles to himself. This has been the most Pip has talked since he got ill and went quiet.

"Mowzl?"

"Yip?"

"Do you think I'm ever going to get well?"

"You's not deaded yet."

"I don't want to be deaded, I want to be well!"

"You's bein' re-knittd, you's avin to be slow."

"Mowzl, what do you mean 're-knitted'?"

"You's merembrin' wen LuLu knitz wrong, n unduz all she's knut, n knitz it all again?"

"Yes, I know, it's hard to believe it! She undoes hours of work and just knits it again! Well, what about it?"

"Bein' poorly sorted iz wen you's un-knittd, n knut new."

Silence.

"Does that mean I'll be different, Em?"

"You'sll be different, Pippee."

"How? Why?"

"It's a mystry. We's all avin' bad abbits of seein', n we's all needin' re-knittin' now n again."

"Do you mean we get ill because we need to be re-knitted?"

"Xaklee rite."

They are quiet for a bit, thinking or dozing. Mowzl watches the pigeons still dancing on the wire. They must love each other very much.

"Iz you merembrin wen you's seein' me n Scraggy fishin'?"

"I remember only too well, I shall never forget that, Em. I was thinking about it when you started to tell the story of Home Oak."

"You's been poorly sorted evva since, coz you woz un-knittd n nevva got re-knut. Now you's bein' re-knut, n wen you's 'nough betta we'sll go in our pouchiz."

"I want to go in the pouch now, Mowzl. When LuLu gave me my pouch to hold while you were reading the story I felt stronger and happy."

"Pippee, you's not enough well to be dreamin' in yor pouch."

"Can you tell me what they are?"

"Wot wotz iz?"

"The pouches."

"They's littl bags knut bi LuLu."

"Oh, Mowzl! You mischievous mouse! Yes, I know they are little bags crocheted by LuLu, but what is their magic?"

"You's askin' dangerus fingz, Pippee."

"But I want to know!"

"Pouchiz iz speshl coz of wotz inside. Wotz inside iz bein's, but they's invizibl beins."

"Do these invisible beings live in the pouches?"

"They's not livin' in pouchiz xaklee, they's livin' all evry where. Pouchiz iz for mouses to be imaginin' wotz invizibl, oomans iz imaginin' angels. Angels iz'nt really real, but they's ooman's way ov imaginin' invizibl bein's coz you 'as to make 'em look like oomans."

"Angels? Angels look like humans with wings!"

"You's gettin' it! That's wot oomans iz imaginin'. Wot we mouses iz imaginin' iz pouchiz, n wotz inside iz avin' no shape at all nevva, xcept they 'as a glow wot you might be seein' one day."

"How big are they?"

"They's avin' no sizeniss."

"So why the little pouches?"

"Be keepin' up, Pippee! Pouchiz iz Mowzl size, n angels iz ooman size, it's wot you's xpectin', tis all. We's wantin' to be feelin' close wiv invizibl bein's, n we's avin' pouchiz 'oldin' us."

"Why do we want to be with them?"

"Coz they's from before time, n they's wize, n they's seein' all worlds appnin'."

"Em, you'll have to explain that as well!"

"It's unwordabl, coz they's diffrent."

"How do you know all this, Mowzl?"

"You'sll be seein' wen we's in our pouchiz feelin' evry fing."

"Mowzl, when will I be able to go in my pouch?"

"Wen you's abl, you'sll dream in yor pouch n be floatin'.'"

"Will you be with me?"

"I'sll be wiv you, Pippee."

"Em, I need to sleep now."

After a bit, Pip says sleepily, "Mowzl, thank you. Thank you for everything. Thank you for coming to our world."

And with that, he drifts off to sleep.

Mowzl smiles, looking out of the window watching his thoughts running about like little chick-hens.

~

"Hallo, Mowzl!" whispers LuLu, coming quietly into the room, "I've come to see how you two are getting on."

"Allo, LuLu, I's been missin' you, n opin' you's orite, n opin' Muffin's orite too."

"Thanks, Em. Thanks for thinking of us."

"Me's feelin' ov you, LuLu, me's not a finka really."

"Oh, Em, you are lovely."

LuLu sits in a chair next to the window so that she can be close to Mowzl and to Pip. She sees that Pip's expression is lighter than when she last saw him.

"Mowzl, he looks a bit better, don't you think?"

"Yip, e's a littl betta, n e luvd story n woz talkin lotz afta."

"That's good, he's been quiet for too long."

"Anuvva story you's avin' wen e's wakin'.'"

"Oh, Em, I've been missing you too. Are you alright?"

"Fingz iz lookin' up, n Pippee's learnin' lotz n I's appi."

"That's good."

"But itz urtin bein' real in ooman world, LuLu," Mowzl says quietly.

"Oh, Mowzl!"

"You's kno-in' wot I's meanin'?"

"Yes. Being hurts, for some, like you and me."

"N Pippee."

"Yes, and Pip too."

"LuLu, I's kno-in' wot urtz you too."

"Thanks, Em, thank you for being in our world. I know you didn't mean to come here, and it must be very difficult. Remember, Em, we love you very much."

"You's elpin me be real, LuLu, n elpin mi 'eart be nough big to be 'oldin all feelin's, feelin's ov bein' toy mouse wotz real, n missin' 'is ome world."

"Tell me about your family, Mowzl."

"I'sll be tellin' all in stories now Pippee's enough well. I's not merembrin' xcept wen story appns."

"Will you wait for me to come back before you tell another story, Mowzl?"

She pauses. "Look, here's some salad for Pip and chocolate for you. Please make sure he eats, and he must drink lots of water too."

"Fankz for choklit, LuLu. Orite, I'sll feed im. Wen's you returnin'?"

"Soon, you will know."

"LuLu, you's avin' purlniss."

"What's pearlness?"

"Like wot Purl iz."

"Does that make you sad, Em, that I'm like Pearl?"

"Mi 'eart glowz warm."

"I'm glad. I'll come back later, Mowzl."

"Later! Bi!"

~

Mowzl breathes in the smell of the chocolate that LuLu put beside the Gypshun Boat.

Mmm, he thinks, *I wish I could eat it really properly.*

You might be wondering how Mowzl can think in human words; well, he's actually thinking in Mouseze, but we wouldn't understand it at all if Pip wrote in Mouseze, so he writes it all down in human words. Simple. Well, it's not quite so simple, because Pip doesn't know he's doing it, he writes the words when he's asleep! You've heard of sleepwalking — this is sleep-writing!

Pip is asleep now, but he's not writing anything at the moment. Mowzl sits comfortably in the Gypshun Boat looking out of the window and looking into his heart. He thinks of LuLu's question

about her pearlness making him sad. LuLu's pearlness reminds him of Pearl and of his family, and he feels a stab of homesickness, but at the same time he feels good, because it brings Pearl closer.

He lets the thoughts flit about like little chick-hens, and he feels the warmth that has happened in his heart spread through his whole body.

~

Pip dozes and wakes, half in and half out of sleep. He opens his eyes, yawns, and sighs deeply.

"One day I'll sigh like that and it will be my last breath!"

"Ha-ha! Pippee, you's not deaded yet!" Mowzl jumps down from the windowsill onto the bed and scampers over the bedclothes to get close to Pip's face. He jumps up and down on his chest ignoring Pip's shouts of protest, and he sings —

"In yor eerz, in yor eyz, up yor noze,
in yor 'air where yor borld patch growz,
on yor chin, down yor neck n in yor beerd,
you'll nevva catch me coz I's dis appeerd!"

Pippee splutters and laughs — and is awake!

"Mowzl, you little rascal, I'll get you for that, just you wait!"

Mowzl jumps onto Pip's tummy and bounces about.

"Pippee, you's gettin' too fin, not enough pudge for Mowzl to ave a good bounce. You's not eatin' enough, n you's kno-in' choklit iz bestest food."

"I know you live on chocolate fumes, Mowzl, but I must eat healthier things to get me well again."

"Good, n you's rite. Ere's food wot LuLu brung, n you'd betta ave it et before she's returnin'!"

"When's LuLu coming back? Was she here earlier? I don't remember. I'd love to see her."

"Inna mo."

"Oh."

"Inna mo."

"You said that already. How long's a mo?"

"Lastic."

"Like a rubber band?"

"Xaklee. So, a mo iz lookin' like this — " Mowzl stretches his arms out sideways:

"Meanin' a littl bit ov time wot takes agiz to appn. Or a mo iz

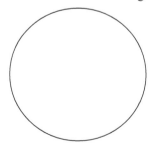

lookin' like this —," Mowzl holds one arm up and one arm down, stretching as high as he can.

"Wotz meanin' a littl bit ov time wot appns before you's kno-in'; or a mo iz lookin' like this —," Mowzl stretches both arms up as high as they will go, bringing them down sideways stretching out making a circle.

"Wot iz a littl bit ov time wotz nevva endin'. Ha-ha!"

"Em, you're a genius. When will LuLu come back?"

"Wen you's et."

"Ah! Alright."

Pip sits up and opens the food box that LuLu left beside the bed. Inside there's a salad and a fork to eat it with. He stirs the salad to mix in the dressing and begins to eat hungrily. It's made with grated carrots and beetroot, chopped apple and celery and spring onions, with feta cheese and sunflower seeds. Mmm! And it's a brilliant zingy dressing! Well done LuLu.

Mowzl has climbed back up to the windowsill and is sitting in the Gypshun Boat, looking out of the window. He has a secret smile on his face.

LuLu taps gently on the door, coming in quietly in case Pip is still asleep. She is happy to find him looking much better.

"Hallo, LuLu!" says Pip. "I'm very happy to see you. Mowzl has been telling me a story about his home world; I'm sorry you missed it. Thanks for bringing me food. I've eaten it all and it was delicious!"

"I'm glad you liked the food, Pip, it's good you've eaten something at last. I didn't miss the story, I was here when Mowzl told it. You've not been well, Pip, and you've not been remembering everything, but you seem much better today."

"LuLu, ow'z Muffin?" asks Mowzl.

"Oh, Muffin!" cries Pip. "How is she? I miss her; I haven't seen her for ages."

Lulu sits down in the chair by the window, taking a few moments to compose herself before speaking.

"Muffin's very poorly today and she's needed company, but she settled down to sleep eventually. She's purring a lot, and sometimes she goes off into a dark corner where she purrs to herself. I'm learning about the different purring sounds that she makes, and some are just for her. I am worried about her; she is so thin, and she eats hardly anything. She's becoming an elemental being."

"LuLu, Muffin's becomin' invizibl one, n she's purrin' wiv invizibl ones."

"How long has Muffin been with you?" asks Pip.

"Nearly twenty years. She was six weeks old when she came to me. I went with a friend to a place where they look after abandoned cats. I didn't mean to end up with a kitten because I wasn't well and thought I wouldn't be able to look after a kitten, but she chose me and sat on my lap. That night, she overcame her fear and scrambled onto my bed; she slept over my heart all night long."

"LuLu, you's not to be worryin' bout Muffin, she's 'ad big luv all er life, n she's becomin' a luminous bein'."

"Thanks, Em, I just can't imagine her not being here. But I don't want to think about it, it hurts too much. Let's talk about Home Oak!"

"We'sll ave to be talkin' 'bout Muffin later, LuLu, let's be merembrin'."

"I will remember, Em, thanks."

Pip has a puzzled look on his face.

"Em, let me get this straight. I've been thinking about your story, and I'm a bit muddled about who's who. Pearl is your sister, Uncle One-Eye is your uncle — and Scraggy —?"

"Scraggz iz mi cousin, who's dad iz Uncle One-Eye; BillBill n Nettl iz mi cousins who's dad iz Burrow Bill."

"Mowzl!" cries LuLu feeling excited. "I want to hear more about them — and everybody! What lovely names! Can we draw a family tree?"

"I's kno-in' wot you's meanin', LuLu, n afta story we'sll make a nametree. Iz you avin' yor pouch?"

"Yes, Mowzl. I've been keeping my pouch with me all the time, and I hold it in my hand; it's like putting on a woolly jumper on a cold day, only better. Is it alright to do that, Em?"

"Orite for a bit, nevva always, coz pouchiz 'as to be livin' in bowl ov fingz sometimes."

"Why's that, Em?" LuLu asks.

"Uncle One-Eye's bowl of little heads!" exclaims Pip.

"You's rite, Pippee, n welcum bak from yor dreamin'! Uncle One-Eye's bowl ov littl eads iz 'is bowl ov fingz, n it's a battree for dreamin'. So pouchiz 'as to be livin' in bowl ov fingz."

"Oh, Mowzl, I'm lost now!" says LuLu.

Pip's eyes are far away. Maybe he understands, maybe he doesn't. Maybe he's asleep with his eyes open!

"LuLu you's not to be urryin', coz you'sll be seein' clear soon."

"Thanks, Mowzl."

Mowzl jumps down from the windowsill onto Pip's chest and

starts leaping about and singing, and soon LuLu is singing too. Pip wakes up from his daydreaming and laughs and protests. Mowzl's song goes like this:

"Duz yor eerz ang low? Duz em wobbl to n fro? Can you ty em in a bow? Duz yor eerz ang low . . .?"

"Alright! I'm back, I'm awake, stop! Stop!" splutters Pip.

Mowzl climbs back to the windowsill and settles in the Gypshun Boat.

"Pippee, 'as you energee nough for story?"

"Yes! I'm awake now, Em, I'd love another story."

"LuLu, pleez be givin' im 'is pouch."

LuLu fetches the pouch and puts it into Pip's hand.

"Thanks, LuLu, that's nice," he murmurs.

Mowzl is silent, gazing out of the window waiting for the story to arrive. LuLu and Pip relax, their pouches in their hands, feeling the strange and lovely warmth spreading through their bodies.

"Be settlin' n openin' yor eerz n yor earts, n be 'oldin yor pouchiz in yor 'ands n I'sll be tellin' ov wen leavz 'as all fallen coz it's winta in mi ome world. Mouses iz inside Burrow Cave keepin' warm n playin' n singin', n outside iz dark n wintry."

Pip and LuLu close their eyes, relaxing with the sound of Mowzl's voice as he begins the story. As they drift into story-sleep, a little magic happens that has something to do with the pouches. Perhaps they go to sleep and hear the story as a dream, but whatever the magic is, they are hearing Mowzl's heartspeak and understanding it like it is their own language.

And the story begins . . .

Chapter Six

Snow!

There's a small window in the wall of Burrow Cave made with red glass; Scribbla says that humans made the glass a very long time ago. When sunbeams find their way through the clouds and shine through the trees, they sometimes find their way through the red window and light up the wall at the back of Burrow Cave. A wobbly bit in the middle of the red glass causes the light to focus into a bright spot on the wall inside the cave.

As summer comes to an end and autumn turns to winter, the morning sun rises a little further towards the South each day, and the days shorten. On mornings when the sun manages to reach Burrow Cave, the bright patch of light on the wall, at the moment of sunrise, moves a little further round each day.

Now, One-Eye knows a thing or two about stars and navigating and Never Eating Snakes. He likes to make a mark on the wall of Burrow Cave with one of his marking sticks — which, some of the mice whisper, is dipped in octopus ink — at the moment of sunrise, and as the year goes on towards winter, the mark moves along the wall, towards the back of the cave.

In the depths of winter there are often such thick clouds that the sun doesn't shine at all, but on days when the wintry skies are blown clear of cloud and the sunbeams can reach the cave, One-Eye will be there, with his marking stick, waiting for sunrise.

Towards the middle of winter One-Eye's marks on the wall advance more slowly and get closer together, until, on a certain day, the marks begin to move back the other way, a little each day. The year has turned! The light is returning! A new year has begun! This is the best news and deserves a special party.

Even so, it is still the middle of winter and though the year has turned, and the sun is climbing a little higher every day, there is more winter still to come and it will be cold for many moons yet. The wood mice sleep a lot in winter, snuggled up in sleeping chambers with lots of dry grass and moss, gathered in the summer. However, wood mice don't hibernate, unlike dormice and hedgehogs who sleep right through the cold until the spring comes — which is why they have to eat so much in the autumn.

Everyone at Burrow Cave is looking forward to Spring coming, and hopes are high, but the winter has a surprise in store. One night it snows and when the snowstorm ends there are deep drifts, and the entrance to Burrow Cave is well and truly buried. When the sun rises in the morning the light coming through the red window is much brighter than usual, reflecting the whiteness of the snow onto the ceiling in an unusual way.

The young mice are very excited, because they have never seen snow before, and they want to go outside and play, but they can't go out yet. The entrance is blocked, and a tunnel will have to be dug through the snow.

The mice begin to tunnel under the snow, starting at the burrow entrance between the buttress roots of Home Oak. They don't want to go out on top of the snow because an owl or a fox, or other cold and hungry hunter, would easily see them. They tunnel by pushing the snow upwards with their backs, slowly making a space big enough to walk along.

It is dangerous to do this, because owls have such good hearing they can hear mice under the snow and locate them exactly. The owl hunts by swooping down and plunging its talons through the snow, gripping a mouse and carrying it away. A fox, too, would hear a mouse under the snow and would pounce. This is not something that our family of mice want to happen.

A few years ago, Burrow Bill was thinking about a story his Dad, Digger Bill, had told, of how an Owl had caught and carried away two of his offspring right outside Burrow Cave. Burrow Bill thought about it for a long time and came up with an idea. He's good at tunnelling, as his name tells us, and he dug a tunnel that opened to the outside world high up on the cliff above the entrance to Burrow Cave. The tunnel twists and turns, following the softer seams and cracks in the rock, until it opens into a little nook in the cliff face. From this place, a mouse can see the whole area in front of Burrow Cave and be safely hidden!

This lookout post is being used today because of the danger of hunters on the prowl. It's a very cold day, so the lookout mouse has to be wrapped up warm with one of Ping Ling's special shawls. Whoever it is on lookout duty, they can't stay outside for long because they would soon get cold; you can't be alert if you are too cold.

BillBill, Nettl's brother, is not the first to be on lookout duty, but when his turn comes he spends a little time checking the alarm. Scribbla, Mowzl's Dad, who is good at inventing things, invented the alarm system, but Digga Bill, who's good at making things, actually made it. There's a wooden peg banged into a crack in the rock in the nook where BillBill is hiding, tied to this wooden peg is a string that dangles down the cliff face, connecting to a bell hanging on another peg in the rock down below.

"Testing, testing!" calls BillBill, jiggling the string, and he hears the bell tinkling down below. *It's working!* he thinks.

"Testing! No alarm!" he shouts again, and then hears the muffled voice of someone calling up to him.

"It's working!"

So that's alright, thinks BillBill, *I wonder who that was, calling up to me?*

He thinks about the mice under the snow making the tunnel knowing that he will have to take his turn soon. He is not looking forward to it, so he makes sure that he is really awake, and looking out for owls and other hungry hunters.

~

Forby and Fivrit, One-Eye's brothers, are the two mice working in the tunnel under the snow, and it is Fivrit that calls up to BillBill to say that the bell is working. They are tired and cold as they've been working in the tunnel for some time, and now they're on their way back to Burrow Cave to rest and warm up.

LaLa, Scraggy's mother, has been putting things to eat on table rock, so that anyone coming in cold and hungry can help themselves. The table in Burrow Cave isn't really a table like in the human world, it's a slab of rock that juts out of the floor of the cave. It is smooth, and almost flat, so it's just right.

"LaLa, why do we have to make this tunnel?" asks Sapphyr.

"We need to be able to get outside, Sapphyr dear, but we have to try to keep the burrow entrance secret. If we just went out from under Home Oak onto the top of the snow, our tracks would tell every passer-by where the entrance is. So, we tunnel under the snow to the bank where the exposed tree roots give us more cover."

LaLa pauses, thinking.

"We should have more than one escape route. There is another that opens onto the hill above us, but it was closed off for some reason, I don't remember why."

"Who's next in the snow tunnel?" asks Star, Scraggy's brother.

"You and me, Star," mumbles Mowzl, with his mouth full. "I'll just finish this hazelnut and be with you."

They set off along the burrow that leads to the oak tree known as Home Oak and come to the familiar place where the burrow emerges between the tree roots into the open air; but now it emerges into a strange tunnel of ice — the snow tunnel! It's late in the day, and a wintry sun sparkles on the snow. In the tunnel, Star and Mowzl can see quite well as the snow above them lets through a glow of sunlight.

They run to the end of the tunnel and begin to work, pushing the snow upwards, first with their noses then with their heads and finally with their backs, as they work their way forward.

"How far since the last side tunnel, Mowzl?" asks Star.

"I didn't notice, we'd better check."

"I'll go!" Star runs back, counting his paces as he goes, until he gets to a short side tunnel.

"Twenty-five!" he calls to Mowzl as he runs back.

"Time for another one, then."

"Alright, I'll do that while you carry on with the main tunnel."

After a while Star calls out, "How far do I have to go?"

"Make just enough room for both of us to hide there, so if someone breaks into the tunnel and looks along, they won't see us."

They work for quite a long time and begin to get cold and tired. The light is fading, and the snow is getting colder and harder. It's slowly freezing up. Star has finished the side tunnel and is back working with Mowzl.

"It's time to stop, don't you reckon, Star?"

Just as Mowzl speaks, the snow in front of them falls away and they can see outside. They've reached the top of the slope, where a tangle of roots sticks out of the ground; over many winters, rain has washed the soil down the hill.

Mowzl sniffs the air. "We made it! Let's have a quick look around before we go back."

He wriggles forward on his tummy and examines the tree roots just below him. He climbs out using the exposed roots to clamber over the edge and under the overhang of the bank. Star is close behind, and together they find a comfortable place to stop and rest. The slope just below them is bowl shaped and smooth with snow.

"Mowzl, do you think the snow is hard enough for us to slide on?" suggests Star.

"Ha! What a good ide — O-oh — Alarm!"

Even as Mowzl is speaking, they hear the alarm bell tinkling.

The two mice react like lightning and in a twinkling, they are hiding in the side tunnel that Star has just made, their hearts racing and their bodies trembling. They're ready to run as fast as they can go, but where to? Which way?

They hear a thump and a sniffing, another thump and a sniffing — it must be a fox!

If they could see what BillBill is seeing from the lookout post, they would have been even more frightened. The fox had been passing by when her sensitive nose noticed mouse smell. The fox has a very good sense of smell and also very sharp ears! She could hunt with her eyes shut if she had to. She uses her nose to plough up the snow, and quickly finds the tunnel the mice have been making. She ploughs her way towards Star and Mowzl and is so excited that she leaps up into the air and pounces down again, making the thump sound. She ploughs along a bit more with her nose, snorting and sniffing, and leaps again yet closer to the terrified mice.

"It's a fox! Star, we'll have to run for it!"

"Come on, Mowzl, let's go-o-o-o!"

"Yeeeeeeeeeee — yaaaaaaaaaaaaa!" they scream, running from their hiding place along the tunnel towards the opening. The fox hears them, and in one bound is close enough to pounce. The two mice run as they have never run before, and when they reach the end of the tunnel they pop out like corks from a bottle just as the fox's paws land on the very edge of the slope.

Finding nothing, the fox looks up to see the two mice on the surface of the snow, sliding and spinning down the side of the 'snow bowl' that Mowzl and Star had been looking at just a moment ago. The fox leaps into the snow bowl, landing in the middle where the snow has drifted deep, and she sinks in because she is so heavy. The mice have been sliding so fast that they are already whizzing up the far side of the snow bowl, up and over the edge!

"Yiiiiiiikes!" yells Star.

"Hora-a-a-tio-o-o-o-o-o!" yells Mowzl, sailing through the air.

The day's sunshine has melted the surface of the snow a little, but now that the sun has gone it freezes again and the snow has an icy skin on top. This icy skin is not strong enough to hold the weight of the fox, but it is strong enough for the two mice to slide and bounce crazily down the steep hillside.

"Ouch!"

"Mind that tree!"

Sliding fast, they dodge trees and rocks as best they can, thrilled but frightened too.

"Ow — ow!"

"OMG!"

"Look out!"

Suddenly the snow slide comes to an end, and this time it isn't just a little cliff that they fall over, but a big one. Star and Mowzl whiz over the edge, sailing through the air, down, down and down they fall!

"O-n-o-o-o-o-o-o!"

A moment later they tumble through layers of snow-covered branches. An old yew tree, growing out from the cliff face, is slowing their fall.

"Oooof!" cries Star.

"Uggghhh!" grunts Mowzl.

The springy branches cushion their fall, slowing them bit-by-bit until at last they stop falling. They scramble along the branch to the trunk and climb down to where the tree is rooted. Finding a place to rest, safe from the risk of falling further, they pant and gasp, catching their breath.

"Star, I'm aching all over, and my hands and feet really hurt."

"Me too, but we're not Foxy's dinner yet!"

"That's true. I wonder where she is," Mowzl peers down to the bottom of the cliff. "It's not very far to the bottom from here, but if we did climb down there where would we go?"

"We'd have to find our way back up the hill," says Star. "I don't think we could do that with the snow so slippery in the frost and we'd be easily seen by the fox."

"You're right, we might not have the strength to climb up there anyway. We need to find somewhere nearby to shelter and rest and keep warm."

"Look, Mowzl, we can squeeze through this gap in the rock that the tree roots have made!"

"Alright, but it'll be dark in there."

"It's cold and nearly dark out here, and it'll be warmer in there if we can get inside a bit."

They squeeze through the narrow gap in the rock and for a short distance walk along the yew tree root. The root dips downwards disappearing into the ground, but they can carry on because the gap in the rock is a bit wider now and keeps widening the further they go.

Mowzl turns to look back the way they have come, seeing only a little slit of light. When he tries to look deeper into the cave again, he sees only darkness.

"I hope you can see in the dark!" he says.

"Not yet, we'll have to wait until we get used to it. Anyway, I need a rest and my feet hurt."

"Yes, let's have a bit of a sit down," agrees Mowzl.

~

BillBill can't believe his eyes when he sees the fox coming along through the woods, he's so nervous he spins around in circles.

"Oh, dear! What if the fox catches Mowzl and Star and eats them up? Oh, no!" BillBill makes up his mind to sound the alarm as soon as the fox looks like it's heading towards the snow tunnel. At that very moment, the fox stops walking by and stands still, sniffing the air and the ground. Then she moves towards the tunnel.

"Oh, dear me! Oh, no! Oh, no!" BillBill mutters anxiously.

He tugs on the string, hearing the tinkling of the bell down below. The fox looks up, alert and curious, but then carries on hunting. BillBill watches as the fox pounces into the snow ploughing along with its nose. It pounces again, then leaps, landing very near the edge of the steep slope.

Because the light is fading, BillBill can't see well enough to know if his friends have escaped. He thinks he hears a mouse yelling 'Yikes' and 'Horatio', but he doesn't know for sure; he sees the fox jump over the edge and disappear.

He knows that there is nothing more he can do from the lookout place, and he must tell everyone what has happened. He goes back down the tunnel as fast as he can, which is difficult because it is dark, and the tunnel is twisty and squeezy, but he gets to Burrow Cave in good time.

As soon as he arrives he sees the effect of the alarm bell. Everyone is rushing about doing something important, or thinking they should be doing something important, but not knowing what it is.

"BillBill, there you are, lad," Scribbla calls above the all the noise. "Were you on watch at the lookout?"

"Yes, Uncle," replies BillBill, and he begins to tell the story as fast as he can.

"Whoa there, lad!" interrupts Scribbla. "Wait a minute, come over to the table."

Scribbla bangs a stone on table rock and calls for quiet.

"Quiet please! Settle down, quiet please! Now if you can all calm down and listen we'll hear what young BillBill has to say."

BillBill is trembling with the excitement and fear that he's been feeling. Now, as well as that, he is trembling with shyness and his voice is a bit wobbly as he tells of what happened while he was on duty at the lookout.

LaLa breaks the shocked silence that follows BillBill's story.

"Thank you, BillBill, you did well to sound the alarm so quickly." She pauses for a moment before going on. "You all know that I am Star's mother and if he were dead my heart would be heavy, but my heart is not heavy and I'm sure he's alive — and Mowzl, too. Of all our family, there is one who sees with the eye of her heart most clearly, and that is Flimsy. Flimsy dear, will you tell us what you see?"

"Mummy I see only darkness now, but I am sure they are alive. When the fox chased them, I could feel them falling very far. They are inside the mountain."

"Thank you, Flimsy," says Scribbla. "Now we need to make a plan. BillBill, please fetch your Dad and Grandpa, if they can be found, and the rest of us must get to work."

BillBill scampers off to find Burrow Bill and Digga Bill, while Scribbla starts to get things organised.

"Let's divide up into two teams," he says. "One to block the burrow entrance under Home Oak, and the other to open up the entrance on the hillside above. Burrow Bill will lead that team, and

I will lead the team blocking the entrance at Home Oak. Please would Pearl, Dreamer and Scraggy come with me, and everyone else help Burrow Bill when he turns up."

"Why do we have to block the burrow?" asks Sapphyr.

"Because the snow tunnel has been discovered and dug up by a fox. As long as the snow lasts, our burrow is too easy for hunters to find. In the Spring we can open the burrow entrance again."

"But, Grandpa, aren't we going to look for Mowzl and Star? They will need help!"

"We all want to do that, Sapphyr, but it's too dangerous for us to go out over the snow to look for them. Let's see what Burrow Bill and Digga Bill have to say about it. Ah! Here they come now!"

'They are inside the mountain' says Flimsy'

Digga Bill is Nettl and BillBill's grandfather. All the young mice think he's a bit fierce because his fur is grizzly grey, and he shouts, but he only shouts because he's a bit deaf.

"BillBill has told us what's happened," says Digga Bill. "What's the plan?"

His voice booms out in the cave, echoing off the walls and bouncing around, and the youngest mice duck their heads and flatten their ears.

Scribbla explains his plan. "I will lead a team to block the Home Oak entrance, and Burrow Bill will lead a team to open the entrance up top, if you will . . .?"

"Yep, sounds good to me!" agrees Burrow Bill.

"Alright then," booms Digga. "I will give my mind to the meaning of Flimsy's words — 'they are inside the mountain'. Flimsy, please fetch your father. We need him and his maps."

"Right then, who will be working with you, Scribbla?" asks Burrow Bill.

"Me, Dreamer and Scraggy," answers Pearl.

"Alright then. BillBill, Nettl, and LaLa, please come with me!"

"Good," booms Digga. "That leaves Sapphyr and Flimsy to help me think!"

~

In the darkness inside the hill, Mowzl and Star are licking their wounds.

"I'm bashed and bruised all over," says Star. "Sliding over the snow has cut my hands and feet. They're sore!"

"Me too, and I bashed my head on a tree! I'm happy that we're alive, Star, we're dead lucky."

"Not so much of the 'dead'! What are we going to do, Em?"

Mowzl pauses for a moment. "We can't go back outside yet. We'd be easy targets for the fox, or an owl, and anyway the hill is too steep to climb with all this slippy snow."

"How about we explore into the cave a little way and see what we find?" suggests Star.

"Alright, I'm ready."

They pick themselves up, stretch their aching bodies and move slowly onwards into the hillside, feeling their way in the dark with all their senses. Their whiskers help them to avoid bumping into things and their ears pick up sounds echoing off the stone walls around them, giving them an idea of where there is something — and where there is nothing. They can feel the space around them with their whole bodies, because mice are very sensitive creatures.

As they move on they hear new sounds. They hear the sound of water trickling and dripping, and they can tell, by how the sounds change, that the cave is getting bigger the further they go. Mowzl stops moving, listening intently.

"Star, can you hear the sound of running water?"

"Yes, sounds like it, Em — be careful not to fall down a hole!"

"Let's stop and think. I'm worried that we might get lost, and not be able to find our way out."

"But we can't just sit here and shiver!"

"No, you're right, Star. But shall we climb up or down if we get a choice of ways?"

"Up."

"That's what I think too. We shall just have to be careful."

Feeling their way forward in the darkness, they find themselves on a narrow ledge; they can hear the sound of flowing water below. They move to the left, following the rock wall. Water drips from above and the rock they walk on is wet and slippery.

"Star, can you feel the air moving?"

"Now you say it, yes, I can! Hmmm . . . I wonder where that's coming from?"

"It's coming from our left."

"Which is left?"

"Oh, Star! And you're the great navigator!"

"Ha! Just joking, Mowzl."

Silence.

"Mowzl?" says Star, suddenly worried in the darkness.

"I'm here, it's alright. I was looking for where this little breeze is coming from and I think I've found it. It's coming out of this gap in the rocks. I'm going in."

"Wait for me!"

It's a very narrow way, but easy going because of the sandy floor and gentle slope. Mowzl brushes the whiskers on the left side of his face along the rock wall to position himself and to free his hands and feet for walking and feeling for dangers.

"Are you there, Star?" he whispers.

"Yes, just about keeping up."

Mowzl stops suddenly and Star bumps into him in the dark.

"Whoops! Ouch!"

"Sorry, I should've said something. Listen!"

They stand stock-still, listening with all their might.

"Hmm," says Star, quietly. "I can hear a sort of rustling. Oh! Did you hear that squeak? And there! Another sort of click!"

"Come on, let's go a bit further," whispers Mowzl.

The sounds begin to bounce about more, and the echoes around them start sounding more like a cave. The rustling and squeaking is louder and is coming from above.

"Can you see anything, Em?"

"Erm . . . no. Wait! What about that over there? Is that a glow, or are my eyes playing tricks on me?"

"Yes, look!" cries Star. "The floor of the cave! Over there, it's glowing! What is that?"

Mowzl strains his eyes, trying to get a good look.

"I don't know, but I remember your Dad telling us something about caves he had been in once that had bats living in them. I think I can hear bats!"

"I remember that too, it must have been one of his lessons. He said that bats are mice with wings, and they hang upside down in caves and hollow trees! I didn't believe him."

"Yes! He's full of tall stories, your Dad; but maybe it's true after all, Star!"

"Let's stop for a rest, Em, I'm tired out. I wish that you had your backpack with some food in it!"

"I wish I did, too. Let's rest here, it's nice and dry."

They snuggle together to keep warm and soon are asleep — except for their ears which stay wide awake, listening and twitching, just in case.

~

Flimsy sets off to fetch her father, One-Eye, as Digga Bill asked her to. When she arrives at One-Eye's den, she tells him what has happened and straight away he knows what to do.

"Alright, me lovely, we'll be needin' a map, 'n me beloved backpack. Ahh! —'n me trusty lantern."

"But Daddy, you always say the lantern is not allowed out of your den . . ."

"We's needin' light, 'tis urgent."

One-Eye lifts the lantern from its hook above the table, and beckons to Flimsy to follow him over to the shelves where the maps are stored. He chooses two map tubes.

"Be 'oldin' lantern, Flimsy."

"Yes, Dad!"

"'Ere's me backpack; ah yes, in go the maps! Let's be movin'!"

They scramble to Burrow Cave as fast as they can go, Flimsy proud to be carrying the lantern. With the help of the light they soon arrive at Burrow Cave where Digga Bill and Sapphyr are waiting.

"Ah! There you are!" thunders Digga. "What ideas have you got, One-Eye?"

"Hold up, hold up, give us a little minute! Let's be gettin' this 'ere map spread out."

He opens a map tube and carefully teases out the map, laying it on the table and unrolling it.

"Flimsy, me lovely, bring the lantern 'ere to light the maps. There, that's it. Is we 'avin' some stones or somethin' to 'old 'em down?"

"I'll get some," Sapphyr volunteers.

"Well-well," says Digga. "It's a long time since I looked at this map, One-Eye, and a long time since we explored the tunnels and caves. What's your plan?"

"As I's rememberin', back in the old days," One-Eye explains, for the benefit of Flimsy and Sapphyr. "Digga'n me's findin' a tunnel goin' down from this very cave we's in now. Back then we's thinkin' we'd better explore before we blocks it up to keep our burrow safe.

"We goes down 'n down 'n we's 'avin' to be comin' back to get ropes as there be a shaft too slippery for climbin'. With the 'elp o' ropes, we be gettin' down at last 'n we goes on a little more to be findin' ourselves in a cave with bats 'angin' upsydown over-'ead 'n squeakin'. We was thinkin' there 'as to be a way out where the bats is flyin', so we set about lookin' for it. It was quite a job, I'm tellin' ye! We finds the way at last, but it be takin' two days! The ways out be in the cliff below Eagle Rock, 'n there be an old yew tree growin' out of cracks in the rock. I been thinkin' that Flimsy's 'inside the mountain' is tellin' us that our Star 'n Mowzl be there!"

"Memories, memories," says Digga. "Brings it all back, One-Eye! But we had better get that tunnel opened up quicker than quick. Where is it? I forget."

"We marked it on this 'ere ol' map. It'll be in the north wall, yep, over there, and a bit east, yep, that's about it, high as you's able to reach, Digga."

"I remember now! I'll start pulling out the wedge stones."

Sapphyr places small stones on the corners of the map, while One-Eye opens the second tube, taking out another map. Sapphyr places stones on the corners of that map too, when One-Eye has unrolled it.

"What's the other map for, Dad?" asks Flimsy.

"Back then, we made drawin's o' the tunnel, all the tricky bits, slopey bits, 'n 'specially dead ends. We was thinkin' it might come in 'andy someday. So, now I's rememberin', 'n lernin' the map over again. We'll be needin' backpacks with food 'n water for the lads; we's needin' ropes 'n all."

"Can we come too, Uncle?" asks Sapphyr.

"You's truly means it?" asks One-Eye, surprised.

"Oh yes! But it sounds scary."

"You'll be alright. I's 'appy you's wantin' to come."

"Thanks, Dad!" cries Flimsy, excited; she usually gets left behind because she's not as strong as the others. Like Sapphyr, she feels apprehensive, but knows she's just got to go.

Digga's voice booms from the other side of the cave, "Will you be gossiping all day? Will I get some help here sometime soon?"

"Right-oh!" calls One-Eye. Then, more quietly, he says, "Be findin' food to take, 'n get yourselves ready. Get over to the tool store 'n grab three ropes, make sure two of 'em be the longest, mind! Be quick! Ah yes, 'n be findin' Wunda, or Threeda, if they's at 'ome, 'n be tellin' 'em what we be doin'."

"AM I ALONE HERE?" roars Digga.

"'Ere I be, give me a go at it!" cries One-Eye, hurrying to help.

Digga has pulled out some small stones that wedge the bigger rocks tight, so tight that they cannot be moved from the other side. With the wedge stones taken out, the bigger stones can be loosened.

"I can remember putting these in. Now that I see them, it all comes back to me; we did a good job, Tooby."

"Yep! Nice 'n tight, but we'sll 'av' it open in a mo."

While One-Eye and Digga work at opening the tunnel entrance, Sapphyr goes looking for Wunda while Flimsy fetches nuts and seeds for the backpacks. Flimsy doesn't want to go to the tool store on her own, so she waits for Sapphyr to come back. When Sapphyr does come back, she is with Threeda, not Wunda.

"I couldn't find Wunda, don't know where she is," she shrugs.

"Digga Bill!" shouts Threeda. "What is the meaning of making these two young mice go down that dangerous tunnel? And with Flimsy only just mending from her fever?"

Digga and One-Eye stop work and turn to look at Threeda in amazement.

"You'd better ask One-Eye," growls Digga.

"Well?"

"Threeda, they's old enough, 'n it's good growin' stuff 'n Flimsy's ready now."

Sapphyr and Flimsy can almost see the steam coming out of Threeda's ears.

"You old pirate! What rubbish you do talk!" she shouts across the cave.

"You be sister t' me, Threeda, you know me well, there'll be no 'arm comin' to little un's."

"Grrrr," says Threeda, knowing she is beaten. Maybe One-Eye is right — the young ones are ready, it's true. "Alright, One-Eye, you win, as you usually do!"

"Aunty Threeda," says Sapphyr. "Would you come with us to the tool store to fetch the three ropes One-Eye's asked for?"

"Of course, I will."

As they make their way along the dark burrows, Flimsy's curiosity gets the better of her. "Aunty, what was my Dad called before he was called One-Eye?"

"His name, when he was a baby, was a number; mine was too, and your mother's too, Sapphyr. There were five of us altogether, brothers and sisters, children of Captain Blunda and Elfrida. The Captain had no time for names and he called us One, Two, Three, Four, and Five! These numbers gradually grew into names: Wunda, Tooby, Threeda, Forby and Fivrit. One-Eye was number two, so he was called Tooby until he went away on one of his adventures and came back with an eye missing — so he got called One-Eye after that!"

"Tooby! Ha-ha!" cries Flimsy, laughing. "I like that. Does he mind being called Tooby?"

"No, he doesn't mind, I think he likes it."

"I wish he would tell us stories about his adventures," Sapphyr says, wistfully.

"Perhaps you could persuade him to one day dear, but not today! Ah! Here we are."

Threeda knows the tool store so well she can lead the other two straight to where the ropes are hanging; she can tell one rope from another by their smell and their feel.

"Ping Ling and I made these ropes. They are the finest ropes we have ever made, and these two are the longest; this one will do for the third one. Could you manage one of these, Sapphyr?"

Sapphyr takes the rope from Threeda, hefting it to feel its weight.

"Yes, I can carry this one."

"May I carry the other one?" pleads Flimsy.

"Flimsy dear, I am sure you could carry it, and thank you for offering, but I am here and so there is no need for you to carry it. You will need all your strength for the journey."

"Can't I carry the short rope then?"

"Oh, alright, if you really want to."

They set off back to Burrow Cave, talking about making ropes.

"Auntie, will you teach us how to make thread, and how to spin and everything?" asks Flimsy.

"Yes, dear, of course, and I'm sure that Ping Ling would like to help giving the classes. But here we are at Burrow Cave, and it looks like Digga and One-Eye are ready to go."

One-Eye takes one long rope and Digga the other; they expertly throw them across their shoulders, and, as they are already wearing their backpacks, they now look like real explorers. Digga stuffs the shorter rope into One-Eye's backpack while One-Eye looks the young ones over carefully.

"If you's wantin' to stay at 'ome, now's the time t' own it," he says, gently but seriously.

"I'm coming," says Flimsy, determinedly.

"I'm coming too," nods Sapphyr.

Digga and One-Eye look pleased and smile at one another.

They turn to face the wall of the cave and the narrow gap that Digga and One-Eye have opened up. Beyond, where the light of the lantern cannot reach, is blackness. Digga climbs through the gap and helps Flimsy and Sapphyr through. As One-Eye climbs through he turns to Threeda.

"Be tellin' everyone what we be up to, when they gets back. It be my bettin' we'll return as the sun is risin'."

"I will, don't worry. Don't forget the lantern!"

"The map's in me 'ead, no need for lantern. Better leave it safe with you, Threeda."

He turns away, disappearing into the blackness of the tunnel.

Threeda suddenly feels very alone. Burrow Cave is silent and empty, and she is glad of the soft light from the lantern. She thinks about her nephews, Star and Mowzl, and she wishes with all her might that they are found soon and brought home safe and sound. It is not so long ago that Beechnut died, taken by an owl while gathering wool; Threeda could not bear to lose Mowzl and Star as well. She thinks about Flimsy, too, and how brave she is to go down into the dark tunnels below Burrow Cave; Flimsy is still quite weak after her terrible fever. *Dear Flimsy,* she thinks, *she is like a little diamond bringing light into our lives.*

Threeda busies herself preparing food for whenever the two tunnel teams should return, for they will be tired and hungry from their labours. She then settles down to wait, letting her wish grow strong.

~

Mowzl is awake, listening to the sounds in the cave. He can hear Star's steady breathing, and he can hear the bats rustling and squeaking. It's a strange sound, like whispering. Star is snuggled close, so he keeps still, not wanting to wake his cousin.

He thinks about their lucky escape from the fox. Mice are hunted by lots of hungry creatures that have families of their own to feed. It would be sad to die in this cave and not be food for a cold and hungry creature. But then he remembers, there are lots of very small creatures that would eat up his body and they would be able to feed their young ones, too. There are probably lots of tiny creatures in this cave.

Mowzl hopes Star will wake up, because he's feeling lonely and sad. Tears sting his eyes as he thinks of his family and friends, and never seeing them again. He sees Flimsy's face, as though he is asleep and dreaming of her; she smiles and says, "We are coming to you."

His heart leaps and his sadness melts away, but the feelings that had brought tears to his eyes are still there. Instead of feeling miserable, he feels wonder, he feels gratitude for being alive, and love for living beings; and he feels a deep respect for death and the mystery of the great wave.

"Are you awake, Star?"

"No."

"Oh."

"Are you awake, Em?"

"I think so, but I must have been dreaming, because I saw Flimsy and she said, 'we are coming to you'."

Star yawns.

"I dreamed about Flimsy too, then I woke up and thought I heard you sobbing, Mowzl."

"You did. I was. I was feeling very small and sad."

"Tell me."

Mowzl tells how his feelings had plunged and soared as his thoughts explored their narrow escape from the fox.

"I do understand, Em, I've been thinking about it too, and we must talk about it, but now we must find our way out of this cave!"

"But Flimsy said, 'we are coming to you'. Doesn't that mean we should stay where we are?"

"Mowzl, Flimsy will be able to find us even if we move; maybe we will get closer to her if we explore a bit."

"Alright."

They move carefully forward towards the strange, glowing mound. When they get near it seems that the glow is moving, but they can't be sure. Mowzl feels something crawling up his tail.

"What's this!?" he exclaims, turning to look. He can only just make it out in the strange light, it's a centipede and it's glowing.

"Off you go, glowing centipede, or I might decide that I'm hungry enough to eat you up," and he shakes the centipede from his tail.

"Let's go around the mound," says Star.

"Can you hear a sound like rain?"

"Yes, it's a sort of pattering sound. I wonder, is it something falling from the bats onto the mound?"

"Something! You mean it's raining bat poo!" laughs Mowzl.

"Yikes! So, this is a pile of bat poo! There must be a lot of bats. Let's try to keep on in a straight line from where we came into this cave, so we keep our sense of direction."

"Your sense of direction maybe, Star. Do you reckon we're going deeper into the hill?"

"Yep."

"Hmm."

"What do you mean, 'Hmm'?"

"Well, we're not going to find our way out if we go deeper in, are we?"

"You never know, Em, come on."

They carry on, walking slowly over the glowing ground taking care not to tread on anything that is moving. Eventually they reach the far side of the cave and move along the wall until they find a narrow gap, and into the gap they go. The narrow passage slopes uphill getting steeper and steeper — it's hard work! They struggle up the slope until it levels out, where they stop for a rest.

As their breathing calms down, the silence grows; they can't hear the bats anymore. Without the bats making their rustling, and without the soft patter of bat poo falling onto the mound, this tunnel is the quietest place the two mice have ever been. They can hear their own hearts beating loud in their ears, but as they rest, even this slowly quietens.

"There's no smell of bats anymore," whispers Star.

"I was thinking that too, I can feel a little breeze coming down this tunnel, and it smells good."

They are silent for a bit. Even with their mouse eyes they can't see anything — it's totally dark.

"Star?"

"Yep?"

"I don't want to die in here."

"Mowzl, be trusting. Catch that thought before it grows any bigger. We won't die in here. The worst that can happen is that we have to retrace our steps, go outside into the snow and find our way back up the hill."

"I like your calmness, Star. I am glad that I'm with you."

Star jumps up saying, "Come on, let's go on a bit further."

On they go, resting from time to time because the going is sometimes steep. At last the narrow passage opens out, and they can tell by the echoes that it might be another cave, but a smaller one. Mowzl decides on a plan.

"Star, would you wait here while I follow the rock to see how far it is round the edge of this cave, or whatever it is?"

"Er, alright, if you don't disappear completely."

"I'll keep talking — no, I'll la laa a little la laa."

Mowzl sets off in the dark, following the wall and singing his little tune so that Star knows where he is. He discovers that the wall curves round quite quickly, in a wiggly sort of way.

"La la laa la laaa laaa! La la laa la laaa laaa!"

Bump.

"Mowzl! You've gone all the way round already! This is a very small cave!"

"Yes, Star, but the echo is wrong for a little cave. Do you think it might just go upwards?"

They realise that there may be no ceiling, and above them is a hole that goes straight up. But they can't see it, they are guessing.

"Maybe this tunnel was made by water," says Mowzl. "I can imagine water finding cracks between the rocks and washing out all the loose stuff — a bit like Burrow Bill making a tunnel — and the water slowly making a bigger and bigger tunnel as it wears away the rock. That could be why the rocks are quite smooth."

"Well, Em, you may be right, but there's no way out; only back."

"What about up?"

"Alright, let's have a go, but the rocks are smooth and will be hard to climb."

Mowzl is eager to climb. "It'll be fine, Star. I'll go first and call when I find a ledge to rest on."

Mowzl loves climbing, and it cheers him up to have something to do. He starts to climb, his claws finding cracks in the stone or just clinging to the few tiny holes in the surface. The wall of stone does go straight up, just as they had thought! He finds a nook in the wall with a ledge just big enough for them both. At last he can stop and relax, allowing his legs to dangle.

He calls down, "I've got to a ledge, Star, come up if you want to! The rock goes straight up; it isn't curving over like a cave roof at all. This is definitely a tunnel that goes upwards!"

"I think that's called a shaft," calls Star. "I'm coming up!"

Mowzl keeps talking, about not very much, just to give Star a sound to guide him. Before long, Star has reached the ledge, and he too takes some time to stretch his limbs to avoid them cramping up after all that clinging on.

"Phew! That was hard work! While you were talking, Mowzl, I thought I could hear an echo; I mean a proper big one. Shall we see if there is one?"

"Good plan. I know — yippeeee!" Mowzl shouts, and they hear the noise bouncing about, and then a little 'yippee' coming down from above.

"Ha-ha!" tries Star.

'ha-ha', comes the response.

"La la laaa la laaa laaaaaa," sings Mowzl.

'. . . la laa laa' comes the echo.

They fall silent and, as the echoes fade away, they feel suddenly lonely and aware of their plight, sitting on a ledge in deep darkness under the ground. They put their arms around each other.

"It's so big, the echo makes it seem a huge emptiness," Mowzl whispers. "Like there is nothing at all except darkness — except I can hear a sort of singing. Well I can't really hear it, it's more of a feeling."

Star shivers. "Mowzl, I've never felt like this before. I've never been so frightened. But it's not only fear — it's wonder too. We are alive in the middle of emptiness. What you can feel is the invisible ones singing! My Dad told me about their singing; he said that if you listen really, really hard, you might hear it."

"The singing makes me feel calm inside," replies Mowzl.

"Are we dying? Is that why we can hear the singing?"

"No, I don't feel so," says Mowzl. "But we are close. It's like getting to the top of a hill and suddenly seeing a new landscape beyond. We are close to the top of that hill, Star."

"You mean the 'dying' hill?"

"Yes, we can feel the singing; and I am feeling Beechnut so close that I expect her to suddenly say 'boo — found you!'"

"But she won't, will she?"

"No, Star, we aren't going to the top of that hill, not just yet."

They are quiet, but the silence grows too big, and Mowzl has to think of something to say.

"Do you think we should go on, or go back, Star?"

"I don't know. Let's wait until we've calmed down, then we'll know."

They sit quietly on the rocky ledge, arms around each other's shoulders, with their feet dangling into dark space. Two mice lost in the middle of the mountain. Each of them has his own thoughts charging around in his head, but neither mouse has a clear feeling about what they should do. If they continue to climb they risk a dangerous fall, and they have no way of knowing that climbing further will lead them to safety. If they go back they face the arduous journey along the narrow passage, through the bat cave and the twisting tunnel. They will then have to climb the steep, snow covered hill and risk being seen by a hunter. They could tunnel under the snow and look for seeds to eat, but they are too tired already. No, going back does not seem like a good idea.

Mowzl's free hand has been playing with a stone he found on the ledge. He rolls it around in his fingers, feeling its shape; it's flattish, and roundish, one side being smooth with a ridge across it, the other side rough with no ridge.

"Star?"

"Em?"

"I've got a little stone I picked up. It's flattish and one side is rough, and the other side is smooth. Let's say that the smooth side is 'we go on' and the rough side is 'we go back'. I'll drop the stone on the ledge behind us, and you feel for it and see which side is facing upwards, and we do whatever it says. What do you think?"

"Alright! Let's do it."

"I'll drop it behind us, so it won't bounce off. Here goes!"

They take their arms from each other's shoulders, and Star turns a little to be able to feel for the stone with his hand. He finds it, and can tell that the top side is rough, but to be sure he picks it up to feel the other side which is smoother with a ridge across it.

"Does the smooth side have a ridge across it?"

"Yep."

"Then this stone is the right one, and it was rough side up."

"That means we go back," says Mowzl quietly.

They settle back and put their arms across each other's shoulders again. They are quiet for a long time.

"Em?"

"Star?"

"We have to go on."

"I know."

Star makes a sound as if to speak but stops and is quiet again. Mowzl realises that he is thinking very hard about something.

"Do you mind if I call you Emmy?" Star asks eventually.

"I like it. Mowzl is a bit serious isn't it?"

"It's not that, Emmy, it's just that I feel close to you in a new way, and I want to call you Emmy. We are real friends now."

"Thank you, Star. I feel the same."

Shivering now, they snuggle together to keep warm.

"Emmy?"

"Star?"

"We'd better make a move."

"Yes, I s'pose so."

They fall silent and remain so for a long time, reluctant to continue climbing the shaft.

"Coooeeee"

"Star?"

"Em?"

"Did you hear something?"

"Well I did, and I didn't."

"Mmm. Exactly."

"Coooeeeeee." The sound comes again.

"It's a cooee call!" cries Mowzl, excitedly. "Let's call back!"

"Cooooooeeeeeee!" They shout together. The sound bounces around in the blackness, slowly disappearing up into the space above them, fading away to silence.

"Coooeee! Coooeee!"

"Yes! It's a reply! It's real. Emmy, it must be Flimsy. Hooray! I wonder who's with her?"

"I bet it's your Dad and Burrow Bill, or Digga Bill. Hooray! Oh! I feel as light as a feather!"

"Ha-haa! I'm all giggly too!" says Star. "Oh me, oh my!"

"It wasn't just an echo, was it?" says Mowzl, uncertain.

"No. Do you think we should start climbing up?"

"No, this time we should stay put!" says Mowzl decisively, "Let's shout a 'coooeee' now and again to help them!"

"Good idea! Ready?"

"Cooooooeeeeeee!"

"Sing a song, Emmy," suggests Star.

"Alright; let's try a bat song."

Emmy starts it off, and Star soon joins in.

"Bats is waking, — bats is waking, — bats is waking, —
    Up from the day,
Bats is going, — Bats is going, — Bats is going, —
    Out for the night,
Bats is coming, — Bats is coming, — Bats is coming, —
    In from the night,
Bats is sleeping, — Bats is sleeping, — Bats is sleeping, —
    All through the day. . ."

"That's nice, Emmy, I feel better now," says Star softly.

They are quiet for a long time.

"Is it time for another 'cooee'?" asks Star.

"Yes, ready?"

"Yep! One, two, three . . ."

"Cooooooeeeeeee!"

They hear something above them; a voice perhaps! When the remains of the "cooeee" have faded, they begin to make out some words.

alright ^/:? ¬"\ comin' :*)^ keep <>;¬_hair on ¬"

"It's Uncle One-Eye! It's your dad, Star, it's your dad!"

"Daddy? Is that you?"

"For sure 'tis me, 'n where be thee?" comes One-Eye's cheerful reply.

"We're on a rock ledge below you!"

"Is you 'urt? Can you be climbin' a rope alright?"

"We can climb! Oh, it's such a relief to hear you! Thanks for coming to find us!"

"Never mind that now," says One-Eye with more urgency. "I'll be droppin' a rope down — mind it!"

Before climbing down the shaft, One-Eye had tied the first long rope around a big rock at the top — where Digga and Flimsy and Sapphyr are waiting — and dropped the coil down the shaft. He then climbed down, remembering that there would be rocky ledges further down, almost reaching the end of the rope before finding a ledge to sit on. He heard the call from Mowzl and Star coming up the shaft, so he knew he must have been getting close.

One-Eye now ties the second rope to the end of the first rope, with hitches he knows so well he can tie them in the dark. He drops the coiled rope, hearing it swish down the shaft.

Emmy and Star hear the rope swishing too.

"Uncle, we heard the rope, but we haven't caught it yet."

"Keep tryin', I'll swing it to 'n fro."

"No, haven't got it yet — ah! It just touched my hand, but I missed it! There it is again — yes! I've got it!" Mowzl holds the rope firmly, to be sure not to drop it.

"Alright me lads, will I be cumin' down, or is you cumin' up?"

"We'll climb up, Dad," calls Star. "Will you go first, Emmy?"

"No, Star, you go first. I'll hold the rope steady for you."

"Take your time lad, take your time," calls One-Eye. "Grip with hands 'n feet both, 'n be movin' 'em one by one, 'n wrap your tail too!"

Star takes hold of the rope and is surprised by how thin it is, but he likes the feel of it and is reassured by its strength. He climbs easily, and before long he is on the ledge beside his father.

"It's so good you've come, Dad, thank you," exclaims Star with relief, as he gives his father a hug.

"You be safe now lad, that's all that matters. Now, where's that Mowzl?"

"Emmy, come on up!" calls Star.

"Coming up!" calls Mowzl from below. He doesn't want to stay there on his own for a moment longer. It's a bit harder for him to climb because the rope keeps flicking around as he moves, but it's still easier than climbing up the rock.

"What's all this 'Emmy', then?" asks One-Eye.

"Oh! That's what I'm going to call my cousin from now on!"

"So, you'll be best of friends is it?"

"Yes, Dad."

"It brings you close, I know it, when adventure 'appens," says

One-Eye warmly.

"It's true, it's been a big day."

"'N it ain't over, neither. Keep alert, lad, keep awake."

One-Eye holds the twitching rope firmly while Mowzl climbs.

"Do you trust those knots, Dad?" asks Star.

"Them's not knots, lad, but 'itches, 'n I be trustin' 'em always; I did use bowlins to join 'em, easily made 'n easily unmade, 'nll never let you down."

"Will you teach us, Dad?"

"If we're ever to be gettin' 'ome! Here's our Mowzl; come on the ledge, lad, 'n 'av a rest."

"Thanks, Uncle, we were getting worried. Thanks for coming for us!"

"Enough o' that now. Star, up you be goin'."

Star starts to climb up into the darkness above, towards the voices of encouragement that he can hear: Digga Bill's gruff, deep voice saying, "Come on, lads, get a move on . . .", and Flimsy and Sapphyr saying "Oh, thank goodness you are safe, I'm so happy we found you!"

Down below, One-Eye asks Mowzl to hold on to the rope that Star is climbing, while he unties the bowlines and coils up the second rope. He ties it off, slinging the coil carefully over his head and shoulder.

"I'll be glad to see a little light," he says. "Even starlight'll seem bright as day after this black place. Now then, I be thinkin' Star's arrivin' at the top, yep, I can 'ear 'em all chatterin' like starlin's. Up ye go, Mowzl, I'll be oldin' rope."

"Uncle, I'd be happy to come last and to hold the rope for you." replies Mowzl.

"You're a good lad, Mowzl, but off with thee!" One-Eye's voice is just a little stern and Mowzl does as he is bid.

He climbs too quickly, and his grip slips a little, frightening him for a moment. *It's no good being in a rush and falling off*, he thinks. At last he reaches the rim of the shaft, and feels a strong hand grip his arm pulling him up and away from the edge. It's Digga Bill.

"Come over here, Mowzl, here's Sapphyr and Flimsy and Star; have a rest, eat something."

"Thanks, Digga."

Digga Bill, practical as ever, goes back to the top of the shaft to help One-Eye.

Emmy has tears stinging his eyes as he hugs Flimsy and

Sapphyr and hears their voices again.

"Flimsy," he says, when the words come. "Thank you for telling us with your dream talk that you were coming to find us. We were feeling very scared and alone and you gave us courage. Thank you both for coming to find us."

Sapphyr and Flimsy hug them both but say nothing. They are glad that the two lost mice have been found safe and sound.

One-Eye reaches the top of the shaft and straightaway unties the rope from the anchor rock, coiling it up.

"They seem to be alright, those two lads, don't you think?" says Digga.

"They be fine. Digga, would you be carryin' this rope?"

"Yes. Don't forget your backpack." replies Digga.

"As if I ever would."

Emmy and Star eat a few seeds from One-Eye's pack, but they are too tired and excited to eat much. They do need to talk, and they babble away excitedly. Digga Bill interrupts them to say they should set off home as soon as everyone is ready.

"Don't be forgettin' anythin'!" calls out One-Eye, so they check they've got everything they should be carrying. Cries of "ready!" reassure One-Eye, and they set off in single file, keeping close to the tip of the tail of the mouse in front. Digga takes the lead, and One-Eye the rear.

Finding the way home is easier than the way out; Digga simply follows the scent they left before. It's just as well that One-Eye had looked carefully at the map before they left Burrow Cave, because the tunnels are labyrinthine. Some tunnels go to dead ends, and some go on and on into the ground — who knows where? One-Eye's map, made many winters before when he and Digga first explored the caves, shows which way to go. Long ago they had explored all the way to the shaft, and along the steep passage to the cave of bats. They know how difficult some of the tunnels are and are surprised, and very pleased, that Star and Mowzl have managed to get so far towards home by themselves.

"We get to a difficult bit soon," says Sapphyr. "It's a narrow squeezy tunnel that goes upwards in a zigzag. After that it's not too bad."

"Do we climb the rock through the zigzag?" asks Star.

"There's a rope to hold on to; the one we used to climb down is still there," answers Digga.

When they arrive at the zigzagging climb, One-Eye climbs first, talking all the time about how good it will be when the bluebells are flowering in the wood, and when the leaves come back on the trees, and when they reach Burrow Cave.

"Up ye come!" he calls down when he reaches the top.

Sapphyr goes first, followed by Star, and then Flimsy. Flimsy has only gone a little way when she calls to Mowzl, "Mowzl — I mean, Emmy, I don't think I am strong enough to climb this alone. Will you help me?"

"Yes — if I climb up below you, you can put your weight on my shoulders."

Mowzl climbs, pushing Flimsy up little by little to make it easier for her.

Digga is the last to climb up.

When they reach the top, and One-Eye has coiled the zigzag rope, Digga leads the way onwards.

"Come on! The last bit, and we're home!"

They walk in single file as before. Everyone is tired now and longing to be home.

"Look! Look! I can see light!" cries Flimsy.

They can see light coming from the opening into Burrow Cave. Arriving at last, breathless from rushing towards it, they tumble noisily through the narrow opening, and into the cave. A cheer goes up from all the mice gathered there who have been waiting anxiously for their return.

"Hooray! Welcome home!"

"Welcome home, Star and Mowzl!"

Dazzled by the morning light, Star and Mowzl are made a fuss of while everyone asks questions all at once. So begins a celebration that will go on for a long time, and Star and Mowzl fall asleep right where they are, in the middle of the happy crowd.

Outside, the world is bright and cold, the snow sparkling in the morning sun.

Chapter Seven

Bowl of Things

Mowzl sits in the Gypshun Boat looking out of the window. His feelings are in a turmoil with the memories that the story of "Snow!" has awakened.

Tears sting his eyes as he thinks about the story; he hadn't remembered any of it until he spoke it just now, and with the memories comes a wave of sadness that sweeps over him. It is a long time that he has been in the human world and, although he has grown to love LuLu and Pip, he is homesick, and the story reminds him of his family and friends.

Suddenly, he remembers Star naming him with a new, special, name — Emmy — in the darkness inside the mountain.

He thinks about how mysterious it is that he is telling these stories. It is only since Pip was able to imagine Emmy's home world that the stories have been arriving.

Tired after all that story-telling, Emmy is ready for a nap. He jumps down from the windowsill, climbs over to the bowl of things and snuggles into his pouch. Before falling asleep, he thinks how lovely it would be to go to the woods, and, with the eye of his heart, he sees a clearing where the sun is shining through the leaves overhead making a pool of light. A million insects buzz about: flies and hoverflies, wood-wasps, butterflies and — oh! — what could be making those bushes wobble about like that?

He falls asleep.

~

Purling in his pouch, Emmy finds himself in a beam of sunshine somewhere in the woods. Butterflies come to investigate and flutter around him showing off their colours.

"You's ticklin' Emmy!" he says, laughing, and the butterflies rustle their wings, whispering to him.

"You are the biggest bee we ever did see, the biggest bee we ever did see . . ."

They flutter in Emmy's face, tickling him, and he laughs again.

"'Nough! Be stoppin' pleez! Now I's kno-in' ow Pippee's feelin' wen I's ticklin' im!"

They stop fluttering in his face and instead flutter around in a cloud of colour that follows him as the pouch moves on.

"I's not a bee, I's a mouse. I's likin' you flutterbys; you's skwizzit."

Emmy surveys the clearing, an open space between the trees probably made some time ago when a big tree fell over; young trees and bushes are growing, racing to get to the sky, and smaller plants and flowers flourish too. This undergrowth is just what insects like, and the air buzzes with the sound of wings.

Nearby, bushes are jiggling and shaking as though a big animal is moving about underneath them.

It's a badger, or a wild boar, thinks Emmy, but then recalls that there are no boar in these woods, or so he's been told.

"Wot ave we ere appnin', me wondaz?" he murmurs out loud as he moves closer to investigate, his pouch moving without him having to do anything in particular. The butterflies drift back to the sunbeams. Above the bushes now, Emmy hears a voice below.

"Ouch! Ow! Oi! Lemme go!"

Emmy is curious and wants to see who it is. He gets close enough to look down through the leaves, and there he sees a young human. It's a boy, and he is trying to free himself from a bramble which has hooked into his T-shirt and simply won't let him go.

"Allo! Mi name iz Emmy, n I's a mouse. 'Ow's I 'elpin'?

"Ow! I wanna get rid of this 'orrible bramble!" says the boy, without looking up.

"I'sll elp but wot you's avin' to be realizin' iz, bramblz iz very clevva n nevva stupid at all, n you's avin' to be lookin' at itz fornz, n be seein' ow they's curvin' bakwudz, n you's avin' to be steppin' bakwudz n sayin' sorry, n brambles'll be lettin' you get ome."

The boy stares up at Emmy in astonishment. Emmy's voice is a surprise at first, but the boy feels soothed by it, even though he's still angry and wants to shout. He wants to shout, 'what's you knowin' 'bout it anyway, you toy mouse, 'n what's you doin' floatin' 'bout in a ol' sock?', but his anger fades, and he looks at the bramble seeing that the mouse is right, so he steps back, unhooks the bramble and lifts it off his T-shirt. He turns away, but then looks back.

"Sorry, bramble."

He is very surprised at himself. He never would have thought he would ever, ever say 'sorry' to a bramble. Freed from the bramble, he pushes on through the bushes and disappears.

Emmy, still floating above, loses sight of him. "Is you lettin' me be comin' wiv you?" he calls out.

"I's 'idin'."

"Wot's you idin' from?"

"Eyes."

"Who's eyz?"

"Anybody's eyes, 'cos I bunked off school."

While they are talking, Emmy comes down lower and follows the boy into a den. It's made with sticks pushed into the ground in a rough circle and bent over to meet at the top, where they are tied with ragged bits of string. Plastic bags have been stretched over the poles to keep off the rain, and there are more branches and twigs over the top to hold it all down, tied here and there with more string. On the ground is a log. The boy sits on the log staring glumly at the ground.

"I'sll be tellin' no body."

"'Ow come you's talkin'?"

"Coz I's learned ooman talk. Wotz yor name?"

"Billy."

"Allo, Billee. I's avin' a cousin called BillBill."

He floats at the height of Billy's eyes.

"'As I gone mad or summat, talkin' with a toy mouse what's floatin' in mid-air in a ol' sock? Is I dreamin'?"

"You's not dreamin', Billee, n you's not mad, wot evva mad iz meanin'. Why's you idin' from skool?"

"I 'ates school, 'cos I gets in trouble, 'n it's all about 'xams 'n not 'bout real things."

"Woodz iz yor skool, Billee."

"Whad'ya mean?"

"Billee, all wotz in wild places iz teachin' you wotz real."

"There ain't no wild places no more. This little bit o' wood is all what's left round 'ere."

"You's findin' Emmy, n Emmy's real."

"You real? What's your name? Emmy? What sort of a name is that? 'N you ain't real 'cos you's a toy mouse."

"You's rite, Billee, me's only toy mouse, n it urtz."

Billy stares at Emmy.

"'Urts? Bein' a toy?"

"It's true, Billee, it urtz bein' a toy, coz me 'as an 'eart wiv real feelin's."

They are quiet for a bit.

"Where's you from, Emmy?"

"Me's from uvva world where I's real mouse, n I's comin' to ooman world n not kno-in' ow to get ome."

"Where's you livin'?"

"I's wiv ooman called Pippee, n e's poorly sorted, n wiv LuLu too, n she's ooman too."

"Where's they at?"

"They's near where all deaded oomans iz berrid in erf."

"Oh — cemetry."

"Yip, semtri."

Billy pauses for a moment. He is still flustered by the idea of a talking mouse, and a toy one at that.

"'N you's floatin' about in a ol' sock?"

"It's notta sok, it's a pouch, wotz knut wiv magic wool."

"Hmm."

Mowzl stops and glances around the impressive structure that is Billy's den.

"Billee?"

"What?"

"Iz you yourself makin' this littl ows?"

"Me 'n a mate."

"Iz e a good frend?"

"E's a she."

"Wotz er name?"

"Larky."

"Iz Larkee feelin' like you's feelin'?"

"What?"

"You's not appi iz you, Billee?"

Billy has never talked like this with anyone, not even with his friends. Not even with his best friend Larky. He looks at Emmy and feels anger rising like a burning heat, and before he can stop himself, words burst out of him.

"It ain't none o' your business!" he yells.

Silence.

"Emmy's sorry, e's leavin'."

Emmy slowly drifts up and away from Billy, and out of the bivouac, which is the name for the shelter that Billy and Larky have made. He hears the sound of a woodpecker drumming and begins to move in that direction.

"Emmy, wait!"

Billy comes out of the bivouac and looks around until he sees Emmy floating in the sunlight in the clearing. He pushes through the bushes towards him.

"I ain't never 'ad talkin' like this before," he admits.

"Billee, I's sorry. I's feelin' you in mi 'eart, n wordz appnz."

"'N I's sorry I's yellin' at ya."

Mowzl smiles down to let Billy know that he forgives him.

"Billee, let's be findin' woodpecker."

"What?"

"Woz you earin drummin'?"

"Never 'eard nuffin," syas Billy gruffly.

"E's nearby, n e can elp."

What Emmy doesn't say is that he is secretly calling the woodpecker. Do you ever have that feeling when you just know someone is looking at you, and the instant you turn and catch them looking, they look away? Well, this is a bit like that only more so, with the magic of the pouch. Emmy can call creatures from far away. He is not as good at it as Flimsy, but he's getting better now he has his pouch. Emmy calls it 'callin' wiv mi 'eart'.

"Be comin', Billee!" he calls as he moves towards the sound of the drumming.

They have not gone far into the trees when a bird flies down, landing on a tree trunk and clinging on with long toes. He hops up the tree a bit, moving as easily as if he were hopping along the ground.

The bird is mostly black and white, but with a bright red patch on the back of his head and another bright red patch under his tail. He is very smart indeed, and he is fidgety and looks mischievous.

"Hallo, Mowzl!" says the bird. "Who is this human cub?"

Billy stares, his eyes wide and mouth open. He can't believe that he has just heard a bird speak.

"Allo, Rattltap, this ooman cub iz Billee. Billee, pleez be meetin' Rattltap who's a woodnpecka."

"Woodpecker, if you please!"

"I's sorry, Rattltap, wood pecka."

"Hallo, Billy," says Rattltap. Billy just stands there gaping. "Mowzl, I think Billy is practising to be a fish."

"E's nevva 'ad talk wiv wild creacha before," explains Emmy.

"Ah! Billy! You are very lucky to have met the flying mouse. Not many humans can hear the wild talk!"

"I ain't believin' what I's 'earin'! I's dreamin' ain't I?"

"Ah, good, Billy, you can talk! You were dreaming before, perhaps, but you are awake now!" declares Rattltap.

Billy watches the bird move about restlessly on the bark of the tree; Rattltap cocks his head this way and that, looking straight into Billy's eyes. Billy notices his powerful beak and thinks that a peck from that would hurt a lot.

"Yes, Billy, my bill is very strong so that I can peck into wood to find the insect larvae that I live on. But don't be worried, I am not going to peck you."

"What's larvee?"

"Larvae is the name for the grubs that burrow inside trees, usually in the dead and rotten bits. Some of them live for many winters and get really big, and when they are ready, they make a chrysalis. When the chrysalis is ready, it hatches into a beetle, or other creature, which burrows its way out of the wood and flies away, leaving a round hole."

Rattltap's voice slowly calms Billy down.

"Is you eatin' these larvee?"

"Yes, Billy I am. I have to peck into the wood and find them, like this — drrrrrrr!"

Rattltap pecks at the bark of the tree with such speed that his head becomes a blur.

"But I won't find anything to eat here, because this is not dead or rotten wood, it's alive and growing."

"'Ow's you drummin', Rattltap?" asks Billy.

"I look for a broken branch up in a tree where the wood is split and hollow, and when I peck on the wood it makes more noise because of the hollowness. Like that! Did you hear?"

"Yeah! I 'eard drummin' from a way off."

"You are awake! That's my beloved Tattlrap! She's calling!"

Rattltap sees a tree nearby with a fallen branch beneath it, he flies up into the tree to investigate. Finding a good sounding board where the wood is torn, he drums, and the sound echoes through the woodland.

Emmy and Billy hear a reply from far away.

"Tattlrap will be coming to find me," says Rattltap. He has flown back to the tree close to Emmy and Billy. "How's your other human, Mowzl? You said he was poorly."

"Pippee's poorly sorted, n I's tellin' im n LuLu stories 'bout mi ome world n e's I' betta littl bi littl, but I's worryin'."

"Get 'im out 'ere, Emmy!" cries Billy. "Get 'im 'earin' Rattltap, 'e'll soon be better!"

"You's rite, Billee, but e's too poorly sorted to be movin', so I's been atchin' a plan — I's wantin' you to come n be listenin' to stories, n you be comin' wiv Larkee."

"Mowzl, young Billy is calling you 'Emmy'; are you a different mouse?" asks Rattltap, sounding surprised.

"I's same mouse, Rattltap, but I's merembrin' mi Emmy name wen I's tellin' Pippee a story 'bout mi ome world."

"Ah! Then you shall be Mowzl Emmy, henceforth. Ah, here is Tattlrap!"

They turn to watch her flying between the trees towards them, flapping her wings a few times, then folding them a moment, then flapping her wings a bit more, then folding them again — and so she flies, going up a bit and down a bit, like a wave through the air.

As she arrives she swoops down — then suddenly up again, sticking to the tree like a magnet, just like Rattltap. She looks very like Rattltap except she has no red on the nape of her neck.

"Hallo!" she says. "What have we here? I see a human cub and a flying mouse! Please introduce us, dearly beloved."

"Tattlrap, may I introduce you to Billy, the human cub who can hear and talk the wild talk, and to Mowzl Emmy, the Flying Mouse!"

"Billy, Mowzl Emmy, I am pleased to meet you both and I would like to ask all sorts of questions about where you come from, and what you like to eat, but I am too worried for conversation, I am beside myself with worry."

"What's happened?" says Rattltap, very concerned. "What has upset you, light of my life?"

"The old tree that has been our home for so long fell down in the wind last night and I am very sad and worried, because it will be hard to find another tree that will do for a nest when the spring comes."

"You're right, my dearest. There are no more old trees left in this wood because the humans have taken them all. It's hard to find anywhere to make our nest. You see, Billy, we have to make a hole that is just big enough for us, and then dig out a nest chamber inside the tree, deep enough so that hunters can't reach our babies. We need old trees for that."

"What shall we do?" says Tattlrap. "I am worried, because we must be ready when Spring comes. Will we have to find another wood?"

"Oh no!" cries Billy. "There 'ain't another wood for miles, an' I's only just met ya! You can't be goin' already!"

"Calm down, everyone," says Rattltap. "I have had my eye on a certain tree for some time now. I think I may be able to make a nest chamber, so let's go and see about it before we get too worried."

"Where's it at?" asks Billy.

"Young human cub, I cannot tell you that— not until I know you better. I mean no offence."

"E's rite, Billee," says Emmy. "Wild creachaz iz not appy wiv oomans, n wot oomans iz doin'."

"I 'ain't 'appy with 'umans neither, I 'ates 'umans."

"Now-now, Billy," says Rattltap. "Be careful not to let all that anger make your heart go prickly. Billy, I see you, remember that; I know we shall be friends. Come on now, my beloved," he says, turning to Tattlrap. "We must get to work. Goodbye for now young human cub, we shall meet again, I know. Goodbye, Mowzl Emmy, bring that Pippee to see us soon!"

"Goodbye!" calls Tattlrap, and away they fly.

Billy stands staring in the direction that the birds had flown.

"Iz you orite, Billee?" says Emmy, floating in the air just an arm's length away.

Billy looks at Emmy.

"Emmy, somethin's 'appened. Somethin' feels broke inside, somethin's opened up, 'n I's feelin' cold 'n 'ot, 'n I's feelin' old anger, 'n I's feelin' 'appy where I's never been feelin' before."

Tears come to his eyes. He takes a deep breath.

"What's 'appnin', Emmy? I's feelin' broke open."

"Billee, az I's been sayin' to Pippee, I' betta at feelin' iz urtin' lotz."

They are quiet and just look at each other. A smile begins to spread across Billy's face.

"Billee, I's watchin' you atchin' out ov yor krisalis!"

"We's only met a minute ago, 'n you's changed me life already," grins Billy.

"You's bein' Billee, you's bein' wot you's iz. We's all avin' to be birfd lotz ov times, Billee."

Billy takes some deep breaths, waiting for his feelings to calm down. It slowly dawns on him that his world has changed and will never be the same again.

"I's scared Emmy."

"I's 'ere wiv you, Billee."

Emmy watches over him, staying close. Billy thinks about the human that Emmy was talking about with Rattltap just now. *Pip, wasn't it? Or Pippee? Maybe I could talk to him,* he thinks. *I need to talk to someone!* He asks Emmy about him.

"Who's this 'uman you's talkin' about? Pippee, was it? Where's 'e livin'? Cemetry wasn't it?"

"You'sll be kno-in wen itz time," says Emmy mysteriously.

"You's goin' now, ain't ya?"

"You's rite, Billee, I's goin' wen pouch iz goin'."

"Emmy, sorry to yell at ya. 'Ow's I findin' ya?"

"Be callin' wiv yor 'eart."

"'Ow's I doin' that?"

"You'sll be kno-in!"

Emmy moves away, fades, and disappears with a pop. Billy watches him go, the smile spreading across his face again.

~

Emmy wakes in the bowl of things. He yawns, stretches and climbs out of his pouch, and sits quietly on the rim of the bowl.

"Hallo, Emmy!" whispers LuLu. "I've been wondering when you'd wake up. Thank you for the 'Snow!' story, I've got so many questions for you!"

"Iz Pippee sleepin'?"

"Yes, he is, we should wait for him to wake up."

"LuLu?"

"Yes, Em?"

"Dreamin' in mi pouch, I's meetin' a littl ooman called Billee."

"When was this?!" LuLu asks excitedly.

"Before I's wakin' up a minnit ago."

"That's good, Em! Did you like Billy?"

"E's a good un, but e's sad."

LuLu smiles, looking Emmy in the eye.

"I bet you made him smile."

"'Is mowf woz angin' open wen we's meetin' Rattltap!"

"Who's Rattltap?"

"E's a wood pecka you'sll be meetin' wen you's purlin'. I's meetin' im wen I's dreamin' in mi pouch."

"Have you been in your pouch a lot, Emmy?" asks LuLu.

"Evry sleep, n I's meetin' mennee creachaz."

Pip groans, yawns and stretches, but then is silent again.

"LuLu, iz e gettin' betta?"

"Yes, but I think it will be some time yet before he's well enough to get up and go out."

"E might be enough well to be dreamin' in 'is pouch."

LuLu pauses.

"Maybe. We can talk about that with him today."

"We'sll ave a go."

Pip yawns again and this time Emmy jumps onto the bed, runs up to Pip's face and jumps about, singing.

"Allo, Pippee, wakey-up! A-a-a-nd your mowf goze wide n yor eyez goze big, n yor eerz stix owt like theyz orlwayz did!"

"Mowzl! Stop! Please! I'm awake! Stop!" Pip splutters.

Emmy stops jumping about, runs to LuLu and sits in her hand.

"Oh, Mowzl," says Pip. "I just remembered, you're called Emmy now. Why didn't you tell us before?"

"I's forgettin', coz ov fog, n story bringz merembrin'."

"I like your new name, Emmy," LuLu says. "I can see why Star wanted to call you that. You two shared a big adventure and now you're like brothers. Can we write the names down? I'm a bit muddled up about who's who."

LuLu puts Emmy in the Gypshun Boat on the windowsill.

"LuLu, wot you's sayin' iz troof, n Star n me's bruvvaz now. We'sll be ritin' names coz Pippee'z avin' to get 'Wot Appnd' rit."

Pip is very puzzled. "How can you tell the stories if you can't remember anything about what happened to you?" he asks.

"It's appnin' suddn, Pippee, since you's seein' Purl n Scraggy, n since LuLu 'as made pouchiz. I's not kno-in' ow, all I's kno-in' iz I's needin' to fank you, Pippee, n fank you, LuLu, too."

"Thank you too, Emmy," says LuLu softly. "We are so happy that you have come to our world, but we know that you are very homesick. It's good for you to remember, can you remember the names of your brothers and sisters?"

"Oldist iz Purl, n Acorn, n Beechnut. Beechnut got deaded."

"Oh, Emmy! What happened?"

"I's not merembrin', xcept I's feelin' a story to be appnin'."

"I'm sure you will remember, Emmy, and when you do I want you to tell us about Beechnut please."

"Fankz, LuLu."

"Em," says Pip. "What we could do is make a family tree, which is like a map of the generations of your family."

Emmy is happy that Pip is joining in. He looks at LuLu and they smile at each other.

"Ow'z we makin' yor tree, Pippee?"

"I'll write down the names, and sort them into some kind of order."

"Good fing we's got for evva!"

"Emmy!" says LuLu, laughing. "Alright, you've said that your sisters and brother are Pearl, Beechnut and Acorn. Who's next?"

"I's birfd wiv Dreamer n Saffyr, so we's same oldniss, n we's feelin' each uvvaz feelinz, n dad iz Scribbla, n mum iz Wunda."

"Stop!" cries LuLu. "I can't keep up! How are you doing, Pip?"

"Yes, little by little we grow's a tree, and then we'll know what names all be," replies Pip, with a cheeky smile.

"Ha! Pippee, you's lernin' Emmy talk!" says Emmy.

"Let's see how this looks," says Pip, turning his notebook sideways, so they can see what he has written.

"From littl akornz mytee oakz iz growin'," says Emmy.

"Tell us about your cousins, Emmy," says LuLu quickly, trying to cover up Emmy's tease. "What are their names?"

"Cousinz iz Scraggy, n Star, n Flimzee, n they's got littl sistaz Scarlitt, n Violit. Their mum'z LaLa, n dad'z Tooby, who's mi Uncle One-Eye."

"Hold on, Emmy! Scarlett and . . .?" cries Pip.

"Violit."

"And what's Uncle One-Eye's proper name?"

"Tooby," says LuLu.

"Thanks, LuLu. Right, here we go!"

"Wunda n Tooby's bein' bruvva n sista."

"Ah, good. We can join them up too! Do they have siblings?"

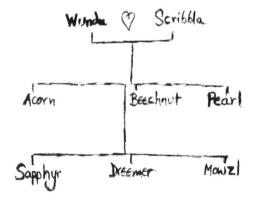

Emmy stares at Pip with a strange frown. "Pippee, siblinz iz soundin' like nastee dizeez, n they's not poorly sorted."

"No, Emmy!" says Pip, laughing. "What I mean is, do they have brothers and sisters?"

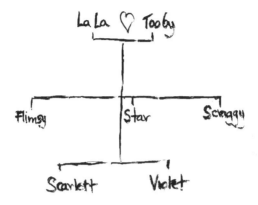

"They's avin' siblinziz, n Captin Blunda, who's themz dad, iz avin' no names so e's givin' em numbaz — Wunda, n Tooby, n Freeda, n Forby, n Fivrit."

"What lovely names!" says LuLu, delighted.

"How's this?"

"Lookin' good, Pippee, if it wozn't sucha mess . . . Wot I's wondrin' iz, wotz appnd to yor tree?"

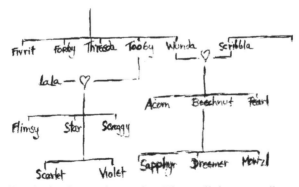

"I'll make it a better shape when I have all the names."

"You'sll nevva be avin' all names, Pippee."

"Well, Emmy, that's why it's a tree — it gets bigger!"

"There are names in the story that we haven't written down yet," LuLu interrupts, to stop them squabbling. "There's Digga Bill and Burrow Bill, and I can't remember who else."

"You's rite, LuLu. I's avin' more cousinz — BillBill, n Littl Garnet — we's callin, 'er Nettl, n they's avin' younga sistaz Marigold, n Rubee. Mum we's callin' Bess, wot iz—"

"Slow down, Em!" cries Pip. "Marigold, Ruby . . . A their Mum? What was her name?"

"Bess, who's Scibblaz sista, n she's me aunt, n dad's bein' Burrow Bill."

"It's getting complicated," sighs Pip. "What about this?"

"Pippee, mi 'eart iz flyin' like a bird coz appyniss iz appnin'."

"I can tell, Emmy," says LuLu. "You're happy to be remembering so much about your home world after so long aren't you? It's telling the stories that's helping you remember, isn't it?"

"N you n Pippee, coz wivout you n Pippee, storeez wouldn't be appnin'."

Pip looks puzzled as he thinks about what Emmy is saying.

"Emmy, I'm not getting this yet. How do we help you to remember?"

"You's learnin' feelin', wot means makin' luv battree."

"What's a love battery, Emmy?" asks LuLu. She doesn't know about what Emmy said to Pip about the love battery when they were walking on the cliffs by the sea. Probably Pip has forgotten all that too because he's not been very well since then.

"I's been tellin' Pippee 'bout makin' bowl ov fingz, to be keepin' littl luv'd fingz wot fillz 'is 'eart wiv warm, littl fingz wot e's found, n luvz."

Emmy pauses; a faraway look comes into his eyes.

"Simpl fingz like littl pebblz from sea, wot merembaz you ov feelin' oshn wind inside you; n like a littl 'eart made wiv red velvit, wot LuLu's givin' Emmy on valuntynz, n mi parsl from Purl n One-Eye, wot comes through portl."

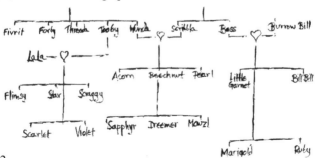

112

The room is very quiet. Emmy stares into space.

"Are you alright, Emmy?" asks LuLu, softly.

"I's merembrin'. LuLu, pleez be gettin' Emmy's bowl ov fingz."

"Of course, Em," says LuLu, going over to get the bowl from the chest of drawers. "Where shall I put it?"

"Pleez be dumpin' all out on Pippee's bed."

"Hey! What's going on!" cries Pip, pretending to be surprised.

"It's orite, Pippee."

LuLu empties the bowl of things onto the bed. Emmy jumps down from the windowsill and rummages about in the jumble, he finds a very small book.

"LuLu, iz you merememberin' littl book you's makin' for Emmy?"

"Yes! Have you written in it?"

"Wiv Pippee's elp, I's ritin' wot e's callin' invntree, wot iz list ov fingz, n it's avin' big 'M' in front wot iz Mowzl, n inside it's sayin': bowl ov fingz invntree (wot iz list):

'1(wun) 'nvlope wiv red velvit 'eart, wot iz valuntynz secrit from LuLu.'"

"Oh, Emmy, you kept it!" says LuLu, clapping with delight.

"Cors me's keepin' it, LuLu, n we's next avin':

'2 (too) tiny pensil, wot I's nickin' off Pippee.'"

"That's where it went!" says Pip.

"'3 (free) I's forgot

4 (for) littl bit ov bloo tak

5 (fiv) square buttn, wotz missin

6 (syx) lympic gold meddl rappa, wot woz choklit wotz bin et

7 (sevn) lablz from One-Eye n Purl's parsl, wot maykz me cryin

8 (ate) cumpas from One-Eye, wot might point ome wen it deesydz

9 (nyn) mi crest made bi LuLu wiv wull fredz . . . n mor.'"

"Emmy, that's so lovely," says LuLu.

"How does this make a 'love battery', Emmy?" asks Pip.

"These iz just words, n we's needin' unwords. It's ways of merembrin' wotz in yor 'eart, fingz wot witniss yor feelin's. It's yor 'eart wot iz luv battree, n we's forgettin' to be lookin', so I's sayin' we's avin' to be makin' bowl ov fingz az an xasize, n we's all avin' to be doin' it."

"Emmy," says LuLu. "I think I understand what you mean. I've got a bowl of things at my place — you know, you like to sleep in it when you come over. I've got all sorts of things that I love in that bowl reminding me of places and people and special moments that have happened. Sometimes, I just like to pick up one of them and hold it in my hand. It might be a stone that reminds me of a time or a place where something important happened, or it might be a little poem folded up, or a beautifully coloured feather. I feel peaceful when I do that."

"I's sleepin' in yor bowl ov fingz, LuLu, coz it's luv battree n I's needin' it n I's feelin' appi n getz energee."

Pip doesn't want to get left behind. "In my bowl of things," he says, "I've got a little cowrie shell I found on a beach in Cornwall when I was little, a bit of string too short to use, and a rusty paper clip that used to hold a photo of . . ."

"Pip! You've got loads of things in there!" cries LuLu. "You must have some things in there that you love!"

"Well, you're right, LuLu, but I do love these little things too, because they remind me not to be too big for my boots."

"Oh, Pippee, you's gettin' deep ere," says Mowzl, teasingly.

Pip frowns at Emmy for a moment, then goes on.

"I have a stone that was given to me by someone very special, and a broken dunnock's egg, which was once a beautiful blue but has faded now; I have some little heads that I made and like to hold sometimes; a bit of rock, given to me by LuLu, which might be gneiss, or schist, so I call it "nice shist", and it reminds me of being in mountains; and there's a ring with a pearl in it that was my mother's, and a tiny diamond given me by someone who died . . ."

"Pippee, I'sll be cryin' inna mo," says Emmy.

"Sorry, Em."

"Not ennee need for sorry, coz you's avin' all ov yor feelin's, n not just eezee ones."

"Pip," says LuLu. "We keep some things because they mean a lot to us, like your little heads, but some things are too big to go into a bowl of things. They are just as important, aren't they? So, we keep something that reminds us of them."

"You's rite, Lulu."

"Hey, Emmy!" cries Pip. "I've just remembered, in your story of 'Home Oak' you talk about going with Pearl to see your Uncle One-Eye."

"I's merembrin."

"And you looked into One-Eye's bowl of things, and there were little heads, and you went into a daydream?"

"One-Eye's bowl ov littl eads 'as big magic."

"Emmy, do the little heads that I make look the same?"

Emmy moves closer to Pip's bowl to inspect them more carefully.

"They's simila."

"How is that possible?"

"Wordz iz nevva kno-in'."

"You mean nobody knows?"

"I's meanin' kno-in' iz where wordz izn't goin', wordz iz stoppin' oomans seein' n feelin' wotz real. Wordz iz not real, wordz iz toolz, powaful toolz."

"You talk in riddles!" gasps Pip.

"He's saying that the mystery cannot be told in words, but can be felt," LuLu explains. "You will understand when you dream into your pouch."

"LuLu, you's rite. Pippee must be purlin' soon."

"What's 'purling', Em?" asks Pip.

"Purlin's wen you's wiv invizibl ones, n in yor pouchiz."

Pip strokes his beard thoughtfully.

"Why do you call it purling?"

"Coz it appnd."

"Emmy!" says LuLu. "You just made it up! You made up 'purlniss' too didn't you?"

"You's not wrong, LuLu, but I's nevva doin' it, I's givn it."

Pip scratches his head. "I'll never understand you, Emmy! But what were you saying just now about the bowl of things?"

"Bowl ov fingz iz luv battree wotz growin' purlniss in yor 'eart, so you'sll be purlin' n feelin' unwordz."

Pip looks just as confused,

"Pip, if I understand Emmy right," says LuLu, "we need the bowl of things because we humans are out of touch with the invisible ones, who don't use words. They communicate directly with feeling — or intuition we could call it. Emmy calls it 'purlniss', because of his sister Pearl. Our pouches help us to be closer to the invisible ones and more open to the unwords, and for the pouches to work they must be kept in the bowl of things."

"LuLu, you's clevva wiv wordz," says Emmy.

Pip still looks puzzled.

"LuLu, how can you understand so quickly? Emmy's told me all this stuff before, and I'm still not getting it."

"LuLu's kno-in' already, coz she 'as purlniss."

"You know already too, Pip," says Lulu. "Otherwise you would never have been able to see Pearl and Scraggy the other day, but you must stop trying to think about it. It can't be 'thought'. You are trying so hard to understand it that you are making yourself ill."

"Oh, what can I do?" moans Pip, unhappily.

"Pippee, we's been ere before. It's nevva a doin', it's a bein'. You'sll be purlin' wen purlin' 'appnz, it'll nevva be 'urrid, n you's avin' to be payshnt. Just be izniss."

"What's isness?" says Pip.

"Izniss iz true bein' ov fingz. Purlniss iz seein' true bein' ov uvva creachaz, n all fingz."

Pip looks downcast.

LuLu breaks the silence that follows. "Well, I'm hungry! Anyone else hungry?"

"LuLu, I's starvin'."

"Emmy! What about you, Pip?"

"Mmm, yes, LuLu, please could I have scrambled eggs with cheese and marmalade?"

"LuLu! E's gettin' betta!" cries Emmy.

"Alright, I'll make us something to eat!" says LuLu, going to the kitchen.

"Emmy?" says Pip, after a quiet time.

"Pippee?"

"Did you and Star think that you would die in that cave?"

"Yip. We's finkin' we'sll be deaded, n we's frit till we's earin' invizibl ones singin'."

Quiet again.

"Pippee, pleez be returnin' fingz to bowl for Emmy."

"Of course, Em."

Emmy climbs back onto the windowsill and sits in the Gypshun Boat. After a bit, when Pip has put everything back into the bowl, and put the bowl back onto the chest of drawers, Emmy speaks again.

"You's avin' to get into yor 'ead, Pippee, that oomans iz finkin' they's seprat, coz of bein' abl to fink. Creachaz, n all Nature iz feelin' belongin', not sepratniss — they's not finkin', they's kno-in'."

"But you 'think', Emmy, and you're a creature!"

"You sez Emmy finks, me sez Emmy's feelin'. In troof, creachaz iz finkin', but they's nevva seprat like oomans iz, they's makin' wild web, they's growin' wild web wiv they's izniss."

"Oh, Emmy! I'm lost again."

"Ere comes LuLu! Ooray!"

"Sit up, Pip," LuLu says, putting a tray on Pip's lap. She picks up a small bowl to take to Emmy.

"Taste Bomz! Mi favrit." Emmy puts his face into the bowl of chocolates and breathes in deeply. "Mmm, fankz, LuLu!"

Pip is already tucking in, and LuLu takes her plate and a fork from the tray and sits down to eat. She and Pip are having scrambled eggs and cheese, though Pip has marmalade too.

"Delicious, LuLu, thanks very much!"

"You's gettin' betta, Pippee."

"Yes, I think I am!"

"You's not to be urryin'. Be keepin' pouch in bowl ov fingz, n not in yor 'and. You'sll ave to be payshnt, coz you izn't reddee."

"Alright, Emmy. Why are you giving me all these instructions?"

"Coz LuLu n me's leavin' you lonesum for a littl bit."

"How long is a little bit, Emmy?" asks Pip, nervous about what Emmy might say next.

"Three sleeps p'raps."

"Oh, no!"

"Pip, Emmy's right," says LuLu. "It's time to get yourself organised again and make your own food and everything."

"Wot I's needin' ov you, Pippee, iz you be lettin' ritin' appn wen wordz iz cummin'."

Pip puts on a voice and pretends to be annoyed.

"Alright, Em, I get the picture. You want me to sort myself out while you two go and have adventures!"

"You's 'bout rite."

"Oh, Emmy, your teasing him!" says LuLu.

"It's alright, LuLu," says Pip. "I'm winding him up too. I know it's time I got myself sorted."

LuLu tidies up the plates, taking the tray back to the kitchen. When she returns, she picks Emmy up from the windowsill and gets his pouch from the bowl of things.

"Goodbye, Pip, see you in three sleeps," she says.

"N you can be doin' woshin' up, Pippee! Bi!"

"Oh, Emmy!" LuLu says, laughing.

And off they go.

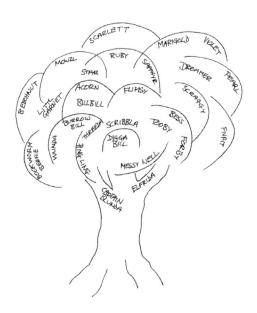

Chapter Eight

Mowzl and Scraggy meet Waggl

After three sleeps, LuLu and Emmy visit Pip again to see how he is. They find him asleep in bed.

"Wake up, Pip!" says LuLu. "Have you been asleep for three days?"

Emmy jumps out of Lulu's pocket and bounces about on Pip's tummy singing one of his wake-up songs.

"In yor eerz, in yor eyz n up yor noze — in yor 'air where yor bald patch growz, — on yor chin, down yor neck n in yor beard, — you'll nevva catch me, coz I's disappeared!"

"Stop, I'm awake! Emmy, stop! Please!" Pip protests.

Emmy jumps up onto the windowsill from where he surveys the room. LuLu is looking around as well, and they see sheets of paper scattered all over the floor.

"It's alright," says Pip, noticing how dismayed they are to see the mess. "I know where everything is! A lot has been written since I saw you last, but I don't have any idea how. It's very mysterious; I wake up, and there it is all over the floor. Oh! I've been missing you both."

"I's been missin' avin' teezabillitee Pippee too!"

"Are you feeling better, Pip?" asks LuLu.

"Yes, much better thanks. I want to get outside again, and I want to —"

"Be slowin down, Pippee, you's urryin' wot's not urryabl," says Emmy, interrupting.

"Have you been eating properly?" asks LuLu, wondering what the kitchen looks like. It's probably piled high with dirty bowls and plates and cutlery waiting to be washed up.

"Yes, thanks, LuLu. But what a poor host I am, are you hungry, or thirsty?"

"I'd like some water, but I'll fetch it," she says. "I'll bring some for you too."

She goes to the kitchen and is pleased to see the washing up all done and the room clean and tidy. Pip must be lots better. She finds a little bowl and some chocolate for Emmy, and she fills two glasses with water from the tap, carrying everything on a tray back to Pip's room.

Emmy is in the Gypshun Boat telling Pip about his adventures. When LuLu places the little bowl of chocolate pieces next to him he breathes in the chocolate fumes. She gives Pip his water and sits down in the chair by the window.

"What has Emmy been saying, Pip?" she says.

"Emmy said thanks for getting lots of writing done, and I said that I didn't do it and I don't know who did. Did you do it, LuLu?"

"No, I didn't."

"Emmy? How is it happening?"

"It's a mystry, Pippee, it's appnin' wen you's sleepin'."

"I don't get it, I really don't. Anyway, LuLu, Emmy then went on to tell me about meeting an oak leaf in the woods."

"Meeting an oak leaf!" cries LuLu, surprised. "What ever do you mean, Emmy?"

"I's been purlin' nearly evry sleep n lotz iz appnin'. I's been seein' Rattltap lotz ov times, n Priklstik too. I's findin' littl ooman called Billee, n e's meetin' Rattltap, n I's meetin' uvva creachaz too who's tellin' 'bout ow oomans iz makin' oles in wild web.

"I's lookin at oak leaf wot's lyin' on the erf, n I's feelin' a funny feelin' appnin' inside. I's merembrin' wen I's lookin' at an oak leaf at ome under Ome Oak, n I's in uvva world — all ov a suddn I's in mi ome world . . ." Emmy falls silent.

"Are you alright, Emmy?" LuLu asks, gently.

"Emmy's feelin' sad in side, LuLu, n feelin' muchly for ome, n I's feelin' story appnin' wotz wantin' to get rit down."

"Have you got a story for us now, Em?" asks Pip.

"I's all full wiv story, n I's avin' to be tellin'."

"We want to hear it, Emmy," says LuLu. "Do tell us!"

"LuLu, pleez be gettin Pippee's pouch for im."

Lulu fetches Pip's pouch from the bowl of things and puts it into his hand.

"Thanks," he says, feeling the mysterious energy flooding in to him from his pouch.

LuLu has been carrying her pouch in her pocket, and now she holds it in her hand and sits down again. Soon they are settled, and the room becomes quiet.

"Wen storys' iz comin' they's iggldeepiggldee, n I's not kno-in' wotz appnin' wen till it appnz."

He looks out of the window waiting for the story to arrive.

"We's goin' bak before 'Snow!', wen Emmy woz Mowzl. Mowzl n Scraggy's explorin' forrist n findin' ollo cherry tree.

They's goin' inside olloniss n climbin' up, n Mowzl iz goin' first coz e's lovin' climbin' n Scraggy's followin' be'ind gettin' dust n bits fallin' on 'is ead."

Emmy's voice and the magic of the pouches, lull Pip and LuLu into story sleep. LuLu pulls a blanket over herself and snuggles down, the scene in Emmy's home world appearing in the eye of her heart as Emmy's voice brings it to life.

~

"'Ow much 'igher you goin', Em?" calls Scraggy, peering upwards inside the hollow tree. At that moment bits of rotten wood, twigs and feathers cascade down on his head, getting dust into his eyes and nose.

"Aaatchooo!"

"You alright, Scraggy?" Mowzl calls, from the darkness above. "You must've got a face full. It was an old nest that fell down, I must've nudged it."

"'Ow much 'igher you goin'?" Scraggy calls again, coughing and spluttering.

"Well, if there's been a nest here, there must be a hole for birds to get in. I'll go a bit higher and look for it. Can't see any light up there yet."

"I'm comin' up!" yells Scraggy, not wanting to be left out of any discoveries. He climbs the crumbly surface inside the tree.

They are on a special mission. Usually, their job is to go out into the woods to gather seeds and other useful things that they find to take home to Burrow Cave; there, everything is sorted out and stored in the storage chambers. Today, they are not gathering food, but are looking out for new nut bushes. One of their tricks is to climb trees to get high enough to see over the undergrowth and, if they are lucky, they can see bushes that might be good for seeds. They are getting good at recognising hazelnut bushes, which are their favourite, and if they do see something worth investigating they have to get down to the ground and go to look at it.

Today they are excited because they have gone a bit further into the wildwood than they would normally go, and have found a special tree, a very old cherry tree, enormous at the bottom with spreading buttress roots. There are holes between the buttress roots going inside the tree, and a dry, brown powder spills out from inside; it is the remains of the middle of the tree which has rotted away leaving a cavity that goes high up inside. The cherry tree is still alive and healthy, it doesn't mind being hollow, in fact it quite likes it because all sorts of creatures come to shelter and sleep in there. Sometimes the visitors hide from whoever is trying to catch them, sometimes visitors make nests and raise their babies inside the tree

The cherry tree likes it when the little cherries that grow on its branches ripen; birds and squirrels come from miles around to eat them, and mice gather the cherrystones that fall to the ground. Some of the cherry pips get eaten, but many are spread around by creatures wanting to store them for winter, and some of these will grow into new cherry trees.

As Mowzl climbs further up inside the tree, he can hear Scraggy below him breathing noisily and shouting out, "Oi!" and 'Not again!' every so often, as rotten wood falls away dustily from Mowzl's paws, showering down onto him.

"I can see light!" calls Mowzl, all of a sudden.

"Good! 'Ow far now? Climin' is 'ard work."

"Not far now."

Mowzl climbs towards the light; his paws feel the edge of a ledge, and he pulls himself up onto a rough, but fairly flat surface. The light is bright, and he is dazzled for a moment. The hole in the tree is a bit above the ledge, and is roundish, where the middle of a broken branch has rotted away.

As Mowzl's eyes get used to the light, he finds himself looking into the face of a very strange bird unlike any bird that he has seen before. It's big, bigger than him, but it must be a baby because it has no feathers.

"Hallo, my name is Mowzl and I'm a mouse," he says, as he usually does when he meets another creature. "What's your name?"

"Quarrk!" shouts the parrot chick, for it is indeed a baby parrot. "Quarrk! Waggl is me, me is Waggl."

"Hallo, Waggl, what sort of a bird are you?"

"Me's an 'alf grow'd parrot bird, and Mummy says one more moon and me'll 'ave feathers and me'll fly," flaps the chick excitedly.

At that moment, Scraggy's front paws and his ears appear as he climbs onto the ledge.

"Quarrk! Quarrk!" Waggl cries in alarm.

Scraggy is dazzled by the light and startled by the baby bird's screeching; he slips backwards and might have fallen, but for Mowzl grabbing his arm.

"'Oo in the world is this?" Scraggy asks.

"'Waggl', so he says."

"Ow come 'e's got no feathers? It'll be winter before 'e's flyin'?"

"I don't know, Scragg, we'll have to ask."

Waggl tilts his fluffy head a little. "Me hear Mummy . . . Mummy cummin. Mummy cummin."

"Is she coming now?" says Mowzl, worried because the Mummy bird might be big and scary and might not like two strangers in her nest.

"Nowcum howcum," squawks the parrot chick.

"D'you always shout, Waggl?" says Scraggy, who is beginning to catch up with himself after nearly falling. But before Waggl can answer they are plunged into semi-darkness and all three peer up towards the hole in the tree; instead of seeing the sky they see the mother bird peering in, blocking out most of the light.

"Hmmmmmm! Now I have three babies! Krrrrrrrk!" The note her hum makes goes up and down again in an interested sort of way, like this:

mmmm

mmm   mmmm

Hmmm   mmmmm!

Only it should look like a smooth curve, but it won't type like that, so we had better draw it:

"Hallo. I'm Mowzl and I'm a mouse," says Mowzl. "I've never seen a bird like you before, where do you come from?"

"Shipwrecked! Shipwrecked!"

"You've got a big curvy beak like an eagle," says Scraggy. "You's not an eagle, is you? Oh, I's Scraggy 'n I's a mouse too."

"Ha! You talk too!" says the mother parrot. "No, me's no eagle."

"Mummee, what's a mows?"

"These two are mowses, so let's ask them!"

She looks Mowzl and Scraggy up and down. "Me see mowses before shipwreck. What are you? Pirate mowses?"

"We live in burrows in the ground under the trees," says Mowzl. "We find seeds and nuts in the wildwood to eat. We are wood mice. We are not pirate mice, whatever they might be."

"Hmmm. Why you in parrot nest?"

Mowzl explains about climbing trees to get a better view when they are searching for food. This tree is unusual because it's hollow and it seemed a good idea to climb up the inside, and that was how they came to be in Waggl's nest!

"Hmm!" hums the mother parrot suspiciously.

"We's never meanin' to give Waggl a fright!" says Scraggy.

"Me's not frit!" cries Waggl. "Me's 'appy to ave friends."

"Waggl's Mum?" says Scraggy.

"Quark?"

"'Ow come Waggl's got no feathers?"

Waggl's mum looks slightly annoyed by the question.

"Waggl is baby parrot, yes."

"But summer is finished, and leaves is beginin' to fall, 'e should be flyin' already!"

"Shipwrecked!"

"We don't understand," says Mowzl. "What do you mean by 'shipwrecked'?"

"When Waggl was egg we see ocean; when Waggl hatch, only trees. Shipwrecked."

"Was your nest on a ship?" asks Mowzl, remembering Uncle One-Eye's talk of ships.

"High up, crow's nest."

"Crows nesting there too?" asks Scraggy.

"No crows, no crows."

Scraggy looks puzzled.

"I don't get it," he says. "'ow did you get 'ere?"

"Mistree, we lost."

"Can we help you to get home?" asks Mowzl.

"Hope so, hope so."

Mowzl thinks for a moment about how they could help.

"Do you have a name, Mother of Waggl?"

"Amazina Loco Sophia, at your service!" she bows.

"Oh dear, what a long name! It does sound lovely, but what do we call you?"

"Gabbee short Gabbee long!"

"Gabbee! I like that. Gabbee, can we have a look out from the nest hole?"

"Come, look now!"

The two mice, and Waggl, shuffle towards the hole in the tree to have a look out, while Gabbee moves along to get out of their way so they can see.

"Weeeeee! Waggl fly soon! Waggl fly soon!" shouts the baby, excited to see the treetops waving in the breeze, the leaves bright in their autumn colours.

"You'd better be growin' some feathers before you's jumpin' out!" says Scraggy.

Mowzl has never before been so high up, except perhaps at Eagle Rock, and the view of the wildwood takes his breath away. He thinks that he can recognise a few of the trees, but the only one he is certain of is the oak tree growing beside Burrow Cave. He is happy to be able to see Home Oak.

"Gabbee, I can see where our family live! Do you see that oak tree over there, with three billowy shapes?" asks Mowzl.

"I see! We go, we go . . ."

"How . . . what?" says Mowzl in confusion.

"Climb Gabbee's back, mowses tight hold" yells Gabbee.

"OMG!" exclaims Mowzl, as he and Scraggy scramble out from the hole in the tree and onto Gabbee's back.

"Oh, you's lucky! Come back see Waggl soon, yes?" cries Waggl.

"We'll come back — woops, I nearly fell off!" cries Mowzl.

"Tight hold mowses, hold feathers!"

And before Scraggy can say 'don't look down!' Gabbee spreads her wings and rolls off the branch into the air.

"Come soon yes!" yells Waggl.

But his voice is drowned out by the screams made by Scraggy and Mowzl, as Gabbee glides and tumbles between the trees.

"Aaaaaaa!" Mowzl squeals.

"Yiiikes!" Scraggy shrieks. Gabbee, of course, takes not the slightest notice, and does just as she pleases.

"Calm down, mowses, tight hold!"

She flaps her wings to gain height, and within moments she is circling high above the trees.

"Mowzl, look," cries Scraggy. "There's our wildwood!"

"Scraggy, it's the best thing I've ever seen, my heart sings!"

The two mice look down at the wildwood spread out below them, stretching away in all directions. The trees are ablaze with the colours of autumn, the leaves luminous in the sunshine.

Gabbee is enjoying flying with the mice on her back. When she hears Mowzl shout 'There's Eagle Rock!' she turns her head a little to see which way he is pointing, and flies that way, flying beyond the cliff and over the valley where the river flows.

"Ooooooo!" says Scraggy. "My tummy feels funny."

Gabbee circles back towards Eagle Rock.

"Gabbee, could you fly to the silver birch trees over there?" asks Mowzl. "That's the hill above Burrow Cave, where we live."

"Kraaaa!"

Gabbee flies over the birch trees, which are like flames in the autumn light.

"Look, Mowzl! We can see where we gathers wool!"

Mowzl looks where Scraggy is pointing. Far away, the pine trees and open heathland of Sandy Heath, where they went to gather wool last autumn, are clearly visible and familiar.

"That's two night's travel away, Scraggy!"

"We fly quick!" says Gabbee.

"No, no, Gabbee, thank you, but no, don't fly all the way over there. Let's go to Home Oak now, please; it's down there, between Eagle Rock and the birch treeeeeeeeeees — yikes!"

As Mowzl is talking, Gabbee swoops down — well, it's more like falling out of the sky — and the mice have to cling on with all their might. Gabbee flaps as she gets close to Home Oak, angling her wings and tail to slow herself down. She settles on a branch in the tree, and peers down to the ground below. She can see moss covered rocks close to the trunk of the tree.

"Are we here? Are we there? Are we aren't we?"

"Yes, we are. Can you fly us down to the ground, please?"

"Yes, fly down — oops!"

Gabbee slips off the branch, and there is hardly time to stretch her wings before she tumbles to the ground, all three of them yelling and screeching.

"Yikes! Oh, my goodness gracious me!" Scraggy cries out.

"Oh em gee gee em!" yells Mowzl.

"Quaaaark!" shouts Gabbee, as the mice roll off her back onto the ground, excited and thrilled to have come home by flying on a parrot's back! What a story to tell everyone!

"Thanks, Gabbee, that was exciting!" says Mowzl. "I was scared but you got us home safe. Can we come and see Waggl again soon?"

"You come, you come. But me see where is it?" says Gabbee, looking around searching for something.

"Where's what?"

"Nest, mowses nest?"

Scraggy runs to the burrow entrance between the tree roots.

"'Ere's a way in, our 'ome is underground," he says, pointing. "It's too small for you, Gabbee, you'll never fit."

"Gabbee want inside," says the bird, tapping her foot eagerly.

"Over here," says Mowzl. "Look, up there in that gap in the rock? There's something red."

"Ah yes, Gabbee see."

"Look through there. You'll see into our burrow!"

Gabbee flies up. Gripping the rock, she peers through the red window into Burrow Cave.

"Ooo! K-k-k-rrrrrrrrrk, Gabbee like mowses nest, Gabbee want inside go!"

"You're too big!" says Scraggy.

"Mowses nest, nice nest, Gabbee want nest in ground."

"Let's look higher up the cliff," suggests Mowzl. "There are bigger cracks in the rocks, one of them might be just right."

Gabbee has already flown up to the top and is looking around, clinging to the rock face while searching in the cracks and crevices.

"Back to Waggl I must! Come soon. Come Waggl soon, bye-bye mowses!" and with these abrupt parting words she flies up and away towards the cherry tree, where Waggl is waiting for her to come home.

"Thanks for the ride, Gabbee!" the mice shout together.

"Why's she's wantin' another nest," says Scraggy, when she's out of sight.

"Mmm. I don't know, Scragg, maybe there's something wrong. She seems to be in a terrible hurry, doesn't she?"

"She's worried 'bout Waggl on 'is lonesome."

"You're right. Come on, let's go in and see who's home."

~

They scamper over to Home Oak, dive between the roots and run along the tunnel to Burrow Cave. As they get near they hear a buzz of excitement caused by the strange bird that had peered through the window, blocking out the light. Bess is trying to get the young ones to calm down.

"Hallo, Bess," says Mowzl. "Hallo, everyone, that was Gabbee and she's a parrot; she carried us on her back all the way from her nest in a hollow tree . . ." Mowzl goes on to tell the story while Scraggy does the "squarks" and "yikes" and other sound effects. The mice gather round to listen, their eyes wide: Bess, Pearl and Beechnut are there, and in front of them the younger ones: Scarlett, Violet, Marigold and Ruby.

"Well, well," says Bess, when the story is told. "I wonder how a parrot came to be in these woods? She must be a long way from home."

"I know," agrees Mowzl. "Gabbee didn't really give us a chance to ask her about anything — although she did say that she and Waggl are 'shipwrecked'. She said that their nest was on a ship, something to do with a crow's nest and surrounded by sea, but when

Waggl hatched from his egg, there was no sea, only trees. She seems to be in a terrible hurry all the time."

"'N she says they's lost, and it's a mystry." Scraggy chips in.

"I want to help them get home," says Mowzl.

"Maybe One-Eye would know a bit about what 'shipwrecked' might mean for a parrot," suggests Bess.

"Good idea, Bess, I'll ask him!" says Mowzl.

"Was it scary when you were on her back?" asks Scarlett.

"Really scary," exclaims Scraggy. "I was yellin' a lot but it was the best thing ever, wasn't it, Mowzl?"

"Yes, we had to hold on tight because we couldn't tell when she was going to flap her wings, or turn, or go up or down. We got a bit dizzy, but it was good fun! It was good to see the wildwood from high up! We could see really far away."

"What's you all up to, anyway?" Scraggy asks.

"We're helping to get ready for the wool gathering!" Marigold says proudly, jumping up and down with excitement.

"That's right, Marigold," says Pearl. "We are preparing the backpacks and food and everything that will be needed."

"Who's going?" asks Mowzl.

"Me and Pearl," replies Beechnut.

"Me, of course," says Bess. "And Flimsy and BillBill."

"Do you need more help?"

"I think we'll be alright, Mowzl, thanks. Pearl and Beechnut have done wool gathering before and Flimsy and BillBill are strong enough now and are very keen to come."

"Why can't we come?" asks Ruby, speaking for the four youngest mice.

"Dear ones, I'd love to take you, but it's a difficult journey and hard work. It's dangerous too. When you're bigger you can come, probably the next time we go."

"That'll be ages away, it's not fair!" says Violet, with a little stamp of a foot.

A new voice speaks from the other side of the cave, they all turn to look. It's Ping Ling. She speaks quietly, walking slowly towards the gathered mice.

"It may feel unfair now, dear Violet, but when you do one day go, you will understand."

"Oh, Grandma! How lovely to see you!" cries Ruby. "We were asking Bess about the spinning and everything, and she said we must ask you, Ping Ling, because you know more than anyone.

Please tell us!"

"Oh, my goodness! Tell you what exactly? There is so much to tell, I don't know where to begin, but I don't mind making a start — if you've finished getting ready for tonight, that is."

"Hooray! Ping Ling's going to tell us a story!" cries Violet.

"Alright," agrees Bess. "We are ready now, mother, so if you'd like to tell them a bit of a story, now is a good time."

"I must sit my aching old body down, first of all. Scarlett dear, would you fetch some moss, please? I'll sit here and lean against table rock."

Scarlett and Ruby carry dried moss from the pile in the corner, arranging it to settle Ping Ling before sharing out the rest, so that everyone can get comfortable.

"When I was young, like you are now," begins Ping Ling, looking at each mouse in turn, "I lived with my family in a faraway country, where the creatures and plants are not the same as here. One of the creatures in my homeland is a moth and the moth's babies, called caterpillars, like to eat the leaves of the mulberry tree. The caterpillars eat the mulberry leaves until they get big and fat, ready to hang upside down from twigs and spin cocoons around themselves with a special silk.

Inside each cocoon a transformation happens, and eventually a grown-up moth pushes its way out of the bottom of the cocoon, where the silk thread is not so thickly matted together. The moth's wings are folded up and crinkly at first, slowly filling with blood and expanding to their full size.

"The cocoon that the moth leaves behind is made of a single thread of silk wound round and round, making the little pod. The silk thread can be unwound and used for weaving and making all sorts of things. Silk is very strong. I learned these things from my mother and father, who were very skilled.

"You may know that when I was young I was kidnapped by some rats and held prisoner on a ship; I had given up hope of ever being free again, but, one day, there was a battle between the rats and some mice that had appeared from nowhere, and Captain Blunda rescued me. I don't remember how it happened, but a long time later we came here to Burrow Cave and I have lived here happily ever since.

"Threeda was already making things with wool when I first arrived here, and I helped her with collecting wool from the prickly gorse bushes. I learned from Threeda how to clean the wool and tease it into a fluff before spinning it into thread. And I learned how Threeda did the spinning and how she plied the thread into thicker, stronger threads."

"Ping Ling, what's plied?" says Scarlett.

"Plying wool is when you spin two or more threads together to make a stronger thread. I worked with Threeda, and all the time I was thinking about how to find a way to make use of my skill with silk, and this question did not get answered until one day when something happened.

"There is a place I like to go, when I want to be on my own, up on top of the hill above Burrow Cave. There are silver birch trees growing there, and the ground is covered with bright green moss. One day in autumn I went there, and I could feel the great wave strong in my heart. I found a place to sit, at the bottom of an old birch tree, and got comfy on a cushion of moss.

"The sun was shining, low in the sky, lighting the golden yellow autumn leaves on the birch trees. Leaves fallen to the ground spangled over the green moss like jewels.

"I looked and looked, the beauty filling my heart; time seemed to stop, and everything became very still, completely still, except for one thing: hanging in mid-air, turning gently in the breeze, was a single birch leaf, luminous in the sunlight, drifting to and fro as the breeze quickened or slackened.

"I watched, and again I was lost to time in the beauty of the spinning leaf; suddenly I woke up, realising that the leaf must be hanging on an invisible thread — a thread of spiders' web-silk! How strong that web-silk must've been! Ideas tumbled through my head and I realised that the answer to my question had been given to me — we could use spiders' silk instead of silkworm silk!

"I was excited and wanted to rush home to tell Threeda. Looking again at the birch leaf, at the sunlight and the green moss, I said, 'Thank you!', with my heart and with my voice.

"When I got home, Threeda and I sat and talked about how we could do it. We had some ideas and tried them out over the next few moons, and bit by bit we learned how to make the finest and strongest threads.

"I am too old now to go gathering with you, but I can still teach you what I know. When the gatherers come back, with their packs full of wool and web-silk, we will all practice spinning!"

"Ooo! Thanks, Grandma," says Ruby, happily. "I really do want to learn, and I would love to know more about your family, and Captain Blunda."

Ping Ling smiles. "I think that will have to be for another day, dear. The gatherers should go to rest now."

"Ping Ling is right," says Bess. "Let's all rest now, and meet here after dark."

They troop out, all except Ping Ling, Mowzl and Scraggy; the young mice say 'thank you' to Ping Ling as they go by, looking at her with admiration in their eyes.

"We went last autumn, Granny," Mowzl says after a pause.

"I remember. Do you think that Flimsy and BillBill will be strong enough?"

"They are as strong as we were when we went, and just as keen. They will be alright."

"Good, I am pleased that you think that."

"Granny?"

"Yes, Mowzl dear?"

"Do you miss your family and your home very much?"

Ping Ling pauses and Mowzl sees the sadness in her eyes.

"I do, it is an ache in my heart that never quite goes away."

Mowzl's heart aches for her. "If I got taken away from our family, and our home and the woods, I think I would hurt so much I would die. You are so brave, Ping Ling."

"Never forget what is living in your heart, for however much it might hurt, it is the love with the deepest roots."

Mowzl and Scraggy give Ping Ling a goodnight kiss, and go to rest. Ping Ling sits quietly, waiting for the wool gatherers to come to be fitted with their packs when darkness comes. She has been moved by Mowzl's question, and she wonders if the great wave will ever take her home again.

Chapter Nine

Little Humans

After telling the story of Ping Ling's silk, and the story of Waggl and Gabbee, Emmy sits quietly in the Gypshun Boat on the windowsill, looking out. Pip's bedroom is very quiet; Pip and LuLu are asleep.

Emmy is thinking about Ping Ling's birch tree leaf, and about his oak leaf. Sometimes it is the little things that wake you up!

But he is in the world of humans, and a great sadness comes over him. He thinks of Ping Ling's gentleness, and her wisdom, and tears sting his eyes. He wonders if she is still alive. The tears that well up surprise him, and he worries that he is getting more real — too real — and in the wrong world!

"I's gettin' more real!" he says out loud. "I's opin' to get ome before I's deaded."

He gazes through the window, watching the chick-hens of his thoughts running about; he waits while they calm down and settle into a heap. He jumps down from the windowsill onto Pip's bed, climbs over to the chest of drawers where the bowl of things is kept, and snuggles into his pouch. Soon he is fast asleep.

~

Priklstik the hedgehog is rummaging through old leaves near the edge of the woods; between the woods and the field beyond is a barbed wire fence. There's not much in the field, just stubble from last years' crop of wheat, or barley; the few plants that have tried to grow have been killed with weed-killer. Priklstik is looking for soft earth with loose, old leaves and bits of grass, where he can scratch the soil up to find earthworms and slugs and other things he likes to eat. Priklstik is always hungry because he has to get big and fat to survive sleeping for the whole winter.

Last night, in darkness, Priklstik went into the field to look for food. He didn't find anything at all, and the ground was too hard for him to plough up with his nose, and it didn't smell nice at all, so he returned to the woods. Now that it's daylight, he has to be more alert to danger.

Hearing a familiar sound coming from above him, he stops what he's doing to look up. His eyes are not very good at looking far away, so he doesn't see what's making the noise until it gets much closer.

"Laa la laa la laa laa!"

It's not very loud, so he waits patiently.

"Laa la laa la laa laa!

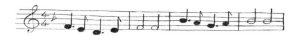

"Ha! It's the flying mouse!" he says, happily, seeing Emmy purling in his pouch. "Hallo, Emmy, how nice to see you!"

"Allo, Priklstik, I's appy seein' you too," says Emmy. "Wotz you doin'?"

"Well, last night I searched in that field for something to eat, and found nothing, so I'm foraging in the woods again."

"Woodz iz good," agrees Emmy.

"Well, you would say that because you're a wood-mouse, but not everyone can find a home in the woods. What do you eat, Emmy?"

"I's livin' on choklit foomz."

"What's that?!"

"Mi oomans iz givin' Emmy choklit, wotz deelishus n made wiv coco beenz."

"Fancy! Give me a nice snail or worm any day," says Priklstik.

Just then, a faraway call can be heard.

"Ehhhhmmeeeee."

"I's earin' some fing," says Emmy.

"Yes, I hear something too!"

"Some one's callin' Emmy's name."

"I think so, too," says Priklstik. "Over here!" he calls.

Emmy floats higher to get a better view.

"It's LuLu! 'Allo, LuLu," he says, when she is near enough. "We's very appy seein' you."

"Hallo, Emmy."

"Pleez be sayin' allo to Priklstik who's mi frend."

"Hallo, Priklstik, I'm LuLu, and I'm very happy to meet you."

"Hallo, LuLu," says Priklstik. "You're a very small human, if you don't mind my saying so — are you sure you're not an Elf?"

"LuLu's ooman, n she's littl coz 'er pouch iz Emmy size,"

Emmy explains.

"Well, well," says Priklstik. "It is a pleasure and an honour to meet you, LuLu, welcome!"

"Thank you, Priklstik," says LuLu excitedly. "I've never talked with a wild creature before, except Emmy of course, and I can't believe that it's happening! Emmy, am I really still sleeping in Pip's house — and here in my pouch at the same time?"

"You's xaklee rite, LuLu."

She looks puzzled. "I woke up floating in my pouch in the woods, and didn't know where to go, but the pouch moved all by itself. I was calling out for you, but I needn't have, because the pouch brought me to you."

"We heard you calling, LuLu," says Priklstik.

"You's not to be worryin'," says Emmy reassuringly. "You's carried bi great wave n invizibl ones."

"Can we ever see them?" asks LuLu.

"The invisible ones?" replies Priklstik. "They are not ever to be seen; they are not creatures like you and me, nor do they have names or faces, or anything at all."

"Oh dear!" says LuLu.

"It's orite, LuLu, you'sll be learnin' more wen . . ." Emmy stops talking, listening to a distant call.

"Emmmeeeee, LuuuLuuuu!"

"What's that?" cries LuLu.

"It's someone calling you both! What fun!" cries Priklstik.

Emmy and LuLu float upwards to see over the bushes. They wait a moment, and then see Pip coming towards them floating in his pouch. Pip is purling!

"Uh-oh," says Emmy. "I's not appy seein' wot I's seein'."

"Hallo, Pip!" LuLu calls. "You're in your pouch, well done!"

"LuLu, thank goodness I've found you! I'm not right, not right at all."

Pip's voice sounds panicky and he looks at them with frightened, far-away eyes. He looks very young, and very small.

"Pippee, you's poorly sorted n you's a bit see-through, coz you's not enough well to be purlin'. Pleez be sayin' allo to Priklstik, who's mi frend."

"Hallo, Priklstik — I'm very happy to meet you, only I'm not feeling well."

"Hallo, Pip, welcome to the wild talk," says Priklstik.

"Pippee, I's avin' to be gettin' you ome kwik," says Emmy.

"You's neither ere nor there. Pleez be sayin' bi, coz we's leavin'."

"Goodbye, Priklstik, Goodbye, LuLu — I'll come back — I will come back — I will . . ."

As Pip says goodbye, he gets more see-through and his voice gets fainter, until he disappears with a pop. At the same moment, Emmy disappears too.

"Well, well, well," exclaims Priklstik. "By the spines on my grandmother's back, never has there been anything so strange in all my life!"

"Yes! Ever since the mouse appeared, everything has been very strange," says LuLu.

"Ah-ha! LuLu, you can still make the wild talk even now the mouse has gone; you are very trusting."

"Trusting? What do you mean, Priklstik?"

Priklstik thinks for a moment about how he can explain it in a way that LuLu will understand.

"It's very hard for humans to make the wild talk because humans no longer listen deeply. LuLu, you are feeling that you are part of the wild web, and so you can make the wild talk. That's how I know that you are very trusting."

"Thank you, Priklstik," says LuLu, smiling. "Does the pouch make a difference?"

"Yes, it has the magic that the mouse brings, but even so, your trust is strong, and . . . shh! — what's that noise? — it sounds like clumsy humans, we must hide quickly!"

Priklstik dives under a bush, burying himself in old leaves, so that only an eye, an ear and the tip of his nose can be seen. A woodpecker drums nearby.

"That might be Rattltap," whispers Priklstik. "Is it a warning or . . ."

"Maybe there's a better view from higher up," murmurs LuLu. "Be careful!"

LuLu floats up high enough to see over the bushes; she sees two children, a boy and a girl, walking through the woods. Then she spies Rattltap clinging to the trunk of a tree, watching the children. He flies a short distance towards LuLu and waits for them to catch

up. LuLu goes back to Priklstik and tells him what she's seen.

"Ah! Human cubs! That's alright then, especially as Rattltap is there; he's leading the children to us. Let's go and say hallo."

~

When Billy goes to school that same morning, he is feeling so excited about his meeting with Emmy and Rattltap in the woods, he just has to tell Larky. Larky is Billy's best friend. When Billy first mentions it to Larky, she thinks he is spinning a yarn — you know, making it all up. She gets impatient with him and says she doesn't believe him. They argue, and don't talk again until lunch-break, when they hide behind the bike sheds while Billy tries to explain.

They don't know that Dungl sees them sneak off. He follows and stands just round the corner of the shed, holding his body flat against the wall, listening with all his might. He has a sly grin on his face. Dungl likes teasing Billy, and this could be something to be teasing him about!

"I needs you to come to the woods after school, Larks, please! There's somethin' special I wants you to see!" Billy pleads.

Larky still doesn't believe him, but something about him makes her want to know more. "Alright, Billy, after school. I'll have to go home for tea and do my homework before Mum will let me go out. I'll meet you at the bivvy later."

"Fanks, Larks, see ya later," says Billy, very relieved.

As soon as Dungl knows what they are planning, he slinks away before they have a chance to see him. He plans to follow them — perhaps he will go early to hide near the bivouac before they get there. He knows exactly where it is.

~

After school Billy is looking forward to proving to Larky that what he has told her is true, about meeting the mouse and everything, but he is also very nervous. What if he takes Larky to the woods and nothing happens? What if Emmy doesn't turn up, or the woodpecker? Larky will never believe him again.

Billy remembers asking Emmy how he could find him. "Billee, you be callin' wiv yor 'eart," Emmy had replied.

"'Ows I doin' that?" Billy had asked.

"You'sll be kno-in'."

Now, Billy has to be very trusting otherwise it might all go wrong and Larky will never believe him. He gobbles down his tea and asks his Nan if he can go out again to meet a friend.

"What about your homework, Billy?" asks Nan.

"I done it already."

"What you mean to say, Billy, is — 'I have done my homework already, Nan'."

"Yeah, alright."

Nan shakes her head.

"Have you really?"

"'Onest, Nan. Last lesson was so borin', I done me 'omework."

"Ha! Alright, off you go, Billy dear, take care and be home by dark, mind."

"Thanks, Nan!" says Billy, and he gives his grandmother a kiss, pulls on his boots and coat, and runs out of the door.

He runs along the lanes and paths to the edge of town, then out into the country where he slows to a walk, making sure that no one is following him. He takes a few detours, so that anyone watching him won't know for sure where he is going. When he gets to the edge of the woods he stops to listen, soon knowing what's going on in the wood. He can hear different birds: wood pigeons, crows and jays, a magpie cackling, a song thrush singing, and, nearer to him, he can hear the busy sound of blue-tits foraging in the treetops. There is nothing out of the ordinary, so Billy sets off again, but keeping alert. He hears a squirrel making a fuss, which they do at almost anything, so it's probably nothing to worry about; even so he is extra careful. It might be that Larky is there already and the squirrel is fussing about her being in the woods.

Billy arrives at the bivouac to find that Larky is not there yet. He sits on the log to wait. Nearby, hiding under a holly bush, Dungl is ready to spy on whatever happens next.

"Hallo, Billy," says Larky.

"Larks! You's makin' me jump! You's really quiet, ain'cha?"

"I like being quiet, so I can listen to the sounds of the woods, and I see more too when I'm quiet."

"Come on, Larky, let's see what we can see."

Larky notices how Billy is fidgeting and continuously looking to his left and right.

"Billy, are you alright?" she asks. "You seem very jumpy."

"I's worried."

"Yes, I can tell. What's up?"

"If nothin' 'appens, you'll think I's lyin'."

"What do you mean, 'if nothing happens'? I thought you were going to show me something."

Billy shrugs. "C'mon."

Billy leads Larky to the tree with the fallen branch.

"Find us a stone, Larks, big as a fist."

"What for?"

"You'll be seein'."

Larky kicks around in the bushes for a minute, finding a stone.

"Here you are," she says, handing the stone to Billy.

"Good 'un, fanks."

Billy has been examining the broken end of the fallen branch; he taps the torn wood with the stone, changes his grip on the stone and tries again. He taps in different places to find the best sound; he taps as fast as he can for a few seconds, then rests. Then he does it again.

"That'll do it, if it's ever goin' to work."

"Billy, what are you doing?"

"Come 'n sit on 'ere with me, 'n we'll wait."

Dungl has crept up behind them and is watching.

A woodpecker flies into the high branches of a nearby tree, looking around suspiciously. He comes nearer, catches sight of Billy and his friend and chuckles to himself, shintering down the trunk of the tree chuckling and whispering as he goes.

"Tchak!"

"Oh, Rattltap, you've come!"

"Tchakka chukkl-chokkl!" cries the bird, but the children don't understand what he says.

"I's not gettin' what your sayin', Rattltap," says Billy.

Billy really wants to be talking with Rattltap to impress Larky, but without Emmy there, he doesn't understand the wild talk. Rattltap knows this and has been saying it, but of course it just sounds like bird chatter to the human cubs.

"What's all this about, Billy?" demands Larky, crossly.

"Ain't you amazed we's callin' a bird like that?"

"So, what? I'm going home!"

Billy feels the moment slipping away.

"Wait, Larks — please!"

But Larky has decided; she's in a huff now and she stomps off.

Rattltap flies in front of her, swooping round and landing on her shoulder. He chatters into her ear for a moment, and flies off.

"Ow! Those claws really hurt!" she yells.

"Don't be like that Larks! 'Ow good is that to have Rattltap on your shoulder?" cries Billy.

"Tchak! Tchak!"

Rattltap has flown to the next tree and is looking back at them. When they look up at him he moves on to another tree.

"Tchak!"

"He's wantin' us to follow 'im!"

"You're having a laugh aren't you, Billy?" says Larky, sounding tired and disappointed.

"C'mon, let's follow 'im!" says Billy, ignoring Larky's huff.

Now that Rattltap knows they are following, he stops 'tchaking' and flies quietly, always waiting for them to see him and catch up, before moving on.

After what seems like a long time — too long for Larky, who's getting fed up again — Rattltap flies up into a tree where he knows of a good sounding board, and he drums loud and clear. Rattltap has led the little humans to the part of the wood where Priklstik and

LuLu are. They hear the drumming and LuLu, in her pouch, floats above the bushes to get a better look. She keeps high enough to be out of reach of the human cubs as she moves towards them.

"Hallo! Are you Billy? My name is LuLu!"

Larky stares, her mouth gaping; she can't move or speak at all. Billy is very surprised to see LuLu and not Emmy, but he keeps himself together.

"'Allo, yeah, I's Billy, 'n this is me friend, Larky," he says with a sense of pride.

With a rustle, Priklstik emerges from the undergrowth always wanting to be in on excitement such as this, and Rattltap flies down to cling to the nearest tree. He and Priklstik greet each other, but of course it just sounds like animal chatter to the children. Larky is hardly noticing because her eyes are fixed on LuLu, who is floating in her pouch talking with Billy; it is the most amazing sight that Larky has ever seen.

Rattltap is very surprised to see LuLu.

"Aha!" he says. "You are a different flying mouse — no! — you are not a mouse at all, you are a very small human!"

"Hallo, Rattltap, my name is LuLu and I am happy to meet you at last. Emmy has spoken of you."

"My word! And you can talk the wild talk. Priklstik, we have strange things happening!" he exclaims.

"Rattltap," says LuLu. "I will translate what you have said so Billy and Larky know — we don't want them to feel left out!"

LuLu tells Billy and Larky what Rattltap has been saying, explaining that without Emmy they won't understand the wild talk.

"You can though, LuLu, can't you?" says Larky, finding the courage to speak.

"That's because of my pouch, Larky."

"What about the pouch? Are you always so small?"

"No, I am not always so small. I'm human just like you. There is so much to tell you, so much to explain, but there will be plenty of time for that. The pouch is made from special wool, which came from Emmy's home world. I crocheted the pouch myself. It has magic."

Larky is still astonished, but she gathers herself quickly.

"I believe you now, Billy but — but — I can't believe what my eyes are seeing!" she cries.

"Clukltikkrrr pikn stiki zik!"

"Rattltap suggests you just feel the truth of it," translates LuLu.

LuLu goes on translating for the human cubs but keeping up is hard work and she has to stop every now and again to rest. This is what is said:

"Listen to me, young human cubs," begins Priklstik. "Very few humans ever feel the wild talk, or even have a whispering of it in their hearts. We wild creatures are not at all happy about it.

"Billy, you were lucky to meet the mouse; you could hear him and you could talk the wild talk as long as he was with you. So, Larky, please believe Billy and please, both of you, find the mouse and learn from him."

"Drrrrrr," Rattltap drills in agreement. "Well said, Priklstik; all the wild creatures will have stories to tell you about the wild web and the great wave, and they will have a lot to tell you about how they feel. We are not happy about what humans are doing and we try to tell them, but they are not hearing us. Will you learn to hear us and tell all the other humans about it?"

After LuLu has translated all this, Billy and Larky are speechless. Billy is watching Larky and realises that she really is listening. *That's the beginning,* he thinks. *That's the first thing — to really listen.*

"LuLu," says Billy. "Thanks for translatin' for us 'n please thank the bird 'n the 'edg'og for us too, 'n say yes, we'll learn, 'n all I's ever wantin' is bein' with creatures."

Rattltap and Priklstik both talk at once saying something like "that's all right young cubs".

"Billy, they understand you."

"Can they understand human words?" asks Billy.

"Klikl ikxl klaklix!"

"Rattltap says they know what's in your heart," smiles LuLu. Rattltap cocks his head to one side, listening intently.

"Do you hear that?" he says.

"'Ow come I's understandin' you, all of a sudden?" says Billy.

"Laa la laa la laa laa!"

"It's Emmy!" cries LuLu.

"Laaa laa laaa laa laaaa laaaa!"

Emmy comes into sight, floating in his pouch.

"Allo mi frendz, I's very appy seein' you all."

"Hallo, Emmy! This is my friend Larky," says Billy.

"Allo, Larkee, mi name's Emmy n I's a mouse comin' from uvva world where I's a real mouse. Ere I's a toy mouse wiv real feelin's, n I's very appy to be meetin' you."

Larky stares at Emmy, her eyes wide and her face excited; she understands everything that he says, even though he has a strange way of talking.

"Er, thanks, Emmy," says Larky, finding her voice at last. "I'm very happy to meet you too. Billy told me about you, but I didn't believe him."

"You's kno-in' in yor 'eart, Larkee or you'd nevva be ere."

"Mowzl Emmy," says Rattltap. "These two human cubs are in need of your help to learn more about wild creatures, can you help them?"

"Yip! I's wantin' to elp ooman cubz, n I's needin' cubz to be elpin' Emmy."

"How can we help?" asks Larky.

"Be comin' to be wiv Pippee n LuLu wen we's avin' stories."

"We'll be comin', Emmy!" cries Billy.

"How is that human of yours, Emmy, that Pip?" asks Priklstik. "He was a bit see-through, wasn't he?"

"'E woz see-through orite Priklstik, neither ere nor there, but e'sll be orite."

Suddenly, Rattltap cocks his head to listen again. "I must go! I can hear my beloved calling! Goodbye! Tchak!" And off he flies.

"Thanks, Rattltap!" cries Larky, then more quietly, "And thank you too, Priklstik. Do you have a family?"

"Thank you for asking, young Larky, but no, I shall be looking for a partner in the spring; now it's time to get ready for the winter sleep, and we hedgehogs move about on our own mostly. And move I must, as there's eating to be done! It is my honour to meet you, human cubs!"

"Thank you, Priklstik, I hope we meet again soon," says Larky.

"We shall!" Priklstik shuffles off into the undergrowth.

"Will you two be able to find your way home?" LuLu asks.

"Oh yeah!" Billy replies. "We's alright."

LuLu and Emmy come close to the children, quietly, just looking into their eyes. Billy and Larky feel happy and sad; sad because they know they are about to be left alone. LuLu and Emmy float in the air in front of the children, slowly fading, becoming more see-through until, with a final wave, they disappear.

"Billy . . . are we dreaming?" whispers Larky, after a quiet.

"No, Larks, we's wide awake."

"No one will believe us."

Billy shakes his head.

"We's not tellin' no one."

"Come on, let's go home."

As they turn around to begin the trudge back the way they came, Larky reflects on what has happened.

"Billy?"

"Larks?"

She looks at him. "Sorry I didn't believe you."

"S'alright."

They make their way back through the woods to the path that leads home. They pass close by a thick holly bush, the prickly leaves scratching at them noisily as they walk by. Hidden behind the holly leaves Dungl has seen everything that has happened, and he doesn't know what to make of it at all.

He is feeling very pleased with himself, but he has a not very nice feeling as well, a sort of 'left out' feeling which he tries to forget about. But he hasn't really been left, out because he wanted to be hiding! Maybe the not very nice feeling is because he's a bit frightened. How can he be frightened of two little fairies floating about in old socks?

He waits before moving, so that Billy and Larky get well ahead and won't see him as he makes his own way home.

~

Pip wakes up, yawns and stretches. *Hmm, I wonder what's for breakfast,* he thinks.

He looks around seeing LuLu asleep in the armchair, but he can't see Emmy anywhere. Perhaps he's in the bowl of things having a bit of a lie down.

Pip suddenly remembers his dream, and a cold prickle of fear ripples over his skin. He had dreamed that he was floating in mid-air in the woods somewhere, and was feeling panicky because he didn't feel right at all. Everything had been a bit see-through and kept disappearing and he couldn't hear anything. Then he had seen Emmy talking to him, but he couldn't hear what he said, and then Emmy disappeared; then everything disappeared. Pip felt the same as when he had first seen Emmy and Scraggy fishing. He felt empty; like he didn't have a middle. He felt sick and horrible.

"And now I'm waking up feeling alright and wanting breakfast!" he says out-loud. "I wonder what happened . . . Emmy? Are you there? Are you awake?"

"Emmy's sleepin'," comes the reply.

"Oh, alright." Pip waits for a bit. "Thanks for rescuing me."

"Ah-ha! You's merembrin' iz you?"

"I'm remembering being in the woods, floating in mid-air, but everything was see-through, and I couldn't hear anything, and I was frightened."

Emmy climbs out of the bowl of things, scrambles over to Pip and sits on his tummy.

"Pippee, you's dreamin' in yor pouch wen you's not enough well for purlin'."

"When will I be ready, Emmy? I'm missing everything!"

"You'sll be ready innabit, Pippee, coz you's much weller. I's finkin' best fing iz for you to get 'Wot Appnd' rit. Wiv out you ritin' 'Wot Appnd', nothin' would be appnin'."

"I don't see why I have to be ill to write about what happens!" says Pip, starting to get frustrated.

"You'sll be gettin' betta kwikka."

LuLu has woken up, and hears them talking.

"Hallo! Did we really meet Billy and Larky?" she asks excitedly.

"Yip! N Priklstik n Rattltap."

She smiles and turns to Pip.

"Pip, are you alright?"

"I feel much better now. Emmy's just been telling me that I've got to stay ill and write 'Wot Appnd'."

"Pip!" exclaims LuLu. "I heard Emmy too, and he didn't mean that! Remember, without you, none of this would be happening."

"Alright, I'll get on with the writing while you have all the fun. Now leave me alone so I can concentrate, and please bring me something nice later!"

A mischievous smile spreads across Emmy's face.

"LuLu, e's milkin' it izn't e? Orite, Pippee, wotz you wontin'? Choklit?"

"No, Em, I mean proper food! Well . . . and some chocolate too maybe."

"Alright, Pip, we'll see you a bit later," says LuLu, as she scoops Emmy up and goes out, leaving Pip wondering what happened to breakfast.

~

Larky just cannot believe her eyes or her ears! She smiles when she remembers the strange and wonderful things that happened in the woods, when she and Billy met LuLu and Priklstik, Emmy and Rattltap. She's still wondering if it can be true, or if it was just a dream.

Larky and Billy meet up whenever they can after school, or after they've been home for tea, and if they have enough time they go to the bivouac in the woods. There they can talk about things with nobody hearing them. They both want to find out more about Emmy, and they remember the invitation to visit Pip — whoever he might be — but all they know is that Pip lives somewhere near the cemetery. They go looking, but in the many streets of houses they don't know which house is his, and they don't dare knock on all the doors.

One day, during break at school, Larky is talking with her best friend Stomper. Like all best friends they like to share secrets, and Larky has been telling Stomper about what happened in the woods. Stomper isn't sure what to believe, so she just listens and says "fantastic" and "ooooo" and "amazing" to encourage her friend to carry on.

Larky and Stomper don't notice two boys standing nearby pretending not to be listening. It's Dungl, and his friend Bottl.

The bell rings and the children go to their classrooms. Larky and Stomper are in the same class and share a desk. Dungl is in Larky's class too, but Billy is older than Larky and is in a different class, with Bottl. Larky's teacher, Mr Weatherstone, is about to begin a lesson about papermaking. Dungl puts his hand up.

"Please, Sir . . ."

"What is it, David?" says Mr Weatherstone, using Dungl's proper name.

"Larky's been talkin' with fairies, Sir."

The whole class turns to look at him. A stunned silence falls upon the room.

"What on earth do you mean?"

"I saw 'er with me own eyes."

"You mean you saw the fairies, David?"

A ripple of laughter goes around the classroom, and Dungl begins to look flustered.

"Erm, no, Sir. What I saw was 'er 'n Billy talkin' to thin air."

Larky panics; she looks at Stomper, a look that says — 'help!' Stomper sticks her hand up.

"Sir, Dungl's a peeper and he's a liar, Sir!" she says boldly.

"That's enough. Quiet, all of you!" shouts Mr Weatherstone severely. "I don't want to hear any more about this. We will begin our lesson, and today we begin looking at how paper is made. You all know, I'm sure, that paper is made from trees . . ."

As Mr Weatherstone talks about forests, trees, pulp and paper mills, Larky is thinking hard. Dungl has spied on them. He must have seen her and Billy in the woods and now the whole class knows that something is up; that means the whole school will know by dinner break. Oh dear.

~

After school, Larky meets up with Billy at the school gates and they walk together, as they usually do. Larky doesn't say much until they have gone far enough to be away from the others.

"What's up, Larks? You ain't right," says Billy.

Larky tells Billy about Dungl and what happened in class

"Is he following us, Billy?" she asks.

"'Ang on, don't look back yet; we'll go a different way 'n see if we can see 'im followin'."

"I know!" says Larky. "That path by the allotments would be perfect, 'cos we can see across."

"Good thinkin', Larks."

They walk on, chattering away, trying to look as they always do. When they get to the far side of the allotments, they stop where the tall fence is thick with old-man's beard that has grown up right to the top. They know that they can't be seen from the other side of the allotments. Carefully, they move aside old leaves and fluffy seed heads, so they can peep through. Sure enough, Dungl and Bottl are following them.

"Alright," says Billy. "Let's 'ead off for the woods 'n lose 'em. I's not wontin' a fight."

He and Larky jog along, dodging down small roads and alleyways trying to keep clear of Dungl and Bottl.

"Hey, Billy, there's the cemetery gate, let's go through there," says Larky, trying to whisper even though she's a bit out of breath.

"Good thinkin', Larks. I wish we knowed where Pip's livin'."

"We don't want to lead Dungl there."

"Yep, true." Billy nods.

Halfway through the cemetery, Billy hears a woodpecker drumming and he takes a different path towards the sound.

"Might be Rattltap!"

They hear the drumming again and follow it.

"If it's Rattltap, he's taking us in circles!" says Larky, as they turn down another path.

"He'll 'ave 'is reasons."

They pop out of the cemetery through a different gateway, and a moment later they hear the drumming again.

"Look!" cries Larky. "On that lectrickery pole — it's Rattltap!"

"Come on, let's follow," says Billy decisively.

They jog down the road as Rattltap flies from one pole to the next. At a road junction, he disappears round the corner.

"I think we've lost Dungl," says Larky, looking back.

"We've lost Rattltap 'n all."

They turn the corner into the side street.

"Look! There, on that door knocker," cries Larky.

Sure enough, Rattltap is clinging to a doorknocker. He taps on the door with his beak and flies away with a brief 'Tchak'.

"Larks, we's found Pip's place," declares Billy. "Thanks, Rattltap!"

~

Billy is wondering if he should knock again in case Rattltap's tapping was not enough for Pip to hear, but the door opens and a scruffy old man peers out at the two children standing there.

"Hallo, is it Halloween or something?" he says.

"'Scuse us, but is you Mr Pip?" Billy asks.

"I is, I mean I am, and what can I do for you?"

"I's Billy, 'n this is Larky, 'n we's needin' to come in quick."

Pip notices that Billy and Larky are out of breath.

"Why have you knocked on my door?" he says.

"Emmy and LuLu said we should find you, and Rattltap showed us the way," says Larky.

"Ah! Why didn't you say so? Come in, come in, kick off those wet shoes and let's get you in the warm and dry."

"Thank you, Mr Pip," says Larky, gratefully. "We've been running to get away from two children who are spying on us."

"I wonder why they would do that? Well, come in and tell me all about it while I make you a warm drink."

Pip is suddenly full of energy; he makes them hot chocolate while they sit at the kitchen table telling him about meeting Emmy and Rattltap, Priklstik and LuLu. Then they tell him about Dungl spying on them in the woods and telling teacher.

"I haven't met Rattltap or Priklstik," says Pip. "You're really lucky. I wish I'd been there. Could you understand them? Could you talk with them?"

"I was able to first time, 'cos Emmy was there 'n 'e 'as the magic," explains Billy. "But when me 'n Larks was there, 'n Emmy weren't, we's not understandin', so LuLu 'terpreted."

"Was LuLu a bit like Emmy, floating in a pouch?" Pip asks.

"Yes! She could've been a fairy!" says Larky, her eyes shining. "Which is exactly what Dungl said."

"I think Dungl is jealous and he feels left out of something special," says Pip. "That can make people a bit mean when they don't want to be. You be careful you don't get spiky and mean as well!"

"What's the story with the mouse, Mr Pip?" asks Billy. "He's always sayin' we 'as to be seein' you."

"Well, Billy, I don't really know. Everything about Emmy is mysterious, and even he doesn't know most of the time. He wants me to write his story, which he calls 'Wot Appnd', so that he can remember how to get home. But he can't remember much about his home world. I had no idea that Emmy had met you two. You see, I've not been very well recently, and LuLu looks after me. Emmy has started to tell me stories about his home world."

"If he can't remember, how can he tell stories?" asks Larky.

"Good question, Larky, even he doesn't know the answer. He talks of the great wave, but I don't really know what that means."

Pip pauses for a moment, looking into the distance.

"It's a funny thing; my memory is not so good, but after Emmy has told a story I have a little sleep — a 'story-sleep', if you know what I mean — and when I wake up the story is written on bits of paper scattered all over the floor. Once, a story got written while I was asleep that Emmy had not even told! Really odd, but then everything is rather odd, now that the mouse is here."

"Mr Pip, will you tell us Emmy's story please — pleeeeease?" pleads Larky.

"I was thinking just that, Larky; the best thing would be to start at the beginning, so I will read you the first story, called 'Typhoon'. That's the one that got written without Emmy telling it. Emmy doesn't remember how he came to be in the human world, so when I read this to him he was very excited and loved being reminded of his friends, Baloop, Wandering Wings and Snugweed. I'll read chapter two as well, where Emmy introduces himself. It's called, 'Allo!'."

"That sounds like Emmy talkin'!" says Billy.

Pip tells Billy and Larky the story of the '*Wreckless*' and the typhoon, of how Emmy arrives in the human world pulled through the fog by a thread — pulled by Pip himself! This story is followed by 'Allo!', which, as you will remember, is about how Pip tried to imagine Mowzl's home world and how he saw Pearl, and Scraggy and Mowzl fishing, and of course, how he became ill because of it; and how LuLu started to make the magic pouches.

Larky is thrilled. "Mr Pip! Please can we have the next story, please!" she cries.

"Larky, the next story is called 'Time Capsules', and I can't read that to you until Emmy says I can. I haven't read that one to anyone yet, not even LuLu. I think it was that adventure that made me ill after all the strange happenings, and I don't want you two to get ill as well."

"'Ow's stories makin' us ill, Mr Pip?" asks Billy.

"Let's talk about that when I read it to you, then you will understand I think. But right now, I'm very happy that you've come. You've really cheered me up, thank you!"

"Was it you that pulled Emmy through the fog?" says Larky.

"That's what Emmy tells me, Larky, but I didn't know at the time. All I knew was that I was looking for a Christmas present for LuLu, and Emmy jumped into my hand!"

"'E's needin' you to get 'imself 'ome, 'n you's needin' 'im for what, Mr Pip?"

"Good question, Billy, I need Emmy to help me get well. Like the story says, I have to get better at feeling or I won't be able to help him."

Billy pauses, thinking. He has other issues on his mind.

"I doesn't know 'ow it all works, 'n it don't matter," he says. "What I's wantin' is to be talkin' with creatures."

"Why, Billy?" asks Pip. "Have you always liked animals?"

"Yeah, they's real 'n never let's me down. They makes me 'appy."

"Do you like getting out of town?"

"Yeah, me 'n Larks 'as made a bivwak 'n we goes there lots."

Pip smiles. "We're lucky living here, aren't we?" he says. "The countryside is close enough for a walk to the woods and fields."

"I's feelin' sorry for folks what can't get to woods, 'n I's meanin' real woods, not some dogs' toilet."

"Billy!" Larky scolds.

"Don't worry, I know what Billy means. Shouldn't you two be at school?"

Larky glances at Billy sheepishly, then stares at the floor. Billy, however, is proud that he's been listening to Emmy.

"We bunk off 'n gets a tellin' off for it. Emmy says everythin' in the wild wood is real 'n that's my school — when 'e says that I's wakin' up."

"Please, can you tell us more of 'Wot Appnd'?" asks Larky, changing the subject.

Pip is quiet, looking at them sitting there at his kitchen table. *Why not? He thinks, why shouldn't they hear more?*

"Alright, let's get comfy in the other room. I'll make another hot drink before we start. Could you two light a fire? Have a look and see if you can work out how to do it, it's through there," Pip points down the hallway.

Billy and Larky go through to the front room, see the wood burning stove, kindling and matches, and soon have the fire started. Pip brings the drinks in on a tray. He checks the wood-burner and sits in the armchair. Billy and Larky curl up on the sofa.

"I'll skip chapter three and go straight to chapter four, which is called 'Home Oak', and it's about Mowzl's home world."

"Why is he called Mowzl in the story, when we call him Emmy?" asks Larky.

"Well, in one of the stories you haven't heard yet, his cousin, Star, gives him a new name, Emmy, and our Emmy had forgotten all about it, until that story happened."

"'Ow weird is that!"

"There are a lot of strange things, Billy, you'll see," says Pip.

He gets up to close the damper on the wood burner, opening it again just a quarter-turn. The flames slow down, beginning their lazy dance inside the glass door. Pip begins reading 'Home Oak', and the children close their eyes, drifting into story-sleep, listening with smiles on their faces. After 'Home Oak' , Pip goes on to read them 'Pouches and Things', and then 'Snow!', where Mowzl gets given a new name by Star. Then he reads 'Bowl of Things', and, finally, about Waggl and Ping Ling. When all that is done, Pip is tired and needs a rest; he sits in silence while the children sleep.

A little later, there's a knock on the front door.

"Door, Mr Pip!" whispers Billy, instantly awake.

"Don't worry, that'll be LuLu, I expect," says Pip quietly, and a moment later LuLu comes into the room.

"What's happening here, Pip? Larky! Billy! How did you two get here? And, Pip! — you're up and about! — you must be feeling better."

Larky and Billy are stretching and yawning.

Pip watches them, as their eyes grow wide with surprise. The last time they saw LuLu, she was purling in her pouch and no bigger than a mouse. Now she is human size!

LuLu laughs. "I can see that you're surprised to see that I'm not always the size of a mouse! I have another surprise for you — look who's here!"

LuLu takes Emmy out of her coat pocket, and holds her hand out so that he can sit in her palm.

"Allo, Larky; Allo, Billy; I's really appy you's findin' Pippee, n I's seein' you's done im good. Pippee, I's appy seein' you up n about. Wotz for brekky?"

"Emmy, it's not breakfast time! We should be eating something though. Let's go through to the kitchen and I'll make a snack."

When they're settled at the kitchen table, Pip asks LuLu if she'd like a drink.

"Just water please, Pip."

"LuLu, thanks for getting in all the groceries and stuff while I've been ill," he says, whilst rummaging about.

"We had to feed you something all these weeks," she smiles.

"Is it weeks already? Here you are, Emmy!"

He puts a small bowl of chocolates on the table and Emmy jumps in, burying his face and breathing deeply.

"Aah! Emmy's nearly starvin'."

"You rascal, Emmy! Here we are folks, tuck in."

Pip brings bread, cheese and salad to the table, then plates, knives and forks, pickle and dressing, everything for a king-size snack.

"Billy, tell Emmy about who followed you," says Pip suddenly, before they start eating.

Billy and Larky tell Emmy about Dungl spying on them in the wood when they met Rattltap, LuLu and Priklstik, and about what happened at school, and about how Rattltap helped them to get away from Dungl and Bottl and find Mr Pip's house.

Emmy is quiet.

"Me's finkin' you's not to be wurryin'," he says eventually. "Nothin's evva all bad, n we'sll be seein' wot appnz."

They begin eating and talking, and soon Billy and Larky are feeling at home and relaxed. Larky feels bold enough to speak directly to Emmy, and she asks him a question.

"Emmy, Mr Pip has been reading 'Wot Appnd' to Billy and me. We really want to hear chapter three, but Mr Pip says he can't tell us without your permission. Please will you let him?"

"You'sll be earin' it soon eenuff, Larkee, n before you's earin' chapta three I's wantin' to be kno-in' you betta. I's not wantin' you poorly sorted, like Pippee woz."

Pip tells Emmy that he has read 'Wot Appnd' to Billy and Larky up to Ping Ling's story, but Emmy seems not to be listening. He's staring into space with a dreamy look.

"Emmy? Are you alright?" says LuLu, quietly.

"Mmm. I's finkin' ov Ping Ling n memoreez iz comin'. I's feelin' story appnin'."

"It's getting late, do you two need to get home yet?" says Pip, looking at Billy and Larky.

"We don't have to go home yet, please can we stay and hear the story? Please!" says Larky. Billy is smiling and looking hopeful.

"Alright. Let's go in the front room and get settled," says LuLu, and she carries Emmy to the front room, putting him in the Gypshun Boat on the windowsill.

Emmy looks out of the window, watching, as he waits for everyone to get settled. He waits for quietness to come to him, so that all his thoughts have stopped running about like little chick-hens and have curled up in a fluffy heap; then he waits for the story to arrive.

"Last rays ov sun iz shinin' through red windo into Burrow Cave. Ping Ling 'as been sittin' finkin' 'bout 'er familee bak ome, n finkin' 'bout xpedishun to gavva wool . . ."

Emmy's voice soon makes the listeners feel dreamy. Billy and Larky snuggle into their cushions and are soon imagining themselves there in Burrow Cave. They are imagining Ping Ling, as she waits for everyone to come to the cave to get ready for the wool gathering expedition. Her heart is uneasy, and she resolves to make sure that all their backpacks are properly strapped on. The sun is going down now, they will be coming soon.

Chapter Ten

Silk and Sad

Soon, the wool gatherers will set off into the night. Everything is ready, and they will be coming to Burrow Cave to collect their backpacks; Ping Ling can hear them chattering as they come towards the cave. Bess sees Ping Ling is waiting, and greets her.

"Hallo, Ping Ling! Have you been here all this time?"

"Yes, I have, Bess. You know, time is different for one as old as me," she says, getting up to meet them.

"Are you alright, Grandma?" asks Beechnut.

"Yes, dear, I am," Ping Ling hugs her granddaughter.

"Right everyone," announces Bess. "Please put on your packs, wearing them as backpacks for travelling; when we get to Sandy Heath we will wear them as front packs for the gathering."

"What's a 'heath', Mum?" asks BillBill.

"It's what we call the place we are going to where heather and gorse bushes grow."

"Why do we go there and not just up the hill here?" asks Flimsy.

"Because it's the best place we know to gather wool. The gorse bushes are prickly, and when animals pass by the prickles rub against their fur collecting bits of wool and hair. It's autumn now, and the spiders are big and fat; they will be making webs all over the bushes. You see, we can collect wool and spider's silk at the same time."

Flimsy is concerned for the spiders. "Do the spiders mind?"

"They do get cross, Flimsy, and we always say sorry, but they have to repair their webs, or make new ones, most days anyway. I don't think they mind all that much, but they do like to make a fuss."

"Are we all ready?" asks Pearl.

"I can't tie this strap properly," says BillBill.

Ping Ling helps him, and then checks all their packs to make sure they are properly strapped on.

"All ready!" she declares.

"I'll go first," says Bess. "Then BillBill, then Beechnut, then Flimsy, then Pearl. Alright?"

"Yes, Bess!" they chorus.

"Goodbye everyone, have a safe journey and come home soon!" says Ping Ling.

With a final kiss from Ping Ling they file out of Burrow Cave and along the burrow to Home Oak, where they emerge between the great buttress roots of the tree. It is almost dark now and the brightest stars can be seen.

"Shh," whispers Bess, sniffing the air, reminding everyone to listen and to be alert with all their senses.

She leads the way up the hill behind Burrow Cave, over the mossy ground under the birch trees and onwards, walking steadily but not hurrying.

She marks the trail from time to time using stones. She does this to teach the young ones and also as a guide in case they get lost on the way home.

Flimsy and BillBill soon feel tired because they are not used to travelling far. They don't say anything, but eventually Flimsy looks to Pearl for comfort.

"I'm getting tired, Pearl, will we be resting soon?"

"Yes, Flimsy; Bess knows that you and BillBill will be getting tired, and it's not just you, we all are. We will stop soon, when she finds somewhere safe to rest."

Bess finds a good resting place under a rock. Before going in, she sniffs the air and listens intently making sure that there is no one lurking under the rock. Inside, all she finds is a scatter of empty nutshells left there by other creatures. The mice flop down.

"Oh! I'm aching all over!" moans BillBill.

"You'll soon get used it, BillBill," Beechnut tells him. "Don't worry, you're doing fine."

They relax, eating a little; Beechnut had collected some seeds while they had been walking.

"Would you like to try a beechnut?" she says.

"Ha-ha! Beechnut's found some beechnuts!" sings Flimsy. "Yes please!"

"They're a lot easier to get into than hazelnuts; mmm, lovely," says BillBill. "Thanks, Beechnut."

"Have you two been noticing the woodland?" asks Pearl.

"Not really, Pearl," answers BillBill. "I've been trying so hard to keep up and not trip over, I haven't been looking around much."

"Me too," says Flimsy.

"Well, I know it's tiring, but do relax and look around. There will be some moonlight later tonight and you should be able to see a lot more."

"Thanks, Pearl, we'll try," says Flimsy.

After a rest they set off again and this time the two young mice feel more relaxed; they are getting into their stride. Looking around, they realise that they have already travelled beyond the part of the wood that they know, and are now deep into the wildwood.

The ground is fairly flat and wet; the trees are a familiar mixture of oak and ash, with an under story of rowan and hazel. On the ground there are the autumn remains of dog's mercury and wood-rush, and a thick layer of old leaves and twigs. There are huge glades where trees have fallen, and here and there fallen branches are tangled in the undergrowth. Bess looks for animal trails to follow, to make it easier getting through the tangle.

"I think this is a badger trail," says Bess. "Yes, here are some paw prints."

The oak trees are huge and spooky in the moonlight. The ash trees have already lost their leaves, which lie in pale patterns on the ground.

The trail gets tougher as they come to an uphill slope, and the ground changes. It's drier now, and steep; the ground is covered with the oval leaves of the beech trees that grow here. Where the moon shines through, the trunks shine silvery grey — smooth, slender and spacious. Flimsy and BillBill have not seen trees like this before, and even though they are struggling to keep up on this hill, they are entranced.

"These are beech trees," says Bess. "You may see their seeds on the ground, they might still be in their husks, which are prickly, so be careful."

They stop to rest; BillBill and Flimsy take the opportunity to gather some beechnuts which they stuff into their backpacks. Soon on the march again, they get to the top of the hill where the trees are not so close together and the ground becomes rockier. They arrive at Tumble Cave where they will sleep for the day. The cave is so called because of the tumble of rocks at the bottom of the cliff, where it is hidden. Tumble Cave is about half way between Burrow Cave and the heathland, their destination.

Bess and Beechnut go into the cave first to make sure there is nothing lying in wait that might jump out and eat them up. There is no sign of any other creatures, except a pile of dry leaves and moss right at the back. Soon they are all inside; they take off their packs and relax, eating nuts and seeds.

"Ooo, I'm going to be stiff as a stick after a sleep," says Flimsy.

The sun is rising in the eastern sky, brightening the clouds as a new day begins. The five mice snuggle down to sleep, Bess, Pearl and Beechnut keeping their ears and eyes and noses alert all the time, just in case.

~

The mice wake up, stretch, and prepare to march again. During the day, while they slept, there were clouds in the sky, but now the sky is clear, and they set off with the glow of a rising moon in the East.

The ground changes again, sloping gently uphill, and the trees are more spread out. The moon is bright, and the mice stop for a moment, turning to look at the view behind them. The moonlit woodland stretches away as far as they can see.

The ground they are walking on is becoming quite sandy. There are silver birch trees, rowan, ash and oak, but they are smaller and gnarled, and further apart from each other. Here and there a pine tree grows, and as they go further, there are more and more of them. Flimsy and BillBill have never seen pine trees before before. The ground is mostly covered with gorse and bracken, making the going quite difficult. Bess tries to find animal trails to use whenever possible even if they aren't going in quite the right direction. She uses stones to mark all the changes of direction that she thinks might be hard to remember.

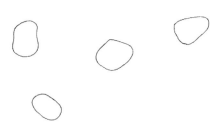

Slowly, as they walk on, the bracken gets patchy and there is more heather and gorse. The soil between the plants is sandy and soft, and where it has not been disturbed it has a skin of lichen and moss. They have arrived at Sandy Heath.

Bess keeps on going until she sees a fallen pine tree, blown over by autumn winds. The roots of the tree have been torn from the ground leaving a crater; there are holes in the sides of this crater formed by roots being pulled out of the ground as the tree fell over. Bess climbs up and explores these holes, and chooses one.

"Come on up," she calls. "We can make this one into a very nice place to sleep."

It's warm and dry inside, but a bit cramped; the root had snapped off not very far into the ground. But as it's sandy soil, the mice can quickly make a larger chamber, pushing the dug sand out of the tunnel entrance. As soon as they are satisfied, they take off their packs and have a bite to eat. The young ones are asleep in no time at all and Pearl goes to sleep too, but Bess and Beechnut are wide awake.

"I'm going to have a look outside," whispers Bess. "Now that it's getting light I would like to see what's there."

"May I come too?" asks Beechnut.

"Of course!"

They walk up the slope further into the heathland. As they get towards the top of the hill the first rays of the morning sun are lighting up the autumn leaves on the birch trees, and the trunks of the pine trees are glowing a warm red. Closer to the ground, the sunshine sparkles in the drops of dew in the heather and gorse bushes, and hundreds of spider's webs are shining like jewels. Looking closely, they see clumps of wool, fogged with dew and shimmering in the sun, caught on the prickles of the gorse.

"Oh! It's beautiful; I have never seen such light," says Beechnut, enchanted and gasping with the wonder of such a sight. "Auntie Bess, it's worth coming here just to see this."

Bess moves to stand closer to Beechnut. "Yes, it is lovely; we're lucky to see such a sunrise. Come now, Beechnut, we must rest. I am very happy to see so many webs, and so much wool. Our work should go well."

"What sorts of creatures leave their wool in the gorse?"

"All sorts of animals come here and brush past the bushes. There are wolves and foxes, lynx, bears and wild boar, deer and badgers and goats, wild horses — everything. Some of the hairs might be too short, but as long as there are enough longer hairs, then, with the spiders' silk, we can make strong thread."

"I hope we don't meet foxes and wolves!" cries Beechnut.

"Me too," agrees Bess.

Bess and Beechnut climb back to their tunnel in the sand, and in two minutes have snuggled in with the others and are fast asleep.

~

When the five mice wake up, only a last little piece of sun can be seen above the horizon. There are ragged clouds in the sky like torn material, lit from underneath by the setting sun. The mice stretch their aching limbs; they have had a good sleep and now breakfast hungrily on the seeds and nuts carried all the way from Burrow Cave. The seeds collected on the way have already been eaten. When they have had enough to eat, the straps of their packs are adjusted to be worn as frontpacks for gathering wool and web-silk. They help each other to get them strapped on properly and they make their way to the heather.

Bess collects some strong twigs , and shows Flimsy and BillBill how to get spider's web silk to stick to a twig, and how to turn the twig to wind the web silk on. Once the twig is covered with sticky web it can be used, with the same twisting, to gather strands of wool and fur from the bushes. It takes ages for Flimsy and BillBill to get the hang of using the 'twizzl-stick', but after they've collected a small ball of spider's web mixed with wool they are feeling very pleased with themselves.

Bess is quick at it, and soon has a big ball of web-wool on her twig; when it's full she puts it into her pack, stick and all, and starts again with a new twizzl-stick.

Pearl and Beechnut have been working hard. They keep close to Flimsy and BillBill, giving them advice and encouragement.

Bess talks to the spiders as she goes. "Please spiders, can we gather some of your web silk? I know you are going to be very cross with us, but please forgive us — we don't mean you any harm! We know that you are so clever that you can make a new web very quickly, and we thank you for helping us."

The spiders are, nevertheless, very cross and scuttle away into the bushes muttering and complaining, but the truth is that they don't really mind, because they are very fat and lazy at this time of year.

The mice stop to rest under a gorse bush.

"Well done everyone," says Bess. "If we do the same amount again we'll have as much as we can carry."

"Will we start for home tonight, then, Mummy?" asks BillBill.

"No, dear, we must rest for the day and travel the next night."

"More to eat anyone?" asks Pearl, who has been handing round nuts and seeds.

"No thanks," comes the response.

They get back to the wool gathering, feeling good. It is going so well! In the distance a Tawny owl hoots and the mice instantly freeze.

"The owl is a long way away," whispers Bess, "but we must keep still for a bit longer and keep listening."

Gathering the wool means that they have to climb about in the gorse bushes quite a lot, which is difficult, but it feels safer than being on the ground. It is when they are on the ground that they are in most danger from hunters. Right now, all the mice are keeping as still as they can. There is no more hooting from the owl.

"Alright, let's get on," murmurs Bess, as she sets to work again.

They work on for a long time, until Bess thinks that her pack is almost full. Bess' pack is bigger than Flimsy and BillBill's packs and she hopes that if her own is nearly full then their smaller ones might be as well; they have been doing really well.

Suddenly, Bess feels a gust of wind shake the gorse twigs she is clinging to, and then . . .

"Shrieeeeeeeek."

Silence.

Flimsy and BillBill freeze into stillness again, fear shivering over their bodies as their fur stands on end. After what seems an age Pearl whispers, "Is everyone alright?"

"Yes, but I'm so frightened I can't stop shaking," says BillBill.

"Yes, Pearl, but what's happened?" Flimsy asks.

"I'm here, Pearl," says Bess.

Silence.

"Beechnut?" Pearl calls softly.

Silence.

"Beechnut?" calls Pearl, louder now, worry for her sister making her careless of making noise.

"Beechnut?" Pearl begins to sob, realising that the owl must have taken Beechnut.

"Come to me, all of you," says Bess, with calm authority. "Who was nearest to Beechnut just now?"

"Me," says Flimsy.

"Show me where."

They go to look but find nothing except Beechnut's twizzl-stick lying on the ground, half full of web-wool. They gather in a tight group and breathe Beechnut's smell on the twig. Pearl is crying; they huddle together. BillBill and Flimsy are crying now, too, as they begin to realise what has happened.

"Come, my darlings, we are not safe here now," says Bess tenderly. "Let's get back to our camp."

Bess coaxes and comforts, leading them back to their tunnel by the fallen tree. She helps them take off their packs, which are now heavy with web-wool. She hugs and comforts the young mice as best she can. Gradually, the sobbing quietens and all four snuggle together and try to sleep, but every few minutes someone sobs, setting them all off again.

After a time, Bess sits herself up and leans against her pack.

"Dear ones, please will you sit up and dry your eyes. Ready yourselves to listen to me."

Pearl, Flimsy and BillBill do as she asks.

Bess prepares herself, breathing deeply and slowly. When she eventually speaks it is in a voice quite unlike her own, and she speaks slowly and gently.

"The great wave has taken one we love, and we feel the pain of loss in our hearts.

"When we are born the great wave lifts us up, carrying us into our lives. We are part of the great wave always, even when we die.

"We feel pain at the loss of Beechnut, but remember, we shall learn to be happy for her too for she lives in our hearts where the great wave dwells. We shall learn even to welcome our sadness because this feeling bears witness to our love. We all give ourselves to the great wave when the time comes, and this gives meaning to our living."

They are quiet for a long time.

"Thank you," says Pearl, gently.

Flimsy and BillBill are sobbing softly. Outside a gentle rain falls and a light wind stirs the bushes and surrounding trees. The breeze brings the smell of rain into their tunnel, and Bess is alerted.

"I suggest that we make a last search for Beechnut and then set off for home. We should go quickly; I feel the weather worsening."

Together they search for Beechnut, looking everywhere and calling her name. It is so sad, speaking her name. It is the hardest thing. Beechnut was here with them, and now she isn't. Her absence is huge — there is a gap in the world where Beechnut used to be.

They find no sign of her. Returning to camp they pack their

things and make ready to leave, setting off into a grey and damp morning with the rain and the wind getting steadily fiercer. Their packs, already heavy with wool, become heavier as the rain soaks into them. Flimsy struggles with the effort, and tears stream from her eyes, but no one would know because of the rain.

"We must march to Tumble Cave," says Bess, in as strong a voice as she can muster. "I know it's a lot to ask but we must try."

March, they do, and as the day wears on the wind blows harder until it is a gale that bends the trees making them groan and swing about, clashing their branches together.

It is comforting for Bess to think that the weather is *so* horrible, it might put hunters off their hunting. Owls don't like to fly in heavy rain because their feathers get too wet. Foxes, weasels and stoats will hunt in stormy conditions, but this rain is heavy enough to make even these predators think twice about hunting — maybe.

"I'm sorry, Bess, I can't go much further," Flimsy gasps.

"Give me your pack, dear, I've been waiting for you to ask."

Pearl helps to undo the straps, and Bess then carries Flimsy's pack loosely across her shoulders, on top of her own.

"It's not far now. Are you alright, BillBill?"

"Yes, Mum, but fed up," he says, sobbing.

"I know — we're all fed up. Let's get to that cave."

In the gloom and confusion of the storm, Bess worries that she has lost her way. But when she sees the marker stones that she put in place on their outward journey, she is reassured, and before long they come to the tumble of rocks.

"Here we are, at last! Tumble Cave!"

They scramble up to the entrance and squeeze into the dry cave. Flimsy is exhausted and shivering. Everyone is cold, and they huddle together with Flimsy in the middle to keep her warm. No one wants to talk.

After a long quiet, Bess begins to talk very softly, almost a whisper, so that her voice might be mistaken for the rustling of leaves. Outside, the storm has reached its most fierce and noisy, but here in the cave her voice is calm and soothing.

"The long wave of life lifts us into being and when our time comes the long wave of life will dissolve us away, nourishing others who are coming into being. All living things are part of the waters of life which make the great wave."

Pearl feels tears coming again. "Oh, I miss you so much, Beechnut!" she sobs. "I am remembering things we have done together, we had such fun, and you are such a good friend. You have been near me all my life and I don't want you to go, and my heart is aching . . ."

The wind outside howls through the trees, but as the gloomy day comes to an end and darkness falls, the wind begins to die down and the rain at last stops falling.

The mice have slept a little, but fitfully, and as they stretch now they feel tired, sore and cold. Flimsy doesn't get up.

"Aunty Bess?" she whispers, her tiny voice quivering.

"Yes, dear."

"I'm feeling cold and shivery and horrible."

Bess touches Flimsy to check her temperature and pulse, and sure enough, her temperature feels high and her pulse too fast. Flimsy has a fever.

"Flimsy, you have a fever; you feel cold because your body is fighting an illness, but soon the heat of the battle in your body will come out, and you will feel burning hot. I know you are frightened, but I will do everything I can to look after you and I will be with you all the time."

Bess pauses to think. She makes a desparate decision.

"Pearl and BillBill, you must go for help at once. If you take only one pack,, and take it in turns to carry it, you will be able to get to Burrow Cave all the faster. There are a few nuts left to keep you going. Go as fast as you are able and send at least two strong mice back here to carry Flimsy home — no — three strong mice, because we have Flimsy's pack to carry too."

Pearl is concerned for Bess and Flimsy. "Aunty Bess, will you be alright for so long? Is there enough food left?"

"There will be enough. Flimsy will not want to eat until her fever breaks. Will you ask Ping Ling to send one of her special shawls to wrap Flimsy in? Now off you go — go with every care, but go fast."

"Goodbye, Mum," says BillBill, feeling a mixture of worry, fear and excitement. "We will get help as fast as we can."

"Goodbye, Bess, goodbye, Flimsy," says Pearl, tears welling.

In another moment they are gone, and Bess curls up with Flimsy, holding her close.

~

Bess worries that Pearl and BillBill will lose their way and not remember about the way-markers. Perhaps the storm has blown the markers around or covered them up with leaves and twigs. But Bess knows about worry, and she says to herself that worry will not help Pearl and BillBill; what will help them is her trust in them, and in the great wave.

Some time later, Flimsy's shivering stops, and she begins to feel hot, as Bess expected.

"Bess, I'm hot now, and thirsty. It's very quiet; what's happened?"

"The storm is over now, Flimsy, and Pearl and BillBill are running home to send help. We need some strong mice to carry you home!"

"I'm so sorry, Bess," she whimpers.

"Flimsy dear, there is no need for you to be sorry. I'm sorry that you are feeling so ill, as well as feeling the loss of Beechnut."

"Is she dead?"

"Yes, Flimsy, Beechnut is dead."

Flimsy takes deep breaths, finding her courage to speak.

"What's happened to her heart?"

"Her heart is singing inside you, and me, and all of us. Her heart is giving life to others. Now, Flimsy, I will go to find water for you to drink. I won't leave you alone for long."

Bess has remembered that there are some empty hazelnut shells on the floor of the cave, and she takes one outside. The shell has a round hole in it where a mouse has opened it to eat the kernel. She stops to listen to the sounds of the night: the last of the wind sighs in the trees, and she can hear water trickling close by. She sees water creeping down the rock face and dripping over the edge of a small overhang. She holds the hazel nut under the drips until it is about half full, any more than that and it might be too difficult to carry.

Holding the nut so that the water is lapping at the edge of the hole, she offers Flimsy a drink. Bess slowly tilts the nut as Flimsy drinks, to keep the water brimming.

"Thank you, Bess," murmurs Flimsy, slumping back onto the ground.

Bess explores the cave more thoroughly now that she has time. She finds more nutshells which she carries, one by one, to collect more water, bringing them in to store in the cave. She knows that the trickle of water will stop soon and if it doesn't rain again they will be in trouble.

She remembers the pile of the dry leaves and moss at the back of the cave where a creature once made a bed. Perhaps it was a mouse, but it is such a lot of bedding Bess thinks it must have been something bigger, a hedgehog maybe.

"I hope you are not going to come home and eat us up, whoever you are, and I hope that you won't mind if we borrow your bedding," she says out loud as she approaches, just in case there is someone still living there. "Thank you, creature, whoever you are."

Bess makes a good bed for Flimsy and when it is ready, she half carries and half walks Flimsy across the cave, settling her into the bedding and covering her well for warmth.

"Will I die, Auntie Bess?"

"No dear, you will not die, and please don't let that worry steal your strength."

Bess lies down close to Flimsy, gently stroking her forehead. Flimsy falls into feverish dreams, seeing strange things and hearing hollow, far away voices, but she can't make out what the words are saying. Then she hears a voice she knows well. It is Beechnut.

"You know what happened to my heart, Flimsy, because you can feel me in your own heart. My heart will always be part of you, and part of everything."

Flimsy sighs, falling deeply asleep for the first time since the Owl took Beechnut.

~

Pearl and BillBill travel through the night as fast as they can go. Pearl carries her pack until she feels that it is slowing her down too much, then BillBill takes his turn. They know which way to go most of the time, but sometimes it is hard to remember, because they are going the opposite way and everything looks different. The

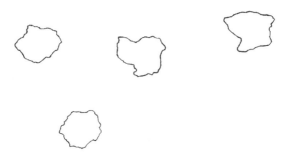

storm has littered the ground with twigs and leaves, which makes it harder too. When they can't decide which is the right way they look for one of the way markers and, so far, they have always found one.

The stones are a simple pattern of four, three in a triangle and one showing the way. Bess had placed the way-markers to show the way to Sandy Heath; now Pearl and BillBill need to go the opposite way. They travel fast and are panting, not able to talk. When they stop for a rest and manage to catch their breath, Pearl speaks first.

"I'm glad to be doing this fast walking. I've been feeling so sad and angry about Beechnut, it's good to let my body work hard and burn up all that anger. I'm feeling her close now."

"I know what you mean, Pearl, everything's happened so fast — I can't believe that Beechnut isn't here. She keeps bursting into my thoughts and I think — oh no! — all those things I would like to say to her and never did!"

"You can say them now, BillBill," says Pearl gently.

"But she's dead!"

Pearl hears the despair in his voice.

"She will hear you, when you let your heart speak."

BillBill hesitates, and then he finds a shaky voice.

"Hallo, Beechnut. I miss you lots, you're like a big sister to me and I wish you were still here."

Pearl hugs him. "She will like that. You can talk to her more as we walk, you know, just under your breath."

"Thanks Pearl. You're like a big sister to me, too."

Pearl smiles. "Come on, let's go!"

They swap the pack often as they get more tired. When they hear the alarm call of a jay, they dive under the roots of a tree, but the sound of the jay moves further away, so after a wait, they carry on.

~

At Burrow Cave, Dreamer is asleep in one of the bedchambers. He is dreaming about someone telling him something very important, and he must listen. He must stop listening to all the other voices in his head. But Dreamer is not good at doing anything except having a head full of dreams.

Suddenly his head clears, and he recognises Flimsy's voice.

He hears Flimsy's words very clearly, so clearly that he wakes up with a thump, his heart pounding in his chest. He looks around

167

to see what has hit him, but there is nothing there. He realises that this must be proper dreaming.

He runs to Burrow Cave where he finds Uncle One-Eye telling a story to the four youngest mice, and Mowzl and Acorn. As Dreamer comes in everyone is laughing at One-Eye's capers, but when they turn to see Dreamer's face the laughter fades away to silence.

"What's 'appened, Dreamer ol' son, you looks like you's seen a ghost!" says One-Eye.

Dreamer explains what has happened in his dream, and how he heard Flimsy's voice clearly.

"What words, exactly, is ye 'earin'?" asks One-Eye.

"Just: 'listen to me' and 'Flimsy, I am Flimsy, listen to me'."

One-Eye understands straight away, and in one second a plan of action is clear to him.

"Alright — 'tween 'ere 'n 'eathland they'll be shelterin' somewheres. 'Tis too far for the likes o' me to be runnin', so it be you three lads must go! Now!"

"Erm, how? What? Where?" Mowzl speaks for them all.

"Wool gatherin' 'appens up by Sandy 'Eath to the north, Bess will 'av laid markers. Git yourselfs ready to be goin'!"

One-Eye's voice is strong and commanding. The youngest mice flatten their ears and pretend not to be there. Mowzl tries his best to meet this new challenge, and begins to get things organised by giving everyone something practical to do.

"Dreamer, please get some food ready to take; Acorn, fetch two short ropes from the tool chamber and my small backpack; Marigold, see if you can find Burrow Bill; Scarlett, see if you can find Elfrida — and, Ruby, please find Ping Ling."

"What about me?" asks Violet, as all the others race off.

"You can help me and Uncle One-Eye with thinking!"

"You'll be rememberin' the trail, Mowzl, you's been before. What matters is — what'll be needed?"

Mowzl tries to remain calm even though he's flustered.

"Maybe the storm . . . Maybe they couldn't find shelter," he suggests.

"Or an accident," suggests Violet. "Someone might be hurt."

"Aye! You's likely right, lass," says One-Eye.

"It could be anything, we had better just go prepared," says Mowzl. "Prepared for anything."

Acorn and Dreamer arrive back with the ropes and food, which they've stuffed into Mowzl's backpack.

"I be thinkin' on what Violet did say," says One-Eye. "If one o' them is injured, you might be carryin' 'em 'ome."

"Ah! You could be right, Uncle. With three of us, we can take it in turns to do the carrying."

"All ready, Mowzl," says Acorn.

"All this because of my dream?" says Dreamer.

It would be good if Dreamer had got it wrong and that there is no emergency, but One-Eye trusts his own instinct that Dreamer has truly dreamed, perhaps for the first time.

"You's 'ad better be right lad!" he says, teasingly.

Mowzl shoulders his pack, hugs One-Eye, and without further ado the three mice set out into the night, heading north.

~

Mowzl knows the way for the first part of the journey and they travel fast. He tries to recall the last time he went wool gathering, and remembers that they spent the daytime in a cave about halfway to the heathland, but he can't remember any details. He thinks to himself that he must take more notice and remember things better.

"Mowzl, are we on the right path?" asks Acorn.

"Sorry, I've been thinking and not watching. You're right, Acorn, this doesn't feel right; let's head over this way a bit."

Suddenly a jay shrieks a harsh warning and the mice duck for cover under some tree roots, where they wait while the sound of the jay gets further away. They wait for quite a long time before cautiously setting out again.

The ground is wet, and the mice are soon covered in mud.

"I recognise these trees," says Mowzl. "We are on the right path now — this way!"

On they go, as the dawn sky brightens and the gloom in the wildwood lifts; the night mist begins to glow magically.

~

Pearl and BillBill are very tired now; making a last big effort, they arrive at Burrow Cave just as the first light of the day strikes the treetops. Staggering through the entrance tunnel, wet, muddy and exhausted, they are welcomed and a great fuss is made of them.

Elfrida, Ping Ling and Burrow Bill are there and have been talking with One-Eye. Now that Pearl and BillBill have arrived home, they all start to ask questions at once, and the young mice are jumping about all over the place, chattering away.

"Let's be 'avin some quiet, please!" calls One-Eye, with not much effect. "Quiet, please!" he shouts.

Everyone stops talking, turning to look at One-Eye in surprise.

"We're all 'avin' questions what are best answered by Pearl 'n BillBill their selves. Pearly — be tellin'."

"Flimsy is really ill in Tumble Cave. Bess asks for three strong mice to hurry there and carry Flimsy home, and carry their backpacks, and to take one of Ping Ling's special shawls to keep Flimsy warm."

"Pearly, I be 'avin' to tell thee — Mowzl, Dreamer 'n Acorn 'as already set off, on account o' Dreamer's dream o' Flimsy 'n all," says One-Eye.

"We must have passed them in the woods," says BillBill.

Everyone is talking at once again now, but they see the tears in Pearl's eyes and they fall silent.

"What is it, Pearl, dear?" asks Ping Ling gently.

"There's something else . . . worse. . ." Pearl chokes back her tears. "Beechnut has been taken by an owl," she says, sobbing.

There is a gasp in every throat, and the sound fills the cave. But with that gasp, Beechnut comes to them, suddenly filling their hearts. Pearl gathers herself, speaking of everything that has happened, until she is too tired to go on.

"Sapphyr, please will you find Wunda and Scribbla and ask them to come here, I am too tired to move," says Pearl, amidst the weeping that has filled the cave.

"Yes, Pearl," replies Sapphyr, scampering away.

"Uncle One-Eye, would you tell them what's happened, when they come?"

"Worry not, Pearl," he nods.

Pearl and BillBill are rubbed with soft, dry moss to clean off the mud and dry their fur as well as possible. They are made comfortable in a bed of moss, and nuts and seeds are brought for them, but they are too tired to eat; soon they are asleep.

Elfrida asks One-Eye if he would call for quiet once again. He does so with a more subdued voice, but just as effective.

"I am old and weak, too weak to even talk loudly enough for you all to hear me properly," begins Elfrida. "I will need your help, please, to prepare a bed for nursing Flimsy when she is brought home. I would like her to be brought to my bedchamber, where I can nurse her and be with her until she is strong again."

Elfrida is respected for her great knowledge of plant medicines, and for her healing skills. Scarlett and Marigold volunteer to do everything that Elfrida needs. They are proud to be allowed in to Elfrida's chamber; they are hoping to be able to help, and to learn, and to be near Flimsy.

"I'm wonderin' ow's we sendin' Ping Ling's shawl?" says One-Eye.

"Where's Scraggy?" says Burrow Bill. "He could go."

"Scraggz would get lost, bless 'im. We's needin' Star."

"I'll find him," says Burrow Bill. "I need something to do."

Having something to do can help when there are difficult feelings needing to be felt. The news of Beechnut's death has been a shock, and everyone is busy with planning the rescue and making preparations for nursing Flimsy. But each mouse needs to have time for crying; time with loved ones, and time with Beechnut.

Burrow Bill finds Star in the Mouseum reading about navigating by the stars.

"True to your birth-name, eh?" says Burrow Bill.

When Star was born, with his siblings Flimsy and Scraggy, there were lots of shooting stars in the sky and LaLa wanted to name one of her babies "Star". Well, one of her babies was a bit scraggy, another was a bit flimsy, so the third one had to be Star!

"Hallo, Burrow Bill," he says, looking up. I was just reading about 'dead reckoning'."

"You'll wish you hadn't said that — I bring sad news . . ."

Burrow Bill relates the story of Beechnut being taken by the owl, and of Flimsy's rescue that is happening now and the need for Star to run like the wind with Ping Ling's shawl. As Burrow Bill speaks, Star's eyes fill with tears.

"I can feel her, feel her in here," says Star, banging his chest with his fist. "I miss her so much, it's like I'm cut open . . ."

Burrow Bill holds Star close until his sobbing subsides.

"Thank you, Bill," Star whispers. "Let's go."

They return to Burrow Cave, where Ping Ling is ready with her most special shawl. Before the shawl is folded, Elfrida sprinkles herbs onto it rubbing them gently into the wool. She has also prepared honey with medicine mixed in and this she puts into an empty hazelnut shell, sealing the hole with beeswax. The hazelnut, wrapped in moss and tied into a little bundle, is placed in the middle of the shawl, which Ping Ling then folds into a neat parcel and ties with string; she adds some extra bits of string for tying the parcel to Star's shoulders.

Everything is explained to Star, especially about the hazelnut medicine, so that it won't get lost or forgotten; with his pack tied on, he bids a tearful goodbye and starts out on the trail at a run.

He is a good runner, he can keep going for a long time if he paces himself carefully. It's not like sprinting as fast as you can for a short way, it needs a different sort of energy, a slower, deeper

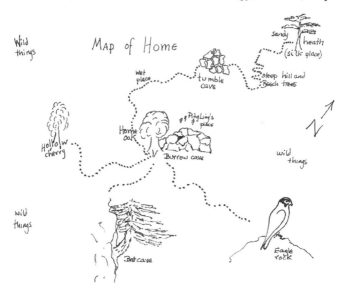

energy that can last for ages.

It's daylight now, and the sky is clear and bright after the storm. The few clouds still in the sky are high up, racing along with the remains of the gale. One-Eye has shown Star the map, made by Pearl and Mowzl. He has been quick to 'find his bearings', as the old books say, and he travels north confident that he will find his way.

Because of the emergency he has to travel in daylight. A hunter might see him at any moment, so he keeps to the shadows whenever he is able to. He thinks of Flimsy, and Beechnut, and he lets his legs run and run.

~

In Tumble Cave, Bess lies cradling Flimsy in the bed of dry moss. She stands to stretch, and, looking at Flimsy she thinks, *poor little one, so small and frail.*

After tucking Flimsy up with moss to keep her warm, Bess goes outside to look and listen. The sun is low in the sky, soon to set. It has been behind cloud, but now, as it sinks lower, the sun escapes the cloud and brilliant light pours into the world. Bess watches as the clouds turn red, lit from beneath, and this gift of beauty fills her heart with joy, and hope for Flimsy.

She listens for the sounds of birds in case an alarm call might warn her of danger. She sees a buzzard circling and mewing high overhead, but she is safe from him; even if he swooped down she would have time to hide in the cave. She hears the cough-like bark of a stag and the piping call of a nuthatch — "Twit! Twit! Twit!", and she hears a squirrel scolding. Everything is as it should be.

Close by, a robin trills, and ticks, tilting her head looking at Bess. "Are you alright?" the robin asks.

"It's a long story . . ." Bess replies, explaining about Flimsy's illness and waiting for help.

"My name is Cheeky," says the robin. "May I help?"

"Thank you, Cheeky, my name is Bess, and it is Flimsy that's ill. I don't know what you could do, but it is good of you to offer."

"I will find Gabbee!" says Cheeky, not to be put off.

"Gabbee? Isn't that the parrot that carried Mowzl and Scraggy on her back?"

"Yes!" says Cheeky excitedly. "We all heard about that! Waggl couldn't help telling the whole world from his nest hole in the cherry tree!"

"Cheeky, do you mean that Gabbee could fly Flimsy home?"

"Oh yes! But you will have to go too, to make sure that she doesn't fall off."

"Oh, my goodness! Yes, please, Cheeky, please try to find Gabbee!" Bess exclaims.

"I will," replies Cheeky, flying off at once.

Bess returns to Flimsy, feeling excited and worried at the same time. She is nervous about riding on the parrot's back, and worried that Flimsy might fall off.

Cheeky isn't very keen on the idea of flying all the way to the hollow cherry tree, so when she hears the nuthatch calling, she flies towards the sound and soon sees Twitwit running down a tree trunk. Twitwit seems to like being upside down — in fact it's normal for him. Twitwit isn't a twit, he's very smart in fact. It's just that whenever he says anything it sounds like 'twit! twit! twit!', so that's how he got his name.

"Hallo, Cheeky! What brings you so far from your favourite place by Tumble Cave?"

Cheeky tells Twitwit about the very ill mouse in Tumble Cave, and how Gabbee could save her life if she is willing to carry her to home to Burrow Cave.

"Would you, please, fly to Gabbee's nest in the old cherry tree, and ask if she would?"

"I will, I will! I'd like to see how many feathers young Waggl has grown. Twit! Off I go!"

And Twitwit flies off like a dart. He knows exactly where the old cherry tree is. He often goes there in search of insect grubs to eat, and there are always a lot to find because it's a very old tree.

When he arrives, he runs down the trunk to peek inside from the top of the nest hole.

"Twit! Twit! Are you there, Waggl?"

"'Allo, Twit! Look at my new fevvers! Me fly soon!"

"Ah ha! Very good feathers, Waggl, they are growing well; but you are not ready to fly yet. You must be patient. It would be good to practice flapping your wings to make the muscles grow strong, but don't jump out of your nest yet. Is your Mum about?"

"Mummee cumin', Mummee's cumin'! Mummeee!"

"Kreee kreee kraaaaaaaa," screeches Gabbee, as she lands.

"Hallo, Gabbee," says Twitwit.

"'Allo, Waggl, 'Allo, Twitwit," says Gabbee, dropping some berries in for Waggl.

Twitwit explains about Tumble Cave, and Flimsy needing to get to Burrow Cave.

"Burrow Cave? Mowses my friends, me help, me help," and away she flies, just like that.

"Well!" says Twitwit. "She didn't take much persuading."

"Mowses my friends too," says Waggl. "They visits Waggl."

"While I'm here, I'll have a look for some grubs."

"Wot Drillbill the woodee pekka is callin' larvee."

Twitwit smiles and shakes his head slightly.

"Drillbill likes using big words; grubs is good enough for me!"

"Twitwit, please come see Waggl again soon."

"I will, Waggl!"

~

The rescue party marching to Tumble Cave — Mowzl, Dreamer and Acorn — travel all day, as fast as they can. Everything goes well until they hear a jay shouting, and they take cover. Peering out from under the roots, Mowzl can see his friend, Dappa the jay, making a terrible fuss, and he can see why. Perched in a nearby tree and staring straight at him, is Sparkeye the sparrow hawk. Dappa screeches and shouts and makes pretend attacks on Sparkeye, and the noise attracts other birds — and squirrels too — and soon there is a terrible racket going on. Sparkeye gets very cross, snapping angrily at whoever comes too close.

After a while Sparkeye gives up; he spreads his broad wings and flies away. Slowly the birds' alarm calls quieten down, as does the squirrels' chattering, and one by one they fly away until only Dappa remains; the squirrels loop away, their tails quivering.

Mowzl, Dreamer and Acorn do not come out of their hiding place until they are sure that Sparkeye has not sneaked back. Dappa the jay is still perched in the tree nearby preening his feathers proudly. Mowzl feels sure that if Sparkeye were sneaking about Dappa would know and sound the alarm again.

"Come on, let's go," says Mowzl, and out they creep, cautious and alert.

"Ah-ha!" cries Dappa. "So that's what Sparkeye was doing! He was hunting you three mice!"

"Thanks for saving us, Dappa," says Mowzl.

"No problem, Mowzl, but really, I didn't know you were there! I just have to make a fuss you see. Where are you off to?"

"We're on a rescue mission to Tumble Cave, where Flimsy is very ill."

"Ah, it's not far to go, I'll fly ahead and make sure Sparkeye isn't lurking. If I see him, I'll shout!"

"Thanks, Dappa!" call all three mice in one voice.

~

Meanwhile, Star has been pacing himself, careful not to run so fast that he has to stop for a breather; he finds a rhythm that he can keep up. He tries to keep out of sight as much as possible, but he knows that he is taking a big risk running over the ground in daylight. He thinks of Flimsy and sets his heart on helping to save her.

He hears a terrible fuss of birds and squirrels mobbing, so he knows there may be trouble ahead, but he keeps going.

At last he sees the tumble of rocks that give Tumble Cave its name, and he can see the cave entrance. Just before he arrives, he sees a parrot glide through the trees towards the tumble of rocks. It's Gabbee!

"Kraaaaakekekekek!" squawks the parrot.

Mowzl, Acorn and Dreamer have also just arrived, and it's a noisy crowd that greets Star when he gets there. Gabbee's voice is so loud in the entrance to the cave, it's impossible to hear anything that's said, but bit by bit things calm down. Bess explains about Cheeky the robin, and about Pearl and BillBill running for help; Gabbee tells of Twitwit the nuthatch, and Dreamer tells of his dream. Eventually, everybody knows what's happened, so they can all start to plan what they should do next. Gabbee is impatient to fly straight away to Burrow Cave, but Flimsy is too weak to hold on by herself.

Star explains about the shawl he has brought from Ping Ling, and that it is important that Flimsy is wrapped up really well to keep her warm. Flimsy is carefully wrapped, carried out of the cave, and tied to Gabbee's back. Star explains about the medicine in the sealed hazelnut; Bess opens it straight away, and helps Flimsy to drink the honey medicine inside.

"Gabbee," says Bess. "I will have to come too to hold Flimsy, these cords will not be enough; will you be able to carry us both?"

"Yes, yes, you two are little and light, little and light! Gabbee carry Mowzl and Scraggy easy. Let's go! Let's go!"

"Ha, Gabbee!" says Mowzl. "You're so impatient! Is Waggl alright, Gabbee?"

"Waggl has new feathers growing, he's warmer now, Waggl fly soon."

Mowzl and Star look at each other, smiling.

"Good, tell him we'll come and see him again soon."

At last everything is ready, and Bess climbs onto Gabbee's back. She holds on to the tying cords and to Gabbee's feathers and to Flimsy all at once, and she hopes that all will be well.

"Gabbee, please fly gently," says Mowzl. "Not too many sudden turns or ups and downs. Remember you have a very sick Flimsy on your back, and Bess is having to hold on for two."

"Mowzl, yes. Gabbee ready, flyaway fly way."

"Bye!" they call, as Gabbee takes to the air.

"Well!" says Acorn. "All that, and now we don't have Flimsy to carry home!"

"We do have four backpacks to carry home," says Star. "These bags are full of the wool and silk that they all gathered. It's even more precious now, because Beechnut died . . ."

A hush falls over them.

"Yes, Star, well said." Mowzl breaks the silence. "I wish we could find her pack as well."

"It's another night's journey to Sandy Heath," says Dreamer.

"I don't think we should go," says Star. "I think we should take these packs back to Burrow Cave."

They all agree. Mowzl opens his small pack, sharing out the food that he has brought with him. After eating they snuggle together, surrounded by packs of wool, and sleep. Later, they wake after dark; wispy clouds drift across the face of the moon.

The mice feel sleepy and stiff from their long march, but after they've stretched their limbs and moved about a bit they feel better. They finish up the food, tie on the backpacks, and set off for home. Cheeky the robin is awake and curious. She watches them go, tinkling a little robin song which floats in the night air like a blessing.

Gabbee arrives at Burrow Cave in quick time, or so it seems to her, but for Bess it's been an eternity, using all her strength to hold on to Flimsy and to Gabbee's feathers at the same time, trying not to fall off.

The parrot lands on the ground under Home Oak, and Bess starts untying the cords. Ruby has been looking out of the red window watching the night, and she calls out to everyone in Burrow Cave that Gabbee has arrived with Bess and Flimsy — well, it looks like Flimsy, but she can't see properly.

Scraggy runs out to help, greeting Gabbee.

"'Allo, Gabz! Thanks for fetchin' 'em 'ome."

"Scraggee welcome, welcome, Scraggee."

As soon as the cords have been untied, Scraggy lifts Flimsy from Gabbee's back. The parrot ruffles her feathers, preening them back into place.

"Home to Waggl, home I go!" she shouts, and off she flies.

"Thank you, Gabbee!" shouts Bess, as loud as she can.

"Bess, get inside quick, you's shakin' like a leaf," says Scraggy.

Scraggy talks softly to Flimsy as he carries her towards the burrow entrance. "Flimsy, my belov'd sister, I's so 'appy you's got 'ome. Threeda's made a bed in 'er chamber 'n she's goin' to nurse you better."

Flimsy says nothing, but she hears everything, and she knows what is happening. She can't move, or open her eyes, or speak — she is very frightened, but it is comforting for her to be carried by Scraggy, and to hear his voice.

Bess has tears in her eyes as they enter Burrow Cave. She hugs Scribbla, Ping Ling and Threeda, and they can tell that she is about to fall down at any moment because she is so exhausted. They settle her into moss bedding, and Ping Ling comforts her.

"Elfrida is ready, Scraggy, would you carry Flimsy to her chamber, please?"

"Straight away, Aunt Threeda."

Now that Bess has fulfilled her task in getting Flimsy home, all her fear and worry comes pouring out in a torrent. She shivers and sobs uncontrollably while Ping Ling holds her close, staying with her until she falls into an exhausted sleep.

~

Scraggy carefully lowers Flimsy onto the bed that has been prepared in Elfrida's chamber.

"Granny, is I takin' the shawl away?" asks Scraggy, in his best voice because he is in awe of Elfrida and a little bit frightened of her, and he wants to do his very best.

"No, dear, please leave it on her for now; it will help to hold her together, like a magic skin, until her body finds itself again."

Elfrida tends to Flimsy with great love and attention. She prepares medicines from dried plants, gathered from the wildwood during the summer, and mixes them into a paste with honey in half a nutshell. Using moss tied into a pad, she dips into the medicine and touches the pad to Flimsy's lips. Flimsy's tongue moves a little and she learns to lick her lips so that the medicine gets into her mouth.

All this time Flimsy has visions. She sees all sorts of things that she knows have not happened in real life, but she has a feeling that they will happen one day. These things that she sees are like stories, but they come to her in random little bits like a storybook with all the pages torn out and muddled up.

But she doesn't dream the bit of story that would tell her if she is going to get better or not. Flimsy begins to understand that her life has changed, and will never be as it was before she became ill. It started with the owl taking Beechnut, and with the terrible sadness that was such a deep pain; then with the storm and endless rain, when the chill got into her bones and the fever wracked her body.

I will never be the same, she thinks to herself. *If I live, my life will not be the same.* But she doesn't yet know what this means.

Elfrida is aware that Flimsy is so very ill that she might die, and that she will be preparing herself to meet that mystery. Elfrida stays close by and attentive. Flimsy will be facing a crossroads: one direction will be to go with the great wave, and the other direction will be to live, but a very different life. Elfrida wants to help Flimsy, because she knows how disappointed Flimsy will be if she can't do all the things normal mice can do; but she will be able to do other things, things that will be gifts of the great wave.

Flimsy slowly gets stronger, and able to open her eyes, but she doesn't speak. She begins to move her limbs, and to stretch; she spends weeks learning how to stand without falling over, and how to walk — she must learn simple things all over again.

At last she is ready to spend a little time each day in Burrow Cave. At first a cousin, or brother, carries her there, but as soon as she is able, she walks there by herself, even though it takes a long time. In Burrow Cave she sits in a bed of moss, watching whatever is happening, enjoying her family giving her hugs. But she doesn't talk; she doesn't say a word.

She is very glad to learn that everyone got back safely from Tumble Cave, and that Bess is all right. It would be so awful if someone else had died that night. Oh, what a terrible night!

The mixed-up pages of the storybook that Flimsy sees inside herself, are still filling her imagination. She never knows if the stories are real or not. She doesn't know if they will ever happen, or have happened already.

Sometimes the bits of story are about her family and familiar places, and sometimes they are about places unknown to her. She realises that she will be shown everything, in time, and she will see things that she would rather not have to see. She feels a sudden chill shivering down her body from her head to her toes — she is feeling the movement of the great wave. She feels the love that the great wave bestows, and she understands that she no longer has to make a choice at all; everything is clear and simple. The gift of the great wave is not to make her better, so that she can live the life she expected to, but a gift of wisdom. Flimsy cries out as her heart contracts in pain, but this pain slowly eases as she accepts what must be.

She spends most of her time with Elfrida, feeling safe and reassured, knowing that Elfrida understands and is there for her, accompanying her.

One day, Flimsy is thinking about her father, One-Eye. He and LaLa, Flimsy's mother, have been coming to see her every day and Flimsy has realised that she has never really 'seen' them properly before. They were just Mum and Dad. But now she sees them properly, and she wants to get to know them better.

She visits One-Eye's den, when she is strong enough to walk there, and they sit quietly together at his table, in the soft glow of the lantern hanging from the ceiling. One-Eye has carried his 'bowl o' little 'eads' to the table, and Flimsy has been looking at some of the wonderful things he keeps there; she holds a shell, or a little head, feeling a mysterious strength flowing into her body. She picks a big shell from the bowl and cradles it in her hands, closing her eyes. She gives herself to 'seeing', and speaks for the first time.

"I am seeing the ocean. It is blue and calm, stretching away to the horizon in all directions. There is nothing but ocean — except there — over there, is mist — no — it's thicker than mist, it's fog. The fog seems closer now, I am inside it and it is cool, and making my face wet. It's not quite dark, but nearly. Now I see a brighter bit, it comes closer and I see the ocean again! And there, through the thinning fog, I see an island with forests and a mountain disappearing up into a misty sky. Close by, in the sea, is a ship at anchor; a human ship. My heart knows that you are there, Daddy, you are there on that ship.

"This shell in my hand comes from there, it comes from that island. I hold it to my ear, and I can hear the sound of waves breaking on the Island's shore. Oh! Now there is a storm, and now I see a great wind tearing at the ship, ripping its sails to shreds. A huge black cloud swirls round and round, howling as it swirls, sucking everything it can lift into the sky — a mast breaks, crashing through the ship's deck, breaking it open; shattered timbers and loose barrels fly upwards, and what is that I see? There! What is that? Who is that? Small, so small, I see a mouse — is it you Daddy? I can't see — no, I don't think it's you, it's not you Daddy. Now it's gone, sucked into the sky by the wind. The mouse has disappeared into the black swirling cloud!"

Flimsy's body shrinks down, her head droops forward.

"Now my seeing has ended," she whispers.

Flimsy's body slumps against the table in One-Eye's den. One-Eye holds her, gently soothing her, a frown deeply furrowing his brow.

"You's safe, lass, never fear, you's safe 'ere in Burrow Cave. You 'as the sight, dear one, for what you's seen be the Island of Mist."

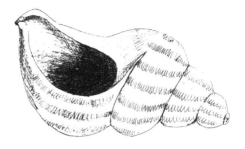

The End
of
Volume One

. . . to be continued

Released in 2019. . .

The Adventures of Horatio Mowzl

Volume Two

First Purlings

Chapter One

Ocean

Springtime in Emmy's home world brings sunshine and flowers
to the woods around Burrow Cave. Wood anemones, violets
and celandines are showing off their colours, and wild garlic and
bluebells are in bud, promising carpets of white flowers and blue
flowers in a week or two. Some of the trees are beginning to unfurl
their leaves, especially the small trees that must get their leaves
going before the taller trees take all the light.

Emmy and Scraggy have been out in the wildwood all day,
finding a new 'lookout' tree. They are on their way home and not
far away from the hollow cherry tree where Gabbee and Waggl
nested when Emmy has an idea.

"Hey, Scragg, let's go and see if Waggl's about, and maybe the
cherry tree will be flowering. I'd love to see the cherry blossom."

"Good plan, Em. I 'ope Waggl's at 'ome 'n I 'ope 'e's flyin' by
now," replies Scraggy.

During the winter they'd visited Waggl a few times giving him
presents of nuts and seeds, and each time they visited they saw that
his feathers had grown a little more. Gabbee would open hazelnuts
with her strong bill and give the kernel to Waggl. The last time they
visited the parrots there was no sign of them whatsoever. Where
could they have gone?

Coming closer to the cherry tree, they hear the humming of bees.
The tree is in full bloom, a fountain of white blossom reaching as
high into the forest canopy. Insects are attracted to the tree by the
nectar that the blossom provides, and while they forage for nectar,
their hairy bodies pick up pollen grains which they carry from
flower to flower, and from tree to tree, helping to fertilise the flowers
and make new seeds.

Emmy and Scraggy climb up inside the hollow trunk. It's
something they've done quite a lot and know how to do. The loose,
dusty stuff has mostly fallen, and they don't get so dirty as the first
time they did it. Scraggy goes first with Emmy following close
behind, and when they arrive, they find the nest empty.

"I wonder where they went?" says Emmy, sadly. "They'll still be
needing a nest for shelter, won't they?"

"Maybe they's outside, branchin'," says Scraggy.

The mice climb up to the hole in the tree and look out.

"Let's call Waggl!" says Emmy, and together they shout Waggl's name.

"Waaaaaaaaaaaaggaaaaaaaaaaall!"

But there's no reply.

From the nest hole, they admire the branches of the cherry tree covered with flowers; foraging bees fill the air with the sound of their wings and there is a delicious smell in the air, a perfume soft and sweet.

"Scraggy, I feel like having a bit of a lie-down. Let's have a nap and see if Waggl turns up."

"Mmm. I's feelin' sleepy too, Em."

They climb back down to Waggl's nest, curl up, and in no time at all they are fast asleep.

~

Emmy yawns and stretches, keeping his eyes closed because the sun is shining directly onto his face. After a bit he yawns again.

"Scraggy?"

"Em?"

"It's bright, isn't it?"

"Yep, it's so bright I can't open my eyes!"

"Me too, let's open our eyes together . . . one, two, three . . .

186

"Yiiiiiiikes! Where are we?" they shout in alarm.

Instead of Waggl's nest inside the cherry tree, what they see when they open their eyes makes them gasp. They can see more blue sky than they have ever seen before, and when they look out from Waggl's nest, they see no trees, no ground, but the sea!

Climbing out from Waggl's nest to get a better view they discover that Waggl's nest is not in the cherry tree in the wildwood but tucked up underneath a wooden platform high on the mast of a human sailing ship. They scramble through the tangle of ropes and timbers that support the platform and climb onto the top.

From here they can see the ocean in all directions, as blue as the sky, but darker and with greenish patches, and there is no land to be seen at all.

"Where's our wildwood?" cries Scraggy.

"Oh, my goodness," says Emmy. "Where are we? How did we get here?"

"We're dreamin', Em."

The two mice are on a platform high on the mainmast of a ship. The mast, the platform and the mice are swaying about in a crazy way as the ship below rolls from side to side with the force of the ocean waves. In ship talk, the platform is called the crows-nest, but our mice don't know that yet. They are worried about how they got here, and how they will get home.

"Pinch me, Scragg, wake me up. Ouch! Not that hard! Oh dear, we're still here."

"If this is a ship it 'as to be a giant's ship."

"Scragg, this is a human ship and it's swaying like a willow in the wind making me feel sick — Oh-oh, I'm going to fall off!"

"'Old tight, Em, 'ere, grab a rope."

"I've never seen so many ropes, and they're huge. We could climb down . . ."

"We don't know what's down there, Em, there might be 'umans, or cats or worse."

"We can't stay here forever."

Just then a bird flies past, squawking.

"Gabbeeeee!" yells Scraggy at the top of his voice. "Em, that was a parrot bird, it must be Gabbee!"

The parrot, which is flying about looking for something to eat, hears the sound 'Gabbee' floating on the wind and that makes him very curious. He flies around the ship looking very carefully for signs of anyone who might have called Gabbee's name, but can see no one, until — ah, yes! — there on the crow's nest platform, two strange-looking mice! He flies down to the platform, landing clumsily and noisily.

"Aaaark — uck — uck — ha!"

"'Allo, Gabbee, oh, dear, you're not Gabbee are you?"

"Me not Gabbee. Who be yoo? Howdyoo know Gabbee name?"

"Please, slow down," says Emmy. "We can't understand when you talk so fast."

"We're mouses 'n my name's Scraggy," says Scraggy.

"Hallo, my name's Emmy, and I'm a mouse."

Emmy always says this when he meets someone new — well, as long as they don't look like they are about to eat him up.

"Ah, meeces," says the parrot. "Allo, allo, welcum abord."

"What's your name, Mr Parrot?" asks Scraggy.

"Parrot name Gobbee!"

"Hallo, Gobbee, we're friends of Gabbee and Waggl, do you know them?" says Emmy.

"My-wife-my-life-my-famillee-vanished-away-I'm-all-at-sea."

Emmy and Scraggy cover their ears, because Gobbee is shouting so loud. When Gobbee stops shouting, Emmy tells the story of how they had met Waggl and Gabbee and of some of their adventures together, and that just before arriving here he and Scraggy had been asleep in Waggl's empty nest.

"Ah emtee emtee. Waggl n Gabbee fly home soon."

"But how did they get there, and how did we get here?" asks Emmy, feeling very confused by all this.

"Mistree mistree timedreem ti —"

"Oh, Gobbee," interrupts Emmy. "What do you mean? And please don't shout so."

Gobbee makes an effort to slow down and be quieter.

"Timedream make porthole, misstree, misstree."

"Gobbee, you talk in riddles."

"Yes, riddl riddl!" shouts Gobbee, forgetting to be quieter.

"Emmy, isn't a porthole like a window in a boat? Is he meanin' it's all a dream?"

"He says it's a mystery, not a dream, Scraggy."

"Misstree misstree yes."

"So, how do Gabbee and Waggl get home? And how do we get home?"

"No do, no do, you follow, you see."

"Gobbee, we don't understand you . . ."

"Mistree."

"Gobbee, what do we do now? Can you help us?"

"Gobbee help meeces — Gobbee fly meeces."

"We isn't flyin'!"

"Meeces fly Gobbeez, back."

"What's down there on the ship, Gobbee? Humans?"

"Oomans-ratses-catsez-meeces."

"Oh, no!"

"Oh-yes! Wotchout, find meeces, Gobbee help you."

Emmy and Scraggy climb on Gobbee's back, gripping his feathers. They have had some practice with Gabbee, but Gobbee is a bit rougher with his passengers. Gobbee leans over the edge of the crow's nest, stretches his wings, and with a great shriek, launches himself into the wind.

"Aaaaarkaaaaaark!"

"Yikes!" cries Scraggy.

"Oh nooooo!" groans Emmy, as Gobbee glides and tumbles between the ropes and masts of the swaying ship until landing on a huge coil of rope on the deck near the bow.

"That was scarier than flying with Gabbee!" exclaims Emmy.

"Gabbee? Fly Gabbee did you? Gobbee want my Gabbee!"

Scraggy explains: "We's climbin' into Waggl's nest by mistake 'n we's makin' friends with Waggl 'n Gabbee, 'n Gabbee's flyin' us 'ome on 'er back."

"Emtee nest? No Waggl?"

"No Waggl," says Emmy. "Waggl and Gabbee have gone away. We don't know where."

"Meeces, hide quick."

"Gobbee, I'm scared, can we call you if we need you?" says Emmy.

"Call Gobbee yes."

Gobbee flies off leaving the anxious mice looking this way and that, trying to see where to hide before being seen

"Scragg, let's not panic, but do something quick!"

"Over there, Em — I's seein' an 'ole in that 'atch,

"Let's go!" yells Emmy, and they jump from coil to coil of the giant anchor rope and scuttle across the deck so fast they hardly touch the boards at all. Just as they disappear through the hole in the hatch a scruffy human comes along; he's on sentry duty and has two cutlasses and two pistols tucked into his belts. He passes by,

189

continuing his patrol round the ship, thinking about what he's going to eat when he gets off duty.

Under the hatch Emmy and Scraggy find themselves at the top of steep wooden steps leading down into the gloom below.

"Emmy, I's feelin' sick from all the rollin' 'n swayin'."

"Yes, Scraggy. We're burrowing mice and there's no ground here! It's no wonder we feel sick. Come on, let's climb down these steps and explore."

They climb down the giant steps to the deck below; Emmy is relieved to find that it isn't as dark as he'd thought it might be. There are cages swinging from beams above them, each one with a flame inside making a yellow light. Emmy remembers seeing a little cage resembling these in Uncle One-Eye's den, but that one was much smaller and the light it made wasn't yellow, it was pale, and there was no flame to be seen inside.

Adjusting to the gloom, they find themselves in a storeroom; piles of boxes and barrels are roped down to iron rings anchored to floor and walls. Everything is very big human stuff; to the mice it is truly a world of giants.

They move forward listening out for danger. Emmy is thinking that they need to find a safe place to hide, and they need to find food and water — and then what? Emmy doesn't like to think about the 'then what'.

"What's that — what's that noise?" says Scraggy, nervously, peering into the shadows.

"Let's have a look," says Emmy, creeping forward. "It may just be the ship creaking as it moves."

"I's 'earin' whisperin'!" Scraggy whispers.

They listen and wait but hear nothing more than the creaking of ropes. The ship rolls from side to side, lifting and falling with the swell of the sea. The flame-cages swing on their hooks, and the ropes holding fast the barrels and crates creak and strain as the ship moves.

"I've just remembered," whispers Emmy. "Uncle One-Eye calls it his lantern."

"What?"

"The light in his den."

The mice move quietly from the shadow of one pile to the shadow of the next, not knowing where to go — except onwards; suddenly they are startled by a shout from above.

"Stand fast, ye scum! Speak the password, or you'll be tastin' the steel of my cutlass, ahhh!"

"Oh, my goodness! Our time has come, Scragg —, oh dear me." Emmy coughs to clear his throat, and speaks in as bold a voice as he can muster. "Er . . . We are Emmy and Scraggy, and we don't know what 'password' means."

"Emmy and Scraggy? Ha-ha! What names! Well now, ye scavenging scum, ye be under arrrest!"

"Oh, gooddee!" says Scraggy. "We's badly needin' a rest, 'n food would be good too, we's not et in ages. Where are you."

The owner of the voice jumps down from the top of a barrel, landing with a thump on the deck.

"Ouch!"

It's a rat! He's wearing two belts with a cutlass stuck under one of the belts, another cutlass in his paw.

"Ha! You be mowses! You mowses be my prisoners! Come along with me 'n no mowsee business or I'll cut off your tails!"

"Why?" says Emmy. "And what's your name?"

"Why what?"

"Why everything? And what's your name?"

"I be Black-Eyed Bart if you must be knowin', 'n why anything? I 'asn't got a clue."

"Hallo, Black-Eyed Bart, my name's Emmy and I'm a mouse, and this is my cousin Scraggy; we woke up in your world and we don't know how to get home."

"Ha-ha! A tall story if ever there were! Never believe mowses, I was always told! This way. Quick march!"

Black-Eyed Bart prods them with his cutlass to make them move towards the dark shadows, where no lanterns swing.

"Why don't you talk to us?" Emmy asks.

"Sentry duty don't allow no chit-chat; git on with you before I skin thee alive!"

They come to a wall of oak timbers and panels. At floor level, in the darkest corner, is a rat-sized hole through the wall.

"Through there — go!"

Emmy goes first, then Scraggy. As soon as Emmy is halfway through the hole, he feels rough paws pulling him to the side, at the same moment he hears a whispered 'shhhhhhhh!'. Scraggy is pulled sideways too, but he is pulled the other way and there is another 'shhhhhhh!' whispered.

The rat, Black-Eyed Bart, follows them through the hole, and when he is halfway through, a voice challenges him.

"Stop there, Bart, or you will surely lose your whiskers!"

Three mice stand close to Bart's head with their cutlasses pushed against his neck.

"Ah —, my dear friends —, how nice to see you!" says Bart.

"Drop your cutlass, Bart. Where's the other one? Bring it out where we can see it!"

Black-Eyed Bart does as he is told, and the leader of the mice kicks each cutlass out of reach.

"Now, come forward slowly, Bart, slowly."

"I mean you no 'arm, Whip-Tail Jack!" says Bart.

"Bart, let us be on our way and we'll be sayin' no more about it, eh? If you be a chasin' after, I'll be tellin'," says Whip-Tail Jack, knowing that Bart doesn't want his fellow rats to know how easily he's been defeated.

"Alright, alright, anything you say, Jack, only a bit of fun . . ."

Black-Eyed Bart crawls through the hole and retreats, picking up his cutlasses and sticking them back into his belts. The three pirate mice back out of the hole, holding Emmy and Scraggy by their arms. They move off swiftly through the shadows, through a doorway where they have to climb over the coaming board, which stops water sloshing through, through a small hole in the floor, onto a beam, through another hole, and another — until Emmy and Scraggy are dizzy and have lost all sense of direction. At last the three pirate mice stop to rest and have a good listen for anyone following them.

"Will the rat chase us?" asks Emmy, looking back.

"No."

"You were all very brave, thank you for rescuing us."

"'Tiz nothin'."

"My name's Emmy and this is Scraggy, we're cousins."

"Talk later."

The mouse with the name Whip-Tail Jack has been muttering these few words while the other two remain silent and watchful. They move on, Jack in front then Emmy and Scraggy followed by the other two pirate mice. After many more twists and turns, they arrive at another hole leading to a narrow space above the galley ceiling. In fact, it's above a store cupboard at one end of the galley. *This is their burrow!* thinks Emmy.

One of the pirate mice stays on guard, and another fetches food and water which Emmy and Scraggy eat and drink eagerly. Whip-Tail Jack watches them intently. At last he speaks:

"Where's you from? Be tellin' 'ow's ye gettin'ere?"

Emmy describes the wildwood at home and the cherry tree with the parrot's nest in, and he tells of what has happened since they went to sleep in Waggl's nest; he says that he doesn't know how he and Scraggy got here to this ship, or to this world, and he says how worried they are about getting back home.

There's a long silence.

"What's in the backpacks?" says Jack, his voice a bit softer than it had been.

"Oh, let me show you," says Emmy. "It's not much because we weren't planning a long journey when we set out this morning. We were just going to map one more tree and visit Waggl on the way home — and I've told you the rest — so let's see what's in here."

Emmy takes off his backpack, undoes the straps and takes out some empty nutshells and seed pods, a compass and two small tubes, each with a cork in the end. Jack gasps.

"Who's Tooby?" he demands suddenly, his voice very serious.

"My Dad, my Dad! Tooby's my Dad!" sings out Scraggy, so happy to hear the sound of his father's name. "He's back 'ome where we's come from."

Emmy explains that the backpack, bamboo tubes and compass were all given to him by his Uncle One-Eye who is helping him learn how to make maps, so he can map the wildwood where they live.

"And he's got a small one of those things that swing from the beams of this ship that make a yellow light, except his makes a pale light and it's got no flame in it. He calls it a lantern."

"Aye, lanterns we's callin' 'em."

"Yes, he's got a lantern in his burrow at home and I always thought it was magic. Do you know Uncle One-Eye?"

"We's all knowin' Tooby. He upp'd 'n vanished. We be missin' 'im."

"What happened?" asks Scraggy.

"Fog there was, when Cap'n Tooby went aloft."

"Do you mean he climbed the mast?" asks Emmy.

"Right enough, in fog thick as soup."

"To the platform high up?"

"Aye! The crow's nest we's callin' it, that's right, 'n 'e climbed up to it."

"Whip-Tail Jack, that's exactly where we woke up!" explains Emmy. "Gobbee said something about a porthole."

"That parrot be crazy, there's no porthole aloft."

"Have you tried going up there when there's a fog?"

"What? 'N vanish meself? Not on your nelly!"

Scraggy looks up, his voice trembles. "I'll do it, when the fog comes! I'll be gettin' 'ome if'n it's the last thing I do!"

Whip-Tail Jack smiles for the first time. "All in good time, young Scraggy! Now we be knowin' who thee be, 'n be trustin' thee, 'tiz time to meet the crew! This 'ere be Black-Boot Bess, 'n this 'ere be Stump-Leg Stew."

"Hallo, Emmy and Scraggy, welcome aboard," says Bess.

"Hallo, Bess, hallo, Stew. Are there more of you?"

"Two more, we be, Emmy," says Stumpy. "Call me Stumpy. Others'll be sentreein', we do turns like. It'll 'av been Cutlass Kate who spied thee on the parrot's back! She come to tell us, leavin' Sieve-Brain Sally to follow when Bart got thee."

"Thank you all for rescuing us!" cries Emmy.

"Thank you!" says Scraggy.

"We were frightened," admits Emmy. "And we still are frightened of the human giants, we've never seen humans before."

"Never seen humans?" cries Jack. "Where in the world have you been?"

"In our home world there's no sign of humans, except for old buried things, and we don't know of any creatures that have seen humans. Do you think it's a different world? Oh dear! How will we get home?"

"Or could it be a different time?" suggests Black-Boot Bess.

"Ooo, that's spooky," says Stumpy, shuddering.

"Never mind yer fancy ideas," snaps Jack. "We 'as work to attend! Get to it!"

Stumpy knows what Whip-Tail Jack means, and he explains.

"What Jack's meanin' is, we 'as our duties to be doin', and now we 'as thee to be mindin' besides. Thee'll 'ave to learn fast, findin' your way's about and deefendin' thyselves. Scraggy, young feller, you be with Bess; Emmy, with me. Keep closer'n yer own shadows!

Emmy puts his things back into the backpack and straps it on. Since his adventure inside the mountain with Star, he takes his backpack with him wherever he goes.

Scraggy gives Emmy a worried look. Emmy smiles.

"See you later, Scraggy; we are in the middle of a mystery, keep your eyes peeled!"

Scraggy and Emmy hug each other as though they might never see each other again.

~

For the next few days the mice are kept busy with the daily patrols and searching for food, but when there is spare time Scraggy and Emmy are given training. There is a lot to learn: how to find their way around, what the dangers are, and where safe hideouts might be. Most important is how to use a cutlass to fight off the rats if they are unlucky enough to bump into them. It's made very clear to Scraggy and Emmy that it's best not to bump into a rat; they are not all so easy to get around as Black-Eyed Bart.

When Scraggy is first given a cutlass, he has no idea what to do with it and he keeps tripping over and getting the blade stuck in the floorboards. One day, when he is in a training session with Cutlass Kate, she suddenly charges at him with a great shout and he has to defend himself. He is frightened but he feels strength fill his body and he finds himself fighting back. Cutlass Kate says she is pleased and that he's a good learner; Scraggy feels very proud and wishes that Emmy had been there.

Emmy is slower to get the hang of it and has to learn little by little, but he, too, feels proud of the cutlass and belt that he's been given to wear.

They do the training in one of the storage holds, a place where the humans hardly ever go. They have a few different escape routes from there in case they are taken by surprise by humans or rats, or the ship's cat. There's noise from the deck above where the sailors are yelling and running about, and that helps to cover the noise they make clashing their cutlasses together.

They always have to be very quiet in the Hideout, or burrow, as Emmy would call it, which is above the ceiling of the ship's larder. It might seem to be a silly place to have the Hideout, but it has one great advantage and that is that the mice don't have to go very far to get the food that they need.

There are several holes through the larder ceiling, tight in the corners where there is no light and where humans are unlikely to look. There are shelves lining the walls of the larder laden with jars, tins and sacks, and everything is held in place by boards fixed along the front edges of the shelves. The mice climb up and down these shelves quite easily, taking care to leave no trace of their comings and goings, creeping into the larder at night when there are no humans about. The mice are careful to take only a small amount of food at a time so that the humans won't notice. Much of the human food is disgusting, things like salted fish and bacon, but there are sacks and barrels of grains and seeds and sometimes dried fruit, which the mice love.

Emmy and Scraggy help with the missions to the larder and learn the quick ways in and out, and they learn the First Rule. The First Rule is that whatever happens, you must not give away the Hideout. If you are seen by a human or are chased by a rat or a cat, you must run away from the Hideout and make your way back later by the secret trails.

Emmy loves learning to navigate around the ship. He has always had a good sense of direction and everything he has learned in the wildwood at home helps him now. As the days go by and Emmy and Scraggy learn the basics of ship life, they begin to get used to the constant movement and to walk more easily without feeling that they are falling over all the time. Stumpy says they are getting their sea-legs.

It's always a surprise to them when they come across a porthole, or hatch, that gives them a view of the sea; they could sit and look at the sea for hours, but it would risk being ambushed by the rats. The sea always makes them feel sad too because it reminds them that their home is unreachable. They couldn't get home even if they were to jump into the sea and swim! The sea is too big, and anyway, they don't know which way to go.

Whenever they get time off they explore somewhere new on the ship. They like to be together and talk, remembering their loved ones and everything back at home in Burrow Cave. One day they make their way to the Quarterdeck, which is the high bit at the back, or stern, of the ship. There is a safe place where they can peep through a split in an oak board and look out over the whole ship, from stem to stern, or front to back. The ship is big, making the mice feel very small, but even bigger than the ship is the sea, and the ship is rolled by the waves, this way and that, and the masts are always moving against the sky.

On the Quarterdeck in front of them is the big, spoked wheel, or helm, that is used to steer the ship. Ship's officers are standing about shouting orders, and the sailors are running about all over the place, climbing the rigging and carrying out those orders. There's always a lot to see and learn about how the ship is sailed. Emmy likes to watch the navigator measuring the angle of the sun, or at night studying the stars. He wants to know how the navigator can be sure which way to go just by looking at the sun or the stars. Star would know, Emmy thinks, and Uncle One-Eye too. Thinking of them makes him feel sad and tears sting his eyes.

"Scragg," he says with a catch in his voice. "I was just thinking of your dad and feeling homesick. I hope we get back one day."

"Me too, Em. This is a good adventure, but there's no land and no trees 'n I's missin' 'ome."

"'Allo, lads!" says a voice behind them, startling them.

"Oh, Stumpy!" exclaims Emmy. "You made us jump!"

"Ah-ha! I crept up on thee!"

"'Ow's you movin' so quiet on a wooden leg, Stumpy?"

"I's learnin' runnin' on all threes, Scraggy!" says Stumpy with a laugh. "Now then, what plots are you two 'atchin'?"

"No plot," says Scraggy. "We's missin' 'ome. I's missin' my Dad. What's you knowin' 'bout 'im?"

"Tooby? We's all missin' 'im. What's not said is 'e's vanish'd before, sudden like, 'n 'e's back when we least 'xpects it. 'E never says a word 'bout it. 'E's always collectin' things 'n when last 'e vanish'd, 'e took some of 'em with 'im."

"What sort of things?" Emmy asks.

"All sorts: like littl' 'eads o' stone, 'n them pipes like yorn."

"I've seen the little heads in his den at Burrow Cave!" cries

Emmy. "They're magic! He said something about dreams — ah yes, he said 'it be full o' magic, that there bowl; nothin' like spells nor troublesome things, but dreams that show the way'."

In the silence that follows, Scraggy looks at Emmy curiously.

"You alright, Em? You looks like you's sleep walkin'."

Emmy shakes his head, trying to snap out of his daydream.

"That was strange," he murmurs. "I was back in One-Eye's den for a moment, hearing him speak those words. Ooo, my fur's standing on end! That's really spooky."

"Ah-ha!" Stumpy exclaims. "This be Tooby alright! He has magic, 'n we be waitin' for 'im."

"Stumpy," asks Emmy. "Have you ever seen when he goes or comes back, or how it happens or where it happens?"

"Nay, lad! 'N me eye be peeled night 'n day, 'n I's seein' nothin'. Even Tooby never did know when or how."

"Even he didn't know?"

"Reckon not."

With a faraway look in his eyes Emmy speaks quietly, almost to himself. "'Dreams that show the way', hmm." He looks at Stumpy. "Are there any of Tooby's things on board this ship?"

"Maybe, maybe not; Cap'n Jack is keepin' Tooby's sea-chest back at the Hideout."

"Let's go back and look inside!" cries Scraggy enthusiastically.

"Not if you's valuin' your life, Jack'll skin thee alive!"

"Maybe we can get Jack to talk about it," says Emmy.

"Hey look! There's Gobbee!" Scraggy cries.

Through the split in the oak board they watch as Gobbee flies about the Quarterdeck getting yelled at by humans when he gets in their way, but the humans don't try to hurt him; it seems they quite like him being around. Gobbee flies towards the ship's bow and the mice lose sight of him amongst the rigging.

Emmy turns to Stumpy. "Is there any way we could talk to Gobbee without being seen or heard by humans? Is there anywhere we could do that, Stumpy? Maybe Gobbee knows more about the 'porthole' than he's told us."

"There be the Fantail."

"What's *that*?" asks Scraggy.

"That'll be aft; the Fantail be where the overhang be, 'n the rudder 'n all. Let's 'ave a look. C'mon, follow!"

Stumpy sets off with the two young mice close behind, going under the floor of the Poop. He knows the gaps in the timbers and holes in the beams where they can squeeze through. At last they see daylight coming through a hole in the stern of the ship; a heavy rope runs through this hole and the rope is moving, first one way and then the other way.

"T'is from the 'elm to rudder, you see. There be two steerin' ropes, one each side o' the ship. When the 'elm is turned, the ropes is pullin' the rudder this way or that."

There is plenty of room to squeeze past the rope and out onto a huge oak beam that holds the top end of the rudder. The wood is old and has been damaged over the years; there are nooks and crannies perfect for the mice to rest in where they don't feel too much in danger of falling into the sea. Above them is the overhang of the Fantail, where the Captain's cabin is. This is the first time that Emmy and Scraggy have been so close to the open water, and the sight of it amazes them. In fact, it's scary.

They watch the wake of the ship for a good long time.

"Gobbee can land on this 'ere beam," says Stumpy.

"How do we call him?" asks Emmy.

"We 'as a code," says Stumpy. "Any old squeak, as 'igh as you can, too 'igh for 'umans to be 'earin'. Let's 'ave a go."

They squeak as high as they can but Stumpy is not satisfied with their efforts and they do it again, and again.

"That'll be alright, now you's knowin'. Gobbee would come if 'ee 'eard us 'n 'ee ain't, so you'll 'ave to be tryin' another time."

"Do you remember there being another parrot?" asks Emmy.

"Aye! She upp'd 'n vanish'd one day, 'n Gobbee's been lookin' for 'er ever since, flyin' everywhere lookin', lookin'."

"She turned up in our world, Stumpy," says Emmy. "She nested in a hollow cherry tree with a baby, called Waggl. She's called Gabbee. Waggl had no feathers because he was too young, but it was autumn in our world and he got cold. During the winter Gabbee and Waggl disappeared; we don't know where they went. We went to their nest to see if they'd come back yet, but they hadn't. We were tired and had a little nap and when we woke up we found ourselves in your world! The cherry tree and the crow's nest must be the 'porthole', as Gobbee calls it."

"Hmm," says Stumpy. "Strange things happen! And stranger things happen at sea!"

"You've got no ideas about what happened?"

"Nope."

"Oh." Emmy feels disappointed.

"Let's go 'n ask Whip-Tail Jack if we can look in my Dad's sea-chest!" says Scraggy.

"Good plan, lad. C'mon!" says Stumpy, and he leads the way back through the labyrinth of secret trails, while Emmy and Scraggy try hard to remember the way so they'll be able to return to the Fantail another time.

~

"Where's you all been for so long?" Whip-Tail Jack sounds cross.

Stump-Leg Stew, Emmy and Scraggy, have returned to the Hideout only to find that they are in trouble already.

"I show'd 'em the Fantail to call the parrot," says Stumpy.

"We'd finished our jobs, Jack," says Emmy.

Sieve-Brain Sally clears her throat before speaking.

"You missed your turn on lookout, and Jack's not happy."

"I's sorry, I never knew," says Scraggy.

"Sorry, Jack," says Emmy.

"It'll be down to me, Cap'n. 'Twas my idea," admits Stumpy.

"Alright, alright, enough!" says Jack, impatiently.

Emmy is thinking this is probably the worst moment to ask Jack if they can look inside Tooby's sea-chest, but he has a feeling that it's got to be now — or never.

"Captain Jack, may we look in Tooby's sea-chest please?"

"Over my dead body!" Jack shouts. "I did swear by my life to guard that chest for Tooby, and that's what I'll do."

"But 'e's my Dad!" pleads Scraggy. "Let me see my Dad's things, please, Jack."

Jack turns away, unrelenting. Emmy takes a deep breath.

"Scraggy and I are newcomers on this ship, Captain Jack. We didn't ask to come here, and we're grateful to you for helping us and for being so generous.

"We have fresh eyes. We can see that the humans are sleepwalking as though they are enchanted. There's a magic that has all of you bewitched. We don't want to fall under the spell. We need to do something, and finding out what happened to Tooby is a good way to start."

There is a long, awkward silence. Jack still has his back turned. He heaves a deep sigh, and at last he speaks.

"We's been 'ere a long time, our lives given to seekin' freedom, but we's forgettin' what freedom is. We's knowin' these humans are trapped in a dream, as you put it; they sail this ship forever in search of — something — they's never findin'. We have our routines, there's no end to it."

Jack's shoulders slump down, defeated.

"How did you get here?" asks Emmy, his voice gentle.

"I's not rememberin'."

"Please, Jack, we are still free, please let us help you."

"You's just wantin' to get 'ome."

"Yes, we want to get home, and we want you to come too, if you will."

"You mean that?"

"Yes! All of you."

Jack turns to face them.

"I'm not against thee, children of Tooby, how could I be?" he says, his voice softer now and beginning to sound interested. "How do we find out what happened to Tooby?"

"It'll be a riddle," says Emmy. "Everything to do with One-Eye'd Tooby is a riddle. But we have the sea-chest and whatever Tooby has left in there will tell us what to do, I feel sure of it."

"Alright, open it."

"Thank you, Jack, but you should be the one to open it."

Jack drags the sea-chest to the centre of the room from the corner where it normally lives. It's a simple box, with a domed lid hinged at the back. It has black lines painted on, pretending to be iron bands, and there is a lock painted on too, but really there is no lock at all.

"Scraggy, you should be the one to look inside," says Jack, lifting the lid.

"Thanks, Jack!"

Scraggy looks inside, reaches in and lifts out an object wrapped in cloth. "It's a map tube, Em!"

Emmy watches intently as Scraggy removes the cloth from the map tube.

"Scragg, don't open the tube yet, put it on the floor, on its cloth. Let's get everything out before we open them, just so we know what there is in there."

"Are you expecting a surprise, Emmy?" says Sally.

"Yes!"

Scraggy takes a larger bundle out of the chest and carefully unwraps it. It's a map tube, but this one is short and fat, whereas the first one had been long and thin. The next bundle is like the first, then comes a collection of small things that turn out to be little heads, just like the ones that Emmy has seen before in One-Eye's den. Emmy remembers One-Eye speaking of the magic of the bowl of little heads, saying about 'dreams that show the way'.

Scraggy has unwrapped everything, placing each thing carefully on the floor on the cloth that had wrapped it. He sweeps his paw around in the sea-chest to check for anything else, finding some seashells. He lifts them out as well and puts them on the floor.

"What's in the big thing?" Stumpy asks.

"You open it, Jack," says Emmy.

Jack hesitates; he picks up the big tube and slowly unbends his body until he is standing up as straight and tall as he is able. He feels calm now, his unease and irritation quite gone. As he eases the plug from the end of the tube a wondrous pale light shines from the opening; he tilts the tube a little and the light pours forth, gathering itself into an Orb which floats in the air.

The mice gasp in astonishment, and with that inrush of breath, something new enters their lives.

To be continued…

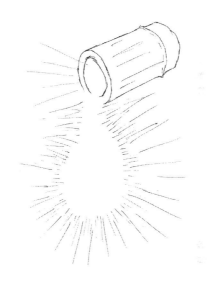

Mowzl's family tree

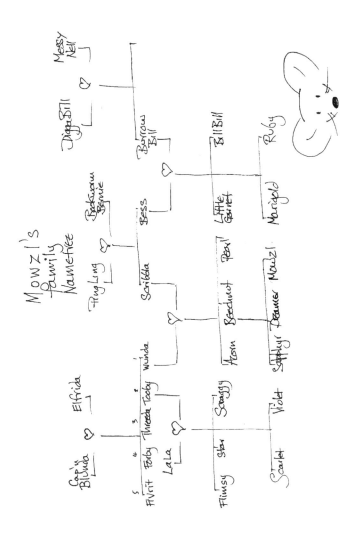

For your notes . . .

Author's notes:

Being outdoors in Nature has been essential to me since childhood; I have spent my working life as much as possible outside. As a student in the 1970's studying biological sciences and ecology, it was clear even then that Nature is in big trouble. Species decline, and habitat loss has escalated since that time to become the industrial scale destruction of the natural environment that we now see happening globally.

Meanwhile, human beings, particularly children, have less and less opportunity to access Nature. These changes have been accompanied by ever more sophisticated means by which children are enclosed, and separated from wild Nature, including the increase of technological substitutes. As successive generations of children and parents benefit less from contact with Nature, they know less about it and hence care less for it, and the continued degradation of the environment goes mostly unchallenged, even unnoticed.

Nature conservation is not an easy subject to make into a story, but when the rewilding of the natural world is extended to include the rewilding of children's hearts and lives, anything can happen!

This novel, to be published in three volumes, is devoted to bringing these issues into the children's domain, inviting children to ask the questions, and to see for themselves — see what it is that is missing that their hearts yearn for, and to support them in creating a platform for rebellion.

Paul Thornycroft. Stroud, Gloucestershire October 2017

~

I wrote the above in October 2017 when preparing the Mowzl manuscripts for publication. Since then there have been exciting developments — Greta Thunberg has triggered global protests by children who have become aware that their futures are being sold for immediate profit by indifferent politicians and wealthy minorities. She began alone, with a simple placard, sitting on the ground outside her school demonstrating against climate crisis inaction. "I have done my homework," she says. "Our house is on fire, you should panic." Now, millions of children all over the world have found their voices, thanks to Greta, and the movement expands everyday.

The floodgates have opened, as though we now have permission to admit what we feel and to speak out. There are many organisations and people finding their voices and shouting truth to power. Notably, Extinction Rebellion, appearing almost overnight during the winter of 2018, shows unprecedented clarity of purpose, tenacity and scrupulous codes of conduct. This is rolling out around the world. It is time! We must all shout louder and yet louder, doing what we can, when we can, how we can. Every tiny detail matters, every action; and every species matters, every fragment of habitat damaged or destroyed matters, however apparently insignificant.

The Mowzl trilogy is written to give support to this wave, and to encourage people young and old to look and taste the wild in order to understand what ecological collapse looks like — what it feels like — and all this while reading adventure stories exploring the implications of there being no quick fix. We find ourselves in a dilemma: we are the dominant species on the planet yet seem to be unable to stop ourselves from destroying life on Earth. What to do? This conversation must happen, is it at last taking centre stage?

It is important to remember that ecological breakdown is not caused solely by climate change and global warming, it is the result of human activity destroying the natural world — on an industrial and global scale in every corner of land, sea and air — by mechanical and chemical elimination of Nature for exclusive human use of land and resources. The changes required to reverse this trend go far beyond reducing carbon emissions, yet even that one thing we seem to find impossible to achieve.

The ecological emergency is real, clear and present. Climate Breakdown is real, and is happening now. These headlines are the only headlines worth talking about. Children know this, and we must all take heed. If we are not alarmed, we should be.

Paul Thornycroft Stroud, June 2019

www.mowzl.co.uk

Nothing in the cry
of cicadas suggests they
are about to die

{ Haiku attributed to Basho 1644 – 1694 }

Printed in Poland
by Amazon Fulfillment
Poland Sp. z o.o., Wrocław